PRAISE FOR
SUSAN KANDEL's

I Dreamed I Married Perry Mason

"A Chandlerian vision of Los Angeles . . .
this first novel straddles, rather elegantly, the genres of
'chick-lit beach book' and 'smart mystery.'"
LA Weekly

"A delightful read with an engaging, savvy, intrepid
heroine who finds mystery in crime fiction history,
Cece Caruso will have you singing the author's praises."
Rochelle Krich, bestselling author of *Dream House*

"If Nancy Drew had a closet full of couture, she'd be
the star of Kandel's pulpy fashion-forward mystery . . .
Kandel demonstrates an equally sharp eye
for dramatic plot twists and creative outfits . . .
With a well-spun plot and clever writing . . .
this quick clip of a novel will appeal to fans of
whodunits and designer duds alike. A-."
Entertainment Weekly

"Wonderful fun. Susan Kandel has written an adventurous, humorous debut novel that takes us on a well-researched romp through California's past and present . . . I finished this book this morning and I'm already longing for Cece's return and another case worthy of her skills."

Barbara Seranella, author of
Unpaid Dues and *Unwilling Accomplice*

"Clever, twisty, and mint original,
I Dreamed I Married Perry Mason will enchant mystery lovers. Susan Kandel depicts West Hollywood with a discerning eye, a tart tongue, and a generous heart."

Carolyn Hart, author of *Murder Walks the Plank*

"The verdict is in,
and *I Dreamed I Married Perry Mason* is a winner. Susan Kandel is guilty of penning an utterly original, artful, and nicely noir novel of murder and intrigue— all dressed up in fabulous vintage Hollywood fashions. Yum!"

Mary Kay Andrews, author of *Hissy Fit*

"A good, quick, entertaining read . . .
With all her delicious foibles and exotic tastes, Cece Caruso is an engaging character readers will want to meet again."

Murder Ink

Books by Susan Kandel

NOT A GIRL DETECTIVE
I DREAMED I MARRIED PERRY MASON

I DREAMED I MARRIED
PERRY MASON

A CECE CARUSO MYSTERY

SUSAN KANDEL

AVON BOOKS
An Imprint of HarperCollinsPublishers

AVON BOOKS
An Imprint of HarperCollins*Publishers*
10 East 53rd Street
New York, New York 10022-5299

Copyright © 2004 by Susan Kandel
Excerpt from *Not a Girl Detective* copyright © 2005 by Susan Kandel
ISBN: 0-06-058106-9
www.avonmystery.com

First Avon Books paperback printing: April 2005
First William Morrow hardcover printing: June 2004

Avon Trademark Reg. U.S. Pat. Off. and in Other Countries, Marca Registrada, Hecho en U.S.A.
HarperCollins® is a trademark of HarperCollins Publishers Inc.

Printed in the U.S.A.

10 9 8 7 6 5 4 3 2 1

FOR MY MOTHER, WHO LOVED A GOOD MYSTERY

ACKNOWLEDGMENTS

I'd like to acknowledge my friends and family for their encouragement and sage advice: Deborah Michel, who helped me around more than a few plot points, more than a few times; my sister, Linda Kandel; Didi Dunphy; Elizabeth Hayt; Bonnie Grossman; Deborah Brown, for sharing her legal expertise; and Tristin Tzimoulis, the best next-door neighbor a person could have. Maja Thomas and Susan Sayre Batton will never know how much their support meant to me, especially early on.

Special thanks go to my tenacious agent, Sandra Dijkstra, and to Joel Pulliam from her office; and to my editor, the clear-sighted Carolyn Marino, as well as Jennifer Civiletto.

Unlike Cece, I am not a biographer. The following sources helped me look a little more like one: Dorothy Hughes's definitive *Erle Stanley Gardner: The Case of the Real Perry Mason* (William Morrow, 1978); Erle Stanley Gardner's own nonfiction work, *The Court of Last Resort* (William Morrow, 1952); and Richard Senate's invaluable *Erle Stanley Gardner's Ventura: Birthplace of Perry Mason* (Charon Press, 1996), illustrated by John Anthony Miller. My appreciation goes out to Senate and Miller, who have devoted themselves to keeping the Gardner flame burning.

Finally, I'd like to thank the people I live with: my daughters, Kyra and Maud, for all their sweet, funny ways; and my husband, Peter Lunenfeld, for everything, and a whole lot more besides.

1

*W*hat a pity my vintage Maud Frizon pumps didn't come with steel-reinforced toes. Lace stilettoes are not the best defense against a case of gourmet cat food moving inexorably toward zero-degree gravity. Why on earth did I ever buy in bulk?

"You okay?" asked my gardener, Javier, who was fixing a downed sprinkler head on my small but velvety front lawn.

"I'm fine, just ignore me," I moaned, rubbing what was left of my foot. "What about the snails?"

Javier checked the bowl of beer I had put out last night. I wasn't being a good hostess (I drew the line at cheese and crackers), but I had tried everything else, including mail-order carnivorous snails bred to destroy their herbivorous cousins. I'd been ready to give up entirely on my ornamental cabbages when I'd heard the mere smell of beer lured the monsters to their deaths.

"Sorry. No bodies."

I kicked the door open with my good foot, greeted Mimi, the cat indirectly responsible for my suffering, and Buster, my teacup poodle, dumped the grocery bags on the kitchen table, and upset a half-drunk cup of cold coffee. I decided against wiping it up just then (that would mean finding the paper towels) and hit the button on the answering machine.

BEEP. "*Hi, it's Lael. You won't believe it—*"

Actually, I would. Lael was my best friend in the world and an extraordinary person, but she had a unique talent for disaster. I'd listen to the rest after a shower and perhaps some meditation. I don't meditate, but I keep thinking I should start.

Sidestepping the coffee now dripping onto the floor, I went into the bedroom and took off my favorite suit, a black Joan Crawford–esque number I'd found at an estate sale with Lael, who'd zeroed in on an almost complete and barely chipped set of Wedgwood lusterware. She'd tried to talk me into removing the suit's shoulder pads, but I liked the line-backer/diva effect—not to mention that you don't mess around with a classic silhouette. But I suppose Lael and I are different that way. I am obsessed with clothes, and she is the kind of beautiful woman who doesn't need to be.

I picked my robe up off the bathroom floor and turned on the water, which took precisely three and a half minutes to warm up.

My West Hollywood bungalow, purchased nine years ago with the proceeds from my divorce settlement, was like a Stradivarius—the 1932 Spanish had amazing art deco details, but woe to she disrespectful of its myriad quirks. Like the temperamental plumbing, for one thing. Or the sloping floor in the kitchen, which meant that anything heated on the stove top would migrate to the right side of the pot. Or the front door's inlaid brass knob, which pulled off pretty much every time you tried to open the door from the inside. Visitors seemed to find this latter idiosyncrasy particularly unnerving.

BEEP. *"This is George at Kleiner's. The new motor for your fountain is in. Listen, the old one was really filthy. You have to clean it out twice a week like I told you, especially when the Santa Anas are blowing all that muck around."*

What George didn't know was that my fountain was of the same vintage as my house, and equally volatile. Also, that the portentous Santa Ana winds were invented by Raymond Chandler purely for literary purposes.

BEEP. *"Call your mother."*

BEEP. *"Please call your mother, dear. I have no idea where you are."*

BEEP. *"Cece, it's Richie. Call Mom, for god's sake. She's cleaning the attic again, and doesn't know what to do with your stuff. Do you want to keep your crown? Joanne and the kids send their love."*

Like all good Italian boys, my brothers, Richie and James Jr., worshiped their mother. I was somewhat more ambivalent. This the boys understood from an early age, which meant I'd spent my childhood at the mercy of a pair of pint-size enforcers. They became cops, just like our dad. I became a beauty queen. But for the record, my reign as Miss Asbury Park, New Jersey, was short-lived and utterly lamentable. Mom could use my crown to plunge the toilet for all I cared. More likely she'd wear it to a church potluck. She'd always harbored the belief that she'd been switched at birth and was really royalty, or Frank Sinatra's sister at least.

BEEP. *"Hello, I'm returning Cece's call. Listen, Cece, if you're there, I have a vagabond virgin, a negligent nymph, a hesitant hostess, and a borrowed brunette for you. So, are you a madam or a mystery buff? But seriously, folks, they're five dollars apiece, paperback reprints."*

Everyone's a comedian.

"I've got a first edition of The Case of the Sleepwalker's Niece, *but I don't think you want it. There's some water damage on the sleeve, but it's still pretty pricey. Ditto* The Case of the Curious Bride, *which is one of the better prewar Masons, not that I'm an expert, like some people. You can order on-line or by phone. We're here until eight P.M., thanks to folks like yourself."*

I suppose that made it official. Even the bozo working the desk at the Mystery Manor could see that Perry Mason had stolen my life. Yes, that would be Perry Mason, the world-famous and much-beloved attorney-at-law.

To wit: I could tell you under what circumstances Perry could be persuaded to take a case (a natural blonde in distress was always a plus); his favorite expletive ("the deuce!"); how he liked his steak (broiled rare); and what he drank when he had to drive (soda water just flavored with Scotch)—in short, as much as Della Street, his perfect jewel of a secretary, ever could. I go to bed marveling at his courtroom moves and wake up mulling his situational ethics. Some might say I'm obsessed. My answer would be it's purely business.

Ever since I left my sorry excuse for a husband, I've made my living writing biographies of mystery writers. For the last twelve months, I've been working on Erle Stanley Gardner, creator of the brilliant, unflappable Perry Mason. Gardner wrote eighty-two full-length Mason novels, which have sold more than 300 million copies worldwide. He also wrote twenty-four mysteries under the pseudonym A. A. Fair, featuring the P.I. Donald Lam and his heavyset partner, Bertha

Cool (love that name), and nine mysteries about the D.A. Doug Selby. Plus a whole lot more. Still, to understand Gardner, you have to understand what makes his alter ego tick. Thus the stolen life to which I alluded earlier and the profusion of Mason books, with their fabulously lurid covers, everywhere I turned: in vertiginous piles on my bedside table; between the seats of my car; and covering the floor of my office like pulp-themed linoleum.

The hot water was ready, and it lasted exactly eight minutes so I hopped right in. Later, after a good dinner, I could give my full attention to Lael. Who can think creatively on an empty stomach? Then I'd settle down on the sofa with my new cashmere throw, which Buster had thus far spared, and finish *The Case of the Sunbather's Diary* even if it killed me. I'd been trying to get through it for a week, but it just wasn't happening. There were too many characters. I spent all my time trying to keep them straight, which meant that every time I picked up the book I basically had to start from scratch. The prewar Gardners were indeed better reads.

I toweled off as I meandered over to the kitchen and riffled through the grocery bags. Toilet paper, laundry detergent, cat litter, cocktail peanuts, basil, garlic croutons—a hundred dollars later, and not a thing to eat for dinner. Typical. I couldn't stand cereal after ten A.M., and Buster needed a walk anyway. I threw on flip-flops and an old cotton sundress and headed back to the market, which was located just around the corner.

The Gelson's on Santa Monica Boulevard six blocks east of La Cienega is the closest West Hollywood gets to a Greek agora. Despite its prices, it is the place where the citizens of the republic convene. They make the journey on foot or by Rolls Royce, armed with platinum credit cards or food stamps, in search of bagfuls of stuff or just a Haas avocado and a Meyer lemon (even the produce at Gelson's is luxury branded). But food is merely the pretext. People go to Gelson's to stimulate the senses, to chitchat with the neighbors, to pay their respects to the all-powerful checkers—in sum, to reconnect with the world.

Today was Thursday, and Thursdays were special at Gelson's. Between five and six, one of the box boys leaves his station, puts on a white apron and chef's toque, and stands up front near the prepared foods, slicing up freshly cooked turkey and tri-tip roast to order. Even the least sociable come out of the woodwork on Thursdays.

Tonight there was Melanie, the loquacious PR lady, with her standard poodle, Scarlett, tied up outside the store and wailing like nobody's business (Buster was sequestered in my purse, feasting on treats I offered every time I sensed a bark coming on).

Then there was Richard, the retired screenwriter, who was now directing (very) amateur theater. This fall, it was an all-male revival of *Guys and Dolls*.

No one even blinked at the preoperative transsexual eyeing the bear claws. That was just Tina.

Nor did they gape at "the ladies," white-haired ex-showgirl twins who live on my corner and make it their business to see that every stray cat in the neighborhood is properly fed. The ladies could charge for seminars on how to milk the system. Most recently, they got the city of West Hollywood to turn the curb in front of their house into a private handicapped zone so they'd always have a place to park their ancient white Mercedes.

Max was there, too, with the latest of his bodacious girl-friends. Max was a Sephardic Jewish community organizer who rented the converted garage next door as his base of operations.

And of course, the usual assortment of budding soap opera actors, who always got a little competitive over the turkey legs, despite their high fat content. Me, I went for the beef.

I got into Brenda's line.

"Hi, sweetie. Back so soon?"

"I missed you. How's your son, by the way?"

Brenda's son wanted to be a rocker, but was working by day as a substitute teacher for L.A. Unified.

"Looking for an agent. How about Annie? I haven't seen her for a while. Is she still living in Topanga Canyon?"

"Yup. Still a Trekkie in Topanga. She's fine, my son-in-law, too."

Like my mother and grandmother before me, I was a child bride and at thirty-nine had a twenty-one-year-old daughter who had inherited the family gene. Only unlike me she wasn't pregnant at her nuptials and, for the record, has far better taste in men. She met her husband, Vincent, in art school, where they discovered a mutual passion for science fiction. He is a big cheese in the world of alternative comics, the creator of *Trash Pimp,* and she works as a set designer for a *Star Trek* clone called *Testament,* now in its third season on network TV.

On the way home, Buster and I encountered a gorgeous Siberian husky, and there was much reciprocal sniffing (between the dogs).

"Excuse me," ventured Mr. Handsome's owner, an elderly gentleman in a track suit, "is your dog fixed?"

"Yes, he is," I answered demurely.

"Not my man Pushkin. I ask because whenever he meets another intact male, Pushkin gets aggressive. Testosterone, you know. It's what makes the male of the species strong, virile. But we don't want strong men anymore. We want them to sit still, to lie there, just to take it, like little girls."

I had no idea what we were talking about, but I didn't think it was Pushkin. Buster was enthralled, but I hurried him along. Some relationships just aren't meant to be.

Back at home I fed my beasts, arranged my dinner on a plate, poured a glass of Cabernet, and returned Lael's call. I got the machine.

"Pick up if you're there, Lael. It's me. Where are you?" I trilled. "Are you in the kitchen, baking something divine?"

Lael was a master baker, a genius actually, but her handiwork was decidedly eccentric. This time of year she was probably making Labor Day gingerbread cookies shaped like striking dockworkers or something.

"Cece, hi, don't hang up, I'm here," she said, out of breath.

"Sorry, hon, did I drag you away from something?"

"No, I'm just sitting here with your daughter."

"Annie? What's she doing there?"

"That's what I wanted to talk to you about. Annie's left Vincent. She says it's over."

Damn it.

I leapt up to look for my car keys and banged my knee on the coffee table. Stifling a scream, I tossed the room, sending old magazines and dirty laundry flying. A push-up bra landed on Buster's head.

"You can stop looking for your car keys."

"Who said I'm looking for my car keys?"

"Cece. Please."

"Lael—"

"Listen to me. Now's not a good time. Annie will call you when she's ready. You know how you are. You'll only make things worse."

"But—"

"I mean it."

As she hung up, Buster trotted over with my keys between his teeth.

Defeated, I sought solace in my tri-tip. It was ice cold.

Tomorrow, I thought, sighing, *had better be another day.*

2

For most people the world over, Beverly Hills is a mythic place, a big-ticket Shangri-La chockablock with diamond-dripping trophy wives and buxom starlets cruising in convertibles on perennially sun-kissed days. For me, Beverly Hills meant only two things: parking hell and Raymond Burr.

Every Friday, like clockwork, I headed to the Museum of Television and Radio on Beverly Drive to watch at least four back-to-back episodes of *Perry Mason*. It was the ultimate in decadence—watching TV and calling it work—especially since I usually stopped at the Candy Baron across the street first to load up on Swedish fish and cinnamon bears. But if I didn't get there by eleven A.M., especially during the Christmas rush (which in Beverly Hills begins in August), I'd be punished by having to circle the block for hours.

My horoscope said that today was a good day to travel. Sure enough, I cruised down Santa Monica Boulevard heading west without hitting a single red light. I turned left onto Beverly and directly into the city-operated lot equidistant from the candy store and the museum. It was a hot, hazy day and by midmorning the air was already thick with the intermingled scents of expensive perfume and iced blended coffee. Everyone seemed to be carrying one of these ostensibly low-fat confections—tourists in search of Rodeo Drive; secretaries on break; affluent young moms, their babies immobilized in strollers. With its lunar module–esque bubble lid (to accommodate the standard-issue squirt of whipped cream), the twelve-ounce to-go cup was a veritable civic icon.

I got one. It seemed unpatriotic not to.

Slurping determinedly, I popped in and out of the candy store, then made my way to the museum, a glass-fronted monstrosity chronically streaked with grime. Catching sight of my reflection, I wondered if I passed for a local. Poised on top of my long dark hair, which I currently wore in a sort of Jaclyn Smith homage, was my favorite pair of Jackie O sunglasses, which in and of itself exemplified my fashion schizophrenia. From the neck down, things became yet more complicated. I was wearing a flowing, circa 1974 Ossie Clark knockoff that, according to Annie, totally rocked. Better yet, it was unwrinkleable. And high-heeled Prada Mary Janes that didn't hurt. But, alas, no Hermès bag. Even on eBay, those babies went for triple my mortgage payment, plus some. Champagne taste and a beer pocketbook, as my mother used to say.

I sidestepped the gift shop, stuffed to the rafters with things I *could* afford but didn't want (*I Love Lucy* lunchboxes and *Three Stooges* backpacks, for example), and went upstairs to get my tapes.

On the menu for today were "The Case of the Moth-Eaten Mink," "The Case of the Howling Dog," "The Case of the Twice-Told Twist," and "The Case of the Dangerous Dowager," the latter of which—had Gardner's publisher had his way—would have been titled "The Case of the Pig-headed Widow," which tells you about how much publishers know. Writing as much as he did, Gardner developed a standard meter for titles: la *la* la la *la* la la *la*. The last word had to be short and naturally emphasized, unless it was a two-syllable word, in which case the first syllable was customarily slurred over, as in "brunette." Gardner took a lot of heat for referring to himself as a "one-man fiction factory," but I admired the economy of it all. When everything is systematized, there is no wasted energy. As the reluctant champion of the chicken-with-her-head-cut-off approach to life, I realized I could learn a thing or two from this guy.

There were twenty-four TV-watching cubicles in the main room, and they were almost always empty. How depressing it must be to work here, kind of like being alone in a movie theater. Today there was a man in a Jackson Five T-shirt two seats over from my favorite cubicle, absorbed in the *Apollo 11* moon landing, and an old lady next to him watching what I guessed was an early episode of *Dragnet*. Everybody loves a mystery.

My daughter had become one, overnight. This was distressing. Ah, well. She'd called from Lael's at the crack of dawn to tell me I could come over later in the afternoon, but only if I swore not to talk, just to listen. Listening is not my best event. But I'd give it a shot. Right now, though, I had to get to work.

I laid out my pens and pencils in neat little rows. I sorted and resorted my note cards. I was in the middle of an exquisite Post-it note collage when I realized just how nervous I was about this project. It was August, the manuscript was due in three months, and it was full of loose ends.

I had the literary analysis all tied up, having sat for years at the feet of the master—my ex, the world's second-most-renowned James Fenimore Cooper scholar. What a dubious honor, not that he'd see it that way. The great so often go unrecognized in their own time. Anyway, I will grudgingly admit that he taught me how to deconstruct a text. And, yes, our endless fights about feminist theory were inspirational. They made me realize I had to dump the misogynist bastard, for one thing. Also, that what had been left out of the Erle Stanley Gardner literature was any discussion of the centrality of women in his books.

After reading a dozen or so, I had become convinced that with the Perry Mason series Gardner had pioneered a new kind of soft-boiled pulp written specifically for a female audience. Which is to say the prurient appeal of all those sulky girls, leggy vixens, and glamorous widows throwing themselves at Perry Mason was merely a ruse. In fact, those dames in distress almost always served to undermine his mastery, in subtle and interesting ways.

No, what was hard-going was not analyzing the work. Nor was it figuring out Mason's place along the continuum of amateur gumshoes, cops, and spies skulking their way across the American mystery landscape. That'd been my turf since I'd turned eleven and discovered Nancy Drew. Nope, what was causing all the trouble was Gardner himself.

Descended from Colonial New Englanders, his parents were members of the Sons and Daughters of the American Revolution. When he was a boy of ten, the family moved out West and he commenced a long and distinguished career as a troublemaker. Erle was suspended from high school; got involved in prizefighting at a time it constituted a felony in California; was shipped off to law school in Indiana and took part in a bottle-smashing incident in the dorm; ducked the cops trying to serve the warrant; took a train to Chicago, then Oregon, then California; apprenticed himself to an Oxnard lawyer who needed help with his two-bit cases; fleeced the D.A. with his legendary ingenuity; and wound up the lawyer of choice in Ventura County, "of all classes except the upper and middle classes," as he once so winningly put it. To make some extra money, he started writing for the pulps. The rest, as they say, is history.

It was thrilling stuff, admittedly, but the bad-boy antics took you only so far. I needed to humanize him, and the key, I had finally decided, lay not in Gardner's writing per se, but in the Court of Last Resort.

Let me explain. With the success of Perry Mason, Gardner had become a magnet for hopeless cases. The letters poured in from prisons nationwide. And every last one of Gardner's pen pals claimed to be innocent: framed by an ex-lover, tripped up by circumstantial evidence, victimized by a prison grapevine. In every single case, the jury had been biased, the D.A. up for reelection, the judge senile, whatever. Gardner was a sympathetic ear, having firsthand experience with the fallibility of the legal system and a weakness for the underdog.

And so, in 1948, he conceived of the Court of Last Resort. Its sole purpose was to persuade the authorities to reopen criminal cases in which men and women had been wrongly convicted of capital offenses. Gardner put together a panel of volunteer experts in various aspects of criminology who reexamined case files, performed polygraphs, and interviewed witnesses, looking for flaws in the evidence. Over the period of a decade or so, he wrote seventy-five articles for *Argosy* magazine in which he described the process and put his findings before the public, whom he deemed the ultimate Court of Last Resort.

In April I had taken a research trip to the University of Texas in Austin, where the Erle Stanley Gardner archive is maintained (unbelievably, nobody in California thought to ask until it was too late). The archive was a beautiful thing to behold. Gardner was a stickler about correspondence and kept every last shred, which was not a problem given that his convoy of secretaries was made up of legendary organizational fiends.

For an entire week I focused on the Court of Last Resort. I had a jolly old time going through the "heartbreak files," Gardner's term for each prisoner's correspondence, trial transcripts, parole board reports, and so on, being extra careful not to spill the coffee I smuggled daily into the fourth-floor library. They made good coffee out there in Texas. Nice and strong. As for the barbecue, no thank you. Too sweet. North Carolina barbecue, now that's the real deal.

Anyway, it wasn't working. The whole thing. I wasn't getting much more of a sense of Erle Stanley Gardner. Not until that magic moment when I stumbled across a dog-eared letter from 1958, handwritten on lined paper. It caught my eye because it had been misfiled, and Gardner's team of obsessive-compulsives just didn't make those kinds of mistakes. Then I read it. It had been written by a man recently convicted of killing his wife. And I read it again.

May 12, 1958

Dear Mr. Erle Stanley Gardner,

You do not know me, but you did know my grandfather, William Albacco of Ventura, California. You represented him briefly in the fall of 1916, when he was accused in an assault case. He was innocent, and you got him off. Thank you. My grandmother always spoke kindly of you. She also remembered how you came to the aid of the many Chinese people in Ventura when they were harassed by the police, including Mr. Wu Chen of Sutton Avenue, who was the husband of one of her oldest friends.

Now I find myself in trouble. I, too, am innocent of any crime. Perhaps you could help my family again. My wife, Jean, was killed last year. I do not know who is responsible. I was convicted because I had no alibi for the time of her murder. I cannot say where I was at that time because to do so would complicate someone else's life, perhaps even destroy it. It would be wrong. So I sit here, and the person who killed my wife is free. I am frustrated, but powerless. Will you find out who the wrongdoer is? Will you help me? I await your reply.

Sincerely yours,

Joseph Albacco Jr.

California Correctional Institution, Tehachapi

I knew Gardner had read the letter because he'd appended a note that read, "L.P.: follow up. Rings a bell/ESG." But there was nothing further in the files. I could find no record of the case ever having been written up in *Argosy*. And Gardner had left the Court of Last Resort not long after the letter had been received. Had he ever investigated? Why had this case rung a bell? Had the real murderer ever been found?

Maybe it was the writer's humility. Maybe it was his willingness to suffer to protect someone else, the unnamed person who could have provided his alibi. So many of the other letters had been so hostile. Joseph Albacco seemed more befuddled than brutal, and convinced, somehow, that Erle Stanley Gardner, a perfect stranger, could straighten everything out. What touched me was his faith. He trusted Gardner enough to place his life in the man's hands.

And then, sitting at that old oak desk in Austin, after a long slug of that good Texas coffee, I had a great idea. When I got back home and laid it on her, Lael thought it was insane, but we always thought each other's great ideas were insane (I tried like the dickens, for example, to dissuade her from helping the father of her youngest child, baby August, with his doomed feng shui business. No one shed tears for him when he hightailed it back to Dusseldorf, except maybe the IRS).

Anyway, I decided on that day that I was going to find Joseph Albacco. Yes, I know it would've made more sense to try to track down one of the people Gardner had actually written about in *Argosy*, someone he'd actually gotten out of jail. That person would be guaranteed to have stories, great ones. It would have been the logical way to proceed. But sometimes you have to go with your gut. Joseph Albacco's letter had spoken to me. And if he was still alive, I wanted to meet him. If Joseph Albacco couldn't put a face on Erle Stanley Gardner, I had a feeling no one could.

Weeks, then months of wrangling with the good people at the California Department of Corrections ensued. Inter-

estingly, not one of them much liked my great idea. Yes, the
prisoner in question was still in their custody. But as I was
neither a lawyer nor a family member, it seemed that I had
no business visiting him or anyone else at any of their facilities. True enough, if you wanted to get technical about it.
Three weeks ago, I managed to get the warden on the phone.

"Your name, how do you pronounce it exactly?" he asked.

"Like the opera singer."

"I'm a bowling sort of guy myself."

"Ca-Ru-So, as in Kaboom, Rude, So What," I said, sighing. "It's Italian."

"I'm Polish," he volunteered. "Tam-Row-Ski, as in Tam
O'Shanter, rowdy, the winter sport."

I thought I might be getting somewhere when he said he
had a nephew living in West Hollywood.

"How fabulous!" I chirped. "Maybe I even know him!
West Hollywood's such a friendly place, and what a Halloween parade, my goodness!"

He harrumphed. It seemed said nephew's "lifestyle" had
broken the kid's mother's heart.

I was fresh out of ideas when someway, somehow, the
chaplain got wind of our conversation and interceded on
my behalf, arranging everything with the warden. The chaplain, it seemed, had come to know Joseph Albacco quite well
over the years, and had something important to say to me
himself. We agreed to talk right after my meeting with
Albacco.

Which, I realized as I popped the last cinnamon bear into
my mouth and the first videotape into the VCR, had been
scheduled for tomorrow.

3

*B*ut before I picked up where Erle Stanley Gardner had left off, I had Annie to deal with. And maybe this whole thing with Vincent was just a big misunderstanding. The girl did have a wicked habit of outfoxing people. This had been true from the very moment she'd come into the world.

"Congratulations!" Dr. Berger had trumpeted, hefting all nine pounds, six ounces of her into my arms. "You have a healthy baby boy . . . oops, I mean, girl!" I swear, Annie cracked up.

It's been like that ever since.

Her first word was *da-da*. Annie's father felt vindicated. Only she was talking about the family dog, not him.

As a child, she looked just like Shirley Temple, all dimples and ringlets. My mother was in seventh heaven. A movie career! Broadway! Greater glory for Grandma at her Friday afternoon haunt of thirty-five years, Sheila's Beauty-to-Go! But I hid the tutu she sent on Annie's third birthday. And the tap shoes she sent on her fourth. Just a reformed beauty queen doing her duty. The kid helped out. She tucked her curls into a baseball cap, pitched like nobody's business, and sent the boys home crying, tails between their legs.

The title of that old Jimmy Cagney movie *Angels with Dirty Faces* always reminded me of Annie. But I didn't really know angels until Vincent came into her life.

So he writes a comic book about a garbageman in the future who recruits spies for alien regimes; it sounds a lot more subversive than it is. So he plays drums in a slash metal band; he wears earplugs during practice. So he's a card-carrying member of PETA; I, too, am willing to boycott leather goods—except for those made in Italy.

You'd never pick Vincent out of a crowd. His hair is long and shaggy, and I'm not sure I could even say what color it is. He wears a big T-shirt, baggy pants, and huge construction boots, the latter even in summer, with equally enormous shorts from the army-navy surplus store. But he has a kindness that radiates around him like a halo. And he makes Annie feel safe without smothering her. When Vincent walks into a room, you can feel a light somewhere inside her turn on. And if that isn't love, I don't know what is.

I wouldn't let them mess this up.

Perry Mason had distracted me for a few hours, but I was getting itchy. At the end of the fourth episode, when the big guy winked at Della after having tricked good ol' Paul Drake into picking up the dinner tab, I was out of there.

With no traffic, I could make it from Beverly Hills to Lael's in less than half an hour. But of course there was traffic. This was L.A. Ducking red lights and the occasional overzealous guy in a Hummer, I zigzagged my way to La Brea and Fountain, where things started to ease up.

When asked for advice by a struggling young actress, Bette Davis had replied, "Darling, always take Fountain." That'd been good enough for me, apocryphal or not. But I could see a nasty accident coming up just past Highland, so I cut up and over to Franklin, cruising past the candle shops, the little theaters, and the coffee shop offering the LAST CAP-PUCINO BEFORE THE 101. Turning left onto Beachwood Canyon, I got a perfect view of the Hollywood sign. It was no longer illuminated at night (too alluring for would-be suicides), but it glowed nonetheless, Tinseltown's very own North Star.

It was actually a misnomer. The fifty-foot-long sign had originally read HOLLYWOODLAND, advertising five-hundred-acre parcels to the droves of Midwesterners who came to L.A. in the 1920s in search of orange trees and sunshine. The "land" had fallen off in the forties, but the fairy-tale gates to the development were still standing. Likewise the tiny English cottage that was its original real estate office.

Lael lived halfway up Beachwood, just past the REINDEER CROSSING sign, on a hillside laced with meandering vines, wild vegetation, and mysterious stairwells cut directly into the rock.

On one side of her was a Moorish fantasy; on the other, a nicely maintained Craftsman. Lael had a French Norman cottage with a small tower attached to the hillside garage, but you'd never have guessed it since you could barely see the place from the road. The front yard was overflowing with junk—rusting tricycles, deflated plastic pools, hoses, buckets, terra-cotta pots bearing miscellaneous plant remains, a dented filing cabinet, scattered liter soda bottles, and piles and piles of old newspapers.

The inside was pretty much the same. Nina, Lael's ten-year-old daughter, once said she'd like to turn the house upside down and let everything fall out the windows.

I rang the bell. Nina's fourteen-year-old half brother, Tommy, opened the door.

As usual, my nose went into overdrive. Tonight the dominant note was nail polish, sharp and acrid, mellowed somewhat by the aroma of caramel wafting from the kitchen. Then the merest soupçon of Play-Doh, finished off by a whiff of Crayola crayon. Perhaps also a stray diaper, ripped off in the heat of the moment.

"Hey, Tommy," I said.

"Hey, Cece," he replied. "She's in my room, sitting in that old beanbag chair she gave me. Mom gave her a piece of pie."

I headed toward the back of the house. Years of neglect followed by some haphazard remodeling had preceded Lael's arrival. But she was entirely responsible for the add-ons and the add-ons to the add-ons, a string of converted closets, enclosed porches, and strange lean-tos patched together with plywood and nails in a fashion that not only defied L.A.'s stringent housing codes but was guaranteed to make a city inspector feel faint. And those guys were hard to impress.

Tommy's room was at the end of the line. I knocked on the door. Annie opened it.

"Hi, Mom," she said, looking down at her bare feet. Her toenails were each polished a different color.

"Hi, baby," I answered, wrapping her up in a hug. I could feel my shoulder getting wet, but I didn't think I should be the one to talk first. I waited for a long time, quietly staring at the skateboard decals on the window.

"I like your shoes, Mom."

"Thanks, honey."

"They're really pretty."

"I like your toenails."

"The Hello Kitty pastel palette. Nina did it."

"What's going on?"

"I know what I'm doing even if you don't think so. I made a mistake and I have to fix it." Annie started to pace, something she always did when she was nervous.

"What mistake? Honey, please. Sit down and we can talk this through."

"You always want to talk it through. Why didn't you and Dad talk it through before you screwed everything up?"

"Where did that come from? We're not talking about me and your dad."

"Exactly how many men have you slept with?"

She was as matter-of-fact as an H&R guy tabulating tax deductions.

Stalling for time, I dropped my purse and went to retrieve it. I considered crawling out of the room while I was down there, but that would have been counterproductive. Time to face the music. Honesty is the best policy. I made my bed, now I had to lie in it.

"Nine."

"Nine! How is that possible?" Annie demanded. "You weren't with anyone before Dad, and after him, there was only Joshua, right?"

"Well, not exactly," I said slowly. "There was somebody before your dad, and there were a few before and after Joshua, but no one significant. Well, not really significant, except maybe for Peter Gambino, but that sort of fizzled.

Oh, and Alex. But he moved back to Milwaukee before we had a chance to find out if there was anything there."

Alex, I reminisced. Thick, curly hair. Muscles in all the right places. The man who loved to spend the weekend in bed. Who loved to laugh. At anything. At Howard Stern. At *Family Circus*. Uproariously. Oh, god, it all comes back. He ran a chain of semisuccessful tanning salons. At the time, the differences between UVB and UVA light seemed far more thrilling than James Fenimore Cooper's use of the simile. What did I know? I'm sure I gave myself melanoma as a result of that relationship.

"You are unbelievable! I can't believe this! Everybody's slept around except me. Even my own mother! Mom, listen to me. I am twenty-one years old. I'm not ready to throw in the towel. I've had only two lovers my whole life—"

"Two!" I interrupted. "You were sleeping with someone in high school?"

"Of course not. You know I could barely speak to anyone without breaking out in hives."

"Well, that's what I thought."

"Aren't you going to ask me when?"

"Fine. When?"

She stared me right in the eye, defiant.

"Last week."

"Is that what this is all about?"

"No."

"Does Vincent know?"

"Yes."

"And what does he have to say about it?"

"That he loves me. That he wants to work it out."

Relieved, I said, "Annie, you have to get a grip here. This

isn't a game. Having sex doesn't turn you into a grown-up."
Then it all became clear.

"Not your father, please. Please say it wasn't him filling
your head with this garbage."

Annie was quiet.

"Oh, this is perfect. Your father, the world's leading
expert on screwing around. Getting advice from him on
commitment—good thinking, Annie."

"Mom, from what I understand, you weren't totally
blameless."

"Is that what he says?"

"Before he knew what was happening, you were moving
him into married student housing."

"I was moving *him* in! Give me a break! If only I had been
that Machiavellian."

"Mother."

"Yes, I was crazy about him. You know that. He was rich
and handsome and a grad student at a famous university no
one from my rinky-dink high school was ever going to go
to. But I wanted his *life* more than I wanted *him*."

"What are you saying?"

"That I hardly aspired to being the wife, the one who
passed on college so she could perfect her mashed potatoes
while everybody else went to great lectures and read great
books and had great conversations about important things."

"You do make amazing mashed potatoes, Mom."

"That's not the point and you know it. Oh, it is so like
your father to twist everything around just to get you to
think *he's* the aggrieved party. And to screw up your own
good marriage in the process!"

"Okay, maybe I was harsh. I'm sorry. But this is exactly

my point. I don't want to make sacrifices, like you had to. Remember how you told me Della Street turned down five marriage proposals because she didn't want to give up her job? I'm with her, Mother. And I'm truly sorry if you don't like it."

"Back up a minute, sister. Della Street is a fictional character. You're not her, and no one is asking you to give anything up. Vincent is not your father. And you are not me. Your life has not been one huge accident, for one thing." Shit. Now I was sorry.

"Thanks a heap, Mother."

"I didn't mean it that way, honey."

"I have a hard time buying that right now," she said, in a tone so like my own it gave me chills.

"Look, all I mean to say is, this is you and Vincent. I know how much you love him. That doesn't happen every day. You can't just give it up."

"I already have. That's why I'm here. I've made up my mind."

The door opened. Zoe, who was seven, was holding a squirmy baby August in her arms.

"Mommy's finished the cake she's been working on. Do you want to see it?" she asked shyly.

"No, sweetie, not right now," I said.

"Yes, right now," Annie said, grabbing the baby from Zoe just as he was about to do a face-plant on the hall carpet.

"This conversation isn't over," I insisted as we followed Zoe back to the kitchen.

"So, what do you think?" Lael asked, her blue eyes opened wide.

Poised on a card table in front of the fridge was a six-tiered wedding cake. It looked like a cascading waterfall. Each tier was covered in the thinnest layer of soft blue marzipan rippled with rings of powdered sugar, as if raindrops had fallen onto the surface. There was a large water lily on each tier, the pastillage petals lightly sprinkled with pink dusting powder. At the base of the waterfall, on either side of the royal icing splashes of water, were piles of rock candy pebbles, tinted grayish blue. At the very top of the cake were two sugar-paste dragonflies so delicate you could make out the veins on their wings.

"Exquisite," I said.

"Amazing," Annie offered.

Zoe looked proud.

Even baby August gurgled with pleasure.

"But Annie and I have to finish something right now," I said.

"Not now. I'm going to lie down."

"Well, let's go back home. You can lie down there."

"I'm staying here, Mom, and please don't make a fuss about it."

"What, and getting marriage counseling from Lael?" I blurted out. "I don't think that's very sensible."

"What's that supposed to mean?" Lael shot back.

"Oh, I don't mean anything, you know that. It's just that you're not exactly in a position to say much, considering you've never bothered getting married."

Lael held her tongue as I should have, especially considering the kids were standing right there. Slamming her pastry bag on the counter, she turned to stomp out of the room. The baby's pacifier fell out of his mouth at precisely that moment. He started to howl.

"I'll get it," I said, feeling contrite. Lael tried to beat me to it, and we collided. Zoe went to help us but slipped on some spilled silver sugar beads. Lael and I both reached for her, but not soon enough. Trying to steady herself, Zoe grabbed on to the flimsy card table, which tipped. As if in slow motion, the cake crashed to the floor.

Zoe gasped.

Tommy murmured, "Oh, man . . ."

Annie shot me a dagger look.

I didn't dare speak.

Even the baby was silent. Not a peep.

"Oh, calm down, everyone," Lael said with her usual aplomb. "It was just a trial run. The wedding's not for two whole weeks."

4

The next morning I woke at dawn. I was in a funk. My
daughter was ruining her life and I had a date with a convicted murderer. Perhaps it was time for a run. People keep
telling me exercise is beneficial. It gets the something flowing. Pheromones? Adrenaline? Something.

I pulled on my ratty blue leggings and a *Testament* T-shirt
Annie had given me featuring the star of the show, the lion-
hearted Fleet Commander Gow. My sneakers, however, were
nowhere to be found. I thought they might be in the car, so
I traipsed across the sopping wet lawn and soaked my socks,
only to remember that I had taken them off at my desk the
day before yesterday.

I tromped back through the house and out the back door,
into the garage that, in a moment of madness, I'd had a couple of Lael's handyman buddies convert into my office. The
guys didn't exactly get the glitter garden theme—Lucite desk,
floors painted apple green and walls hot pink, old Pucci pil-
lows on my whopper of an easy chair—but they pulled it off
in seven weeks, built-in bookshelves and all. Still, I wouldn't

want to be back there during an earthquake. Which meant that working at my computer always felt vaguely life-threatening. Maybe that was a good thing, I don't know.

The shoes were there. So was Mimi the cat, draped across the keyboard like an odalisque. I shooed her off, surely to suffer for it later, and checked my e-mail. There was a message from my editor, Sally, inquiring about my progress. Sly, but not that sly. The woman was obviously starting to shake in her boots. What was she, clairvoyant? For all Sally knew, everything was going fine, just fine. A month ago, she'd read the first twelve chapters and hadn't had any complaints. In fact, she'd raved about the section on Temecula.

Gardner had bought a ranch and settled in Temecula after selling his Hollywood residence in 1936. It was a hunting, fishing, and animals-everywhere kind of place, an outdoors-man's paradise. There was even a pet coyote named Bravo that ESG's buddy Raymond Chandler had been especially fond of. But my editor was allergic to furry things. I think the part that riveted her was Gardner's story about how whenever fellow writers down on their luck showed up in Temecula to borrow money the animals were delighted, but editors, well, when they showed up, the dogs knew to bite them.

I suppose a lot can change in a month. I put Sally's e-mail in my drafts folder, which is where I put everything I don't want to deal with. I keep hoping those messages will simply disappear. Or succumb to bit rot, which sounds so slow and painful.

In my neighborhood, you don't need a Walkman when you go running. A clean outfit is good. A business card, better. In the course of pursuing the ever-elusive goal of physical fitness, I have made the acquaintance of decorators, podiatrists, portrait photographers, and other potentially serviceable types conveniently located within a five-mile radius of my house. But today I kept my head down. And besides, it was barely six A.M. West Hollywood is not a town of early risers. Everyone is either retired, an aspiring actor/ singer/model working the dinner shift, or self-employed. No one emerges until around ten, when the streets become clogged with people heading gamely to the gym, or on their cell phones, cleaning up after their dogs.

I started perspiring after half a mile. Not a good sign. Twenty minutes more and I was sweating like a pig. I turned down a tree-lined street. Rapture. It was shady, almost dark. There was no one around, so I did the unthinkable. I stopped to catch my breath. A lone car cruised down the other side of the street, witness to my shame. The guy inside gave me the eye. I didn't think much of it until he swung a U-turn at the corner and started driving slowly alongside me. Unnerved, I started running again. He stayed with me. I turned at the next corner. He turned, too. Great. Where was everyone? Man, these people were lazy. Home was only two blocks away, but I didn't want him to see where I lived. Alone. And I had left the door unlocked, as usual.

I kept running. Past my house, past my neighbor's house, onto King's Road. He kept following. This was crazy. I was seriously out of breath now. I had a stitch in my side. He was just trying to scare me, I knew that. But it was working. I didn't know what to do. I had no idea. I was afraid to glance his way. Maybe he'd take it as encouragement. There were no alleys to duck into, and all the underground garages along King's had electronic gates that were shut, shut, shut. Finally, I couldn't stop myself. I turned my head. He didn't say a thing. He just gave me a long, lazy smile.

Screw him. There was a minimall half a block away with a Starbucks in it. They'd be open by now. I ran up to Santa Monica, clutching my sides, then crossed against the light. He was stuck on red, but as soon as the light changed, he followed, pulling his beat-up blue Camaro into the parking lot just behind me. I sat down at a table in the corner and watched him get out of the car and come inside. This wasn't happening. He walked right up to me.

"I'm calling the police," I said.

He didn't answer. He went up to the counter and ordered a small cup of coffee. When the girl handed it to him, he mumbled something about changing his mind. He turned to leave, bumping his arm against me on the way out. Hard. That spot would be black and blue by tonight. And no one had noticed a thing. Just another morning in the city of the angels. Nothing out of the ordinary.

I sat there for a while, thinking how easy it is to feel safe when you've never been hurt. Then I picked up a paper someone had left behind and read the comics until I felt a little better, or at least too tired to think anymore, which amounted to the same thing.

I went home and showered until the hot water ran out. I wanted to stay in there, but I had an appointment to keep. It had to be today. Well, it was going to be fine. No one had promised me a walk in the park, but it would be fine.

I considered my wardrobe. According to the visitor handbook I'd downloaded from the Web, conservative attire was recommended. No clothing that in any combination of shades resembled California-issue inmate garb. No law-enforcement or military-type forest green or camouflage-patterned items. No spaghetti straps. No sheer garments. No hats, wigs, or hairpieces, except with prior written approval of the visiting sergeant. No clothing that exposed the chest, genitals, or buttocks. Party poopers.

I wondered what Joseph Albacco would be wearing. Prison blues aren't necessarily blue. I knew. I'd read up on it. They come in orange, red, or white, according to the unit in which the particular prisoner is housed. It helps correctional officers determine if a serial killer, say, isn't where he's supposed to be. That was the principle behind stripes as well, which were worn by convicts well into the first half of the twentieth century. The types of stripes (vertical or horizontal) and their combinations (horizontal on pants, vertical on shirts) likewise signified things like crime committed or time served. It was kind of the reverse of the old saying that clothes make the man.

After mulling it over for a while, I dropped my towel on the floor and put on something that made me feel strong— a brown velvet Chanel suit with lots of white braid trim. I had snagged it from my mother's cousin Drena, who'd bought it at a rummage sale, only to decide it made her look like a three-star general.

She had underestimated the genius of Coco Chanel. That made two of us. I looked less like Patton than a Hostess cupcake, something a convicted felon could polish off in a single bite. Thinking about the creep in the Camaro, I squeezed some gelatinous goo into my hands and slicked my hair into a sadistic ballet-mistress updo. Better. Forbidding. You wouldn't want to mangle a plié within ten yards of me.

Enough with the metaphors. Joseph Albacco, Prisoner #C-36789, currently serving thirty-five to life for murder in the first degree, was waiting. For me.

5

$\mathscr{I}$ knew the court transcript like the back of my hand.

December 13, 1957. It was a Friday. The forecast had predicted rain, but little on that day happened according to plan. By noon, the early-morning clouds had dissipated and the sun was shining. Jean Albacco spent most of the day answering the phone, typing letters, and filing correspondence at the insurance offices of Gilbert, Finster, and Johnson on lower State Street in downtown Ventura, where she had been employed since graduating from high school a year and a half earlier. On December 13, she worked through lunch, having asked her employer, Mr. Douglas Gilbert, if she could leave one hour earlier that evening. It was her first wedding anniversary, and she was preparing a surprise for her husband, Joe.

Jean's coworker and best friend, Miss Madeleine Seaton, remembered Jean being somewhat edgy all day, but that wouldn't have been unusual. Jean was known for being high-strung and particular about things. Miss Seaton recalled her spilling a cup of coffee on a stack of unmailed letters early that morning, and accidentally disconnecting Mr. Gilbert's wife, who had called at 11:00 A.M. to remind her husband about a dentist appointment that afternoon. Perhaps, Miss Seaton speculated, it was just that Jean had errands to do after work and was worried about everything getting done before her husband came home. Joe was expected at approximately 7:15 P.M.

It was only later that everyone realized the day Jean Albacco was murdered had been Friday the thirteenth.

Joseph Albacco Jr. (Class of '55, Ventura City High) worked as a linotype operator at the *Ventura Press,* the area's major weekly. Joe's boss, *Ventura Press* editor and publisher Mr. Anson Burke, remembered December 13 well because he had been preoccupied all day about the looming possibility of a strike. He had meetings with union officials in the morning and an unusual number of phone calls to juggle, as his secretary, Miss Mildred Rose, was out sick. Joe, one of his forty-nine employees, had merited scarcely a thought.

Arriving well before 8:00 A.M., Joe shared a breakfast of doughnuts and coffee with several coworkers. He joked about a baseball game over which he had lost ten dollars the previous night, and complained about an old back injury that seemed to be flaring up. No one at work knew December 13 was his wedding anniversary until reading about it in the paper the following day.

Mr. Thomas Malone, who had known Joe since grade school, worked on the city desk. He and Joe usually bought lunch at the Italian deli on Main and walked through the alley to eat in the park across the street from the San Buenaventura Mission, under the old fig tree. December 13 had been no different. That day they talked about the weather,

Mr. Malone's ailing mother, and the military's increased presence in the county. They also discussed the new freeway, the U.S. 101, which would run from the Conejo Grade to Camarillo, cutting the trip to Los Angeles from five hours to just over two. The paper had been running a series of editorials complaining about how the elevated sections proposed for Ventura proper would block out views and access to the beach in the downtown area.

After lunch, Joe stopped at a phone booth to make a call. It lasted no more than three or four minutes. But, according to Mr. Malone, this was unusual for Joe. There was shouting, and Joe seemed agitated during the short walk back to the office. Despite Mr. Malone's inquiries, Joe wouldn't reveal to whom he had been speaking or the subject of their conversation.

Jean left work at 4:15 P.M. on the dot. On her way out, she wished Miss Seaton a nice weekend and told her that she might have a surprise for her very soon. Miss Seaton testified at trial that Jean's manner was coy, which surprised her, given that Jean was normally a serious sort of girl.

At approximately 4:20 P.M., complaining of a headache, Joe went to see the company nurse, Mrs. Bianca Adair. She gave him two aspirins and sent him home to rest, no follow-up required.

At 4:30 P.M., Jean stopped in at C&M Locksmiths at the corner of Main and Santa Clara. She picked up a set of house keys, explaining that her husband had lost his, and asked after two other keys that weren't yet ready. She chatted amiably with the proprietor, Mr. Lorenzo Calabro, but bustled out when she caught sight of the clock, clearly in a hurry. At approximately 4:40 P.M., she went into the used bookshop on Valdez Alley, browsed in the California section, and purchased a two-volume history of Ventura County. A present for her husband, she explained to Mr. Roger Sorenson, the store manager. On her way to the market on Thompson Boulevard, Jean stopped to chat a moment with a friend, Miss Diana Crisp, who worked at the Be Mine Hair Salon next door. Diana complimented Jean on her suit. Jean laughed and said that she had hidden the receipt from Joe since it wasn't on sale and they were supposed to be saving for a house on a better street. At the market, Jean paid cash for her groceries (a roast, some baking potatoes, and a head of iceberg lettuce), though she had opened a house account just the week before.

At 4:30 P.M., Joe was seen driving above Register Street, heading west, just beyond the county courthouse.

At 5:30 P.M., Jean's neighbor, Mr. Josiah McGruder, a retired plumber, saw Jean approach her house, stop abruptly for a few moments, as if lost in thought, and then go inside. She was loaded down with packages.

At 6:30 P.M., Mr. McGruder thought he heard the screen door swing open at the Albaccos'. He looked out the window and saw a person, whom he could not positively identify, enter the Albacco residence.

At 7:15 P.M., smelling something burning on the stove, Mr. McGruder knocked on the Albaccos' front door. When he got no response, he went around to the back door. He called out and, still getting no response, entered the premises, where he saw the body of Mrs. Albacco on the kitchen floor.

At 7:30 P.M., the police arrived.

At 7:45 P.M., Joseph Albacco came home, with a pack of cigarettes in his hand and dried blood on the cuff of his shirt. He was taken in for questioning, held overnight, and charged, the following morning, with murder in the first degree.

The trial was brief. The cause of death was determined to be blunt trauma to the head. The murder weapon was never found. But that didn't stop the prosecutor. There was trouble in the marriage. Talk of another woman. Joe had left work early for no real reason. That looked bad. There was no sign of forced entry. That looked bad, too. The blood on his shirt tested AB positive—his wife's type. And he had no alibi. No explanation whatsoever of where he had been. It added up. At least, the jury saw it that way. But it was hardly an open-and-shut case.

Sitting in the prison parking lot, too nervous to do anything except pick at the tassels on my suit, I went over the details in my mind again and yet again. Any way you looked at it, there were dozens of lingering questions. What had that frantic phone call been about? If it had been Albacco at the door at 6:30 P.M. that evening, as the prosecution had contended, why had his neighbor been unable to make a positive ID, especially since it wasn't even dark out? And if Albacco had indeed killed his wife, wouldn't he have changed his bloodstained shirt before appearing back at his house at 7:45 P.M.? Why had he been carrying cigarettes when neither he nor Jean was a smoker? Most curious of all was the missing murder weapon. Where was it? I stopped myself short. It was hardly my business. Any of it. Erle Stanley Gardner was my business, and all this case meant to me, all it could ever mean to me, was a chance to get the real dope on an old pro.

Right.

6

$\mathcal{J}$oseph Albacco smiled as he sat down, and I knew right away this would be the strangest conversation of my life.

I smiled back through the thick wall of Plexiglas. A drop of sweat trickled down the inside of my blouse. I wondered if he could see it blazing a trail across the silk. I pulled my jacket tighter around me. I was hot and cold, but colder than I was hot.

"Talk right into the receiver," he said kindly. "The only difference between this and a phone call is we can see each other."

"Oh."

"So, you're Italian. Me, too. There was a Caruso I knew when I was a kid. Ran a grocery store near my house. Any relation?"

"No, I don't think so," I replied. "We're all in New Jersey."

"Except you," he said, grinning.

"Right," I said stupidly.

I had lost control already, probably from the moment I laid eyes on him. Joseph Albacco's hair was silver, thick and coarse, and his face as craggy as a relief map of the Rockies. I had expected something like that: he was a sixty-six-year-old man who had spent most of his life behind bars. But I hadn't expected him to be tall, well over six feet, nor strong—and not from lifting weights, but because that's the way he was made.

I pulled myself together. "Mr. Albacco," I said, clearing my throat, "the warden did explain why I'm here, didn't he?"

"Yes. I understand you're doing some work on Erle Stanley Gardner."

Handsome, too. It spooked me that I noticed. I was supposed to be a neutral observer. No emotions. Cool as a cucumber. That was my whole problem. Even as a kid I'd run fevers so high the doctors wanted to hospitalize me every time I got the flu. It was my mom who was the cool one. I was some sort of mutation.

"That's right," I said self-importantly. "I'm writing a book about him, a biography. And while I was doing research, I came across a letter you wrote him, a long time ago, right after you were . . . incarcerated." That was one of those words I'd never actually used in conversation. "You asked him for help. Do you remember?"

He paused, as if gathering up steam. I thought then that this was a story he had been waiting a long time to tell.

"I remember the day I wrote that letter. Every last detail." The rest came out like a soliloquy.

"I had been here only a few months. I didn't think I was going to make it. I didn't think I would stay sane. I was so angry I'd been punching the wall in my cell for days on end and was starting to make a hole in it. The plaster was loose. Falling in bits. I was afraid they were going to think I was trying to escape. So I panicked. I tried to cover the hole with my pillow, a towel, anything, but it was always there. And so I called the guard to show him. I didn't want to be accused of anything. They thought I was nuts. Totally gone. But I was sent to see the chaplain, not the prison psychiatrist. I don't know why. I cried. I was only twenty years old. I thought I'd be freed any day, and I guess that was the moment it finally dawned on me. That was the day I realized I might never see the ocean again."

"But why had you thought otherwise?" I asked. "You were convicted of first-degree murder, Mr. Albacco. Surely you understood what that meant."

"They didn't have anything on me, not really. But it was an election year. The D.A. had something to prove, and the attorney the court provided was afraid to get in his way. It didn't much matter to me, not at first. I thought it'd all come out in the wash when they found him," he explained. "The person who killed her . . . my wife, I mean." He looked down at a ring on his finger. It looked like a wedding band. I didn't know you could keep those in prison.

And then, softly, "Or that I'd hear something from—"

"From whom?" I asked.

"Not important." He smiled that smile, then shook his head and went on. "You know, Ms. Caruso, what's interesting to me is that the police never did investigate. Never asked anybody a question, not really. They decided I was guilty and that was the end of that. I couldn't say where I had been that night, so I had to be the one responsible."

"So, Erle Stanley Gardner?" I prompted.

"So Erle Stanley Gardner. I wrote him a letter. That same evening. After talking to the chaplain, I knew I needed someone to save me, and no matter how many Hail Marys

I said, it wasn't going to be God. I thought Gardner might be the one."

"Why?"

"It sounds so stupid now. You see, my whole life, I've loved mysteries."

"Me, too!" I exclaimed, horrified at my eagerness.

"Yeah, read every single Perry Mason book, just like every other red-blooded American. Read *Argosy*, too, all that stuff about the Court of Last Resort. Even thought I'd go to law school one day. And I *knew* this man, at least through my family. I thought he'd take me on as a cause. You know, the good kid who's been falsely accused. He'd ask the right questions, do the footwork, and nab the real culprit. Prove me innocent, something like that. I suppose I was arrogant enough, or desperate enough, to think I'd strike him as worth the trouble."

"And you never heard a word from him. That must've been disappointing," I murmured.

"Oh, I did hear from him," Albacco interjected. "The very next week."

I nearly choked. There was no correspondence in the file. Nothing at all.

"Yeah, he called me here at the jail, and we spoke briefly. I was scared out of my wits, of course, but he was encouraging. Patient. Asked me how I was doing and all. We talked about the case, and I gave him Maddy Seaton's phone number. She was Jean's best friend. He thought it'd be worth seeing if she knew anything more about what was going on with Jean those last few months. Something had changed, I knew that. And Maddy and Jean were like sisters. They had no secrets."

"So what did he say when you next spoke?"

"We never spoke again," he said flatly. "That was our one and only conversation. I don't even know if he got in touch with Maddy. And then he abandoned the Court of Last Resort."

"Oh," I said.

"There's not much more to it. So here I am. Here I've been."

I shouldn't be here, I thought to myself. *I should not be here.*

"I'm not an intellectual like you, Ms. Caruso."

"I'm hardly that."

"But if you're alone long enough," he continued, "like I've been these past years, you can't help but think. Constantly. You brood. You wonder. You come up with theories. Theories about everything. I've got a theory about life. It's a maze, full of false starts and wrong turns, blind alleys, dead ends. You know what I'm talking about, Ms. Caruso. You've encountered your share."

I felt myself shivering. It was the sweat.

"There's a path you've got to find, though, and it'll take you right where you were meant to go. I haven't found my path, as it turns out. I know that because this isn't my destination." He looked up. "How about you?"

I was dizzy now. The room was spinning.

"I-I feel somewhat awkward," I stammered, looking down at my hands. I could still see the traces of my own wedding ring. I thought about the day I took it off for good. "I'm afraid I've misled you. I'm here doing research on Erle Stanley Gardner. Trying to get a fix on him. That's all. I'm sorry."

I looked up and our eyes met, and just for that moment I thought I could see the young man he had been—untroubled, in the way of people accustomed to being liked. I had never been untroubled a day in my life, never felt that kind of ease in my own skin. I wondered what it would feel like. And what kind of emotional bruising this man must have taken after all these years.

"Maybe I can help," I heard myself saying. "Maybe I could ask a question or two. I have some more research to do in Ventura anyway."

"You're not obliged," he said. "I didn't mean to railroad you."

"You didn't. I'd be doing it for my book."

And at that moment, I actually thought I would be.

On the way out, I went to see the chaplain as promised. Our visit was brief. Someone was using his office so we met in the chapel. This was unfortunate because houses of worship, even those inside houses of detention, tend to make me feel guilty. This meant I'd be calling my mother back tonight, broken in spirit (which is how she likes me best), and maybe even second-day air-mailing her a box of See's Scotchmallow bars, her favorite candy.

Father Herlihy was one of those ancient Irishmen with a nose the size and hue of a pomegranate. A massive fellow, who seemed to be suffering from gout but beaming all the while (hey, he had it better than his parishioners), he rose from the front pew so slowly I didn't know if he'd make it without toppling over. I offered my arm, which he took gratefully. Then he promptly sat back down. I sat down next to him, directly opposite the pulpit, which was incongruously (given the crime-stained setting) ornamented with bas-relief angels.

With a brusqueness his appearance belied, Father Herlihy asked, "Joseph Albacco is a wronged man, and I'd like to know, Ms. Caruso, as a good Catholic, how will you be assisting him?" I have to admit I was speechless after that one. The last time I'd been a good Catholic Richard Nixon had been president. And a good Quaker.

"Ms. Caruso," he repeated, "something must be done. And soon. Mr. Albacco has a parole hearing scheduled in less than three weeks, and it has to go differently this time. He has suffered long enough."

"For something he did or didn't do?"

He glared at me. "My dear, I made your visit here possible because I have an interest in seeing justice done. Joseph and I came to Tehachapi the same year, soon after it was rebuilt, and we have grown old together. Sadly for him, I might add, because our friendship has come at the expense of his freedom."

"I don't understand why he hasn't been released after all this time."

"He received a sentence of thirty-five years to life. There is no guarantee of parole."

"But it doesn't make sense."

He was impatient now. "There are flaws in the system."

"Such as?"

"To be awarded parole, you must admit culpability. You must accept responsibility and evince regret. This puts those who have been wrongly convicted in a rather difficult position."

"How do you know Joseph didn't kill his wife?"

"You're a smart woman," he answered. "And given that, surely you understand that sometimes the truth never comes out, for whatever reason. Because we are too ashamed to acknowledge our guilt. Because we are trying to prevent others from bearing our pain. Because the forces of evil have too much at stake in keeping it buried. Nonetheless, it remains the truth."

I stopped him right there. "I don't mean to be disrespectful, but I can see you're not telling me everything you know."

"Do I need to remind you that I'm a priest?" he retorted. "I am hardly in a position to divulge privileged information, nor to bring the facts of Jean Albacco's murder to light. Joseph thought Erle Stanley Gardner might be in such a position. But that was a long time ago. Now the burden has fallen to you."

"To me?"

"You are a Catholic. Surely you will understand what I'm trying to say. Joseph Albacco has not committed a mortal sin. Not yet. But for years now, he's been holding on to a long rope, and he's come to the end of it. Listen to what I'm saying to you, Ms. Caruso: there will not be another parole hearing."

The man was speaking in riddles. I was lost. Had Joseph been threatening suicide? Was that what he was trying to tell me? My god.

"Father Herlihy," I finally said, "I'd like to help, truly I would, but it sounds like you have too much faith in me."

"My dear," he said, "it sounds like you don't have enough."

7

On the long drive home, Father Herlihy's words reverberated in my ears. The din was deafening, and I didn't like it. I thought about Joseph Albacco and how desperate he must be. About how big his cell was and when he had last gotten a phone call or eaten a good meal. I thought about his theory of life and about the sorry fact that I had theories about everything under the sun except the things that really mattered.

I fell asleep the minute my head hit the pillow. My ex was always amazed at how I could do that. If he got to talking about James Fenimore Cooper, I could fall asleep even before my head hit the pillow.

I'm a deep sleeper. Comatose. Known to drool. So when the phone rings in the middle of the night, it isn't a good thing. Call it my morbid temperament, but I always assume it means someone has died. The only thing I hate more is being woken up by the doorbell. This means that not only do I wake up frantic, but I have to compose my features into some semblance of normality, and before coffee. It's inhuman.

The doorbell chimed. It was going to be one of those days. I bolted upright and peeled my eyes open. I was wearing the contacts you were supposed to be able to leave in for a week. Another case of false advertising. I pulled on my robe, cursing. It wasn't until I stumbled toward the front door, patting my hair down from its Don King state, that I realized it was not, in fact, the middle of the night. According to the kitchen clock, it was 9:05 A.M.

After looking through the peephole, I opened the door to the woebegone figure of my son-in-law, clutching a pair of plush pink slippers in his large hands.

"Hi," I said.

"Oh, I'm sorry. I woke you up," he said.

"No, no. I've been up for hours, cleaning," I replied quickly. An obvious lie, given the state of the living room, but I expect he appreciated the courtesy.

"Come on in," I said. "I'll make us some coffee."

Wrapping my robe tighter around me, I strode purposefully into the kitchen. The prospect of caffeine gave me strength. I knew this wasn't going to be easy.

Vincent followed me like a puppy and sat down at the table, still holding the slippers.

"These are Annie's," he explained. "She puts them on the minute she wakes up. Her feet get cold. I knew she'd miss them."

"I'll give them to her when I see her," I said gently, pouring what was left of the Hawaiian Hazelnut into the filter and flipping the switch.

"Where is she?" he asked, looking toward the hallway. "Isn't she here?"

"No," I answered with a half smile. "She went to Lael's."

He smiled back. "Oh, that makes sense. It's no big deal. She probably just didn't want to upset you, that's all."

It was classic Vincent. Here he was offering me a shoulder to cry on instead of the other way around.

"You're sweet to say so, Vincent. But I'm more concerned about the two of you. What is this all about?"

Vincent fidgeted uncomfortably. I could tell he was torn between the fear of being disloyal to Annie and the need to talk.

"Listen, Vincent, Annie and I spoke on Friday, but none of it made sense. I love my daughter, but I don't understand why she's acting like this. Is there anything I can do to help?"

"What are you talking about, Cece?" he cried. "She's not acting like anything! Annie isn't that kind of person! You of all people should know that!" He jumped to his wife's defense with a ferocity that was pretty surprising given she was sleeping with another man.

Vincent picked up his coffee, poured in unholy quantities of cream and sugar, and walked over to the couch, trying to regain his composure.

"Look, you obviously don't get it. I'm the one who's responsible for everything that's gone wrong. I'm the one who's a liar, a fool, and a coward. I'm the one who's ruined our lives." He looked up at me, his eyes filling with tears.

I wasn't expecting dramatics. Not from him. Vincent was calm personified, the Buddhist monk type. Once, I had called Vincent and Annie in the middle of the night, hysterical, convinced my house was being taken over by a colony of enormous, prehistoric rats. Vincent came over with a broom and talked me down. I was a city kid—how was I supposed to know those were opossums?

"What are you talking about, Vincent? You're scaring me," I said.

"I scared your daughter, too. That's why she turned to someone else, and then just left. I can hardly blame her. She thought she knew me, and then she found out I was somebody else."

"Okay," I said, playing along for the moment. "Who are you?"

"I'm the father of a kid who's never laid eyes on me, that's who," he answered, and walked out the door.

I poured my cold Hawaiian Hazelnut down the drain and headed straight back to bed.

I woke up for the second time that day just before noon, when my gardener rang the bell.

"Cece, four dead snails!" Javier exclaimed, shoving the evidence in my face. I was finding it hard to revel in our triumph at just that moment, given my empty stomach and the news that I was sort of a grandma.

"Wonderful, Javier," I said.

"No problem," he replied, though I had clearly burst his bubble. "I thought you'd be happier. Say," he said, grinning, "were you still sleeping?"

"Oh, you know us creative types. We can work in our pajamas if we want to. You should try it sometime."

He didn't much like the joke, which came out nastier than I'd intended. It was just that I didn't appreciate his insinuation that I was sleeping the day away, which, of course, I was. But no more. I felt like hell. But this, too, would pass. I took a deep breath. I reached way down into myself. I straightened my spine, sucked in my gut, and produced a horrific, pageant-worthy smile. I turned on the shower. I could do this. I could trust Annie and Vincent to work it out. I could try living my own life for once. And it was a gorgeous day. A perfect day, in fact, for a drive to Ventura.

Half an hour later, I was spanking clean and bedecked in a powder-blue 1940s halter dress and matching patent-leather ankle straps. They gave me blisters only that first time. I opened a can of food for Mimi, poured out a bowl of Buster's low-fat kibble, and emerged into the dazzling sunlight. Without being asked, Javier stopped pulling up weeds and moved his truck out of the driveway. I was off.

It was bumper-to-bumper traffic all the way over Laurel Canyon—me and a phalanx of Valley folk heading for the fabled land of hospitality and convenient parking. It took about twenty-five minutes to get to the 101, but from there it would be a straight shot to Ventura, an hour and a half, max. I'm not exactly a Formula One driver, but I am an old hand at the 101, thanks to a torrid affair I had a while back with a beefy LAPD detective who, like so many of his buddies, lived in the nether reaches of Simi Valley. When I asked him why they were willing to put up with that kind of commute, he said the guys wanted out, way the heck out, after a long day of cleaning up other people's messes. And I'm talking messy messes. Still, there were all those bored skinheads out in the exurbs. I preferred the local gangbangers, not that I was friends with any, of course.

I drove past the San Fernando Valley's endless gated communities, with their faux-tile roofs and faux Spanish names—El Petunia Gargantunita, Los Picadoritos Machos, etc. Then I hit Calabasas, where the horse people live, then Thousand Oaks, home to a passel of big box stores—Ikea, Best Buy—and not much else. From there, it was on to Oxnard, where the air smells like fertilizer. Lots of lettuce in Oxnard.

Just when I started to get that desperate, been-in-the-car-for-too-long feeling, the Pacific Ocean came up on my left, a bolt of blue stretching as far as the eye could see. That meant the next stop would be Ventura. I took the Main Street exit, veering away from the ocean toward the historic downtown district, located at the base of the foothills between the Ventura and Santa Clara Rivers. Once, those hills had been covered with sprays of gray sage, blue lupine, and, east of town, golden mustard. It must have been something. Passengers arriving by stagecoach back in the 1860s and 1870s would have been lured by the area's great beauty, the promise of rich soil and balmy weather, and business opportunities ripe for the picking.

Me, the girl in the silver Camry, I'd been lured by the possibility of answering someone's prayers.

8

*I*t was the Spanish colonizers of Alta California who, early in the eighteenth century, gave Ventura its name, which derives from the Spanish word *buenaventura,* meaning "good fortune" or "good luck." So how come it always took me forever to find a parking space? Good luck was definitely on the wane these days. In fact, as I ambled down Main Street I encountered a world of pain, with every possible disease or misfortune represented by a thrift shop of its own: Child Abuse and Neglect, Pet Abandonment, Battered Women, Disabled Veterans, etc. Not to mention it was freezing, which isn't exactly a plus in late summer in a beach town. I hadn't come equipped for the elements, so I slipped into a shop and bought a sweatshirt with a duck in sunglasses on the front. You should've seen the ones I didn't choose.

Aside from the thrift shops, Main Street boasted your usual assortment of souvenir shops, stocked with suntan lotion and other good-weather paraphernalia; a few high-end garden shops selling marble sundials, hand-painted trellises, and cutesy signs that said things like, I'M THE KING OF THE CASTLE UNTIL THE QUEEN COMES HOME; and some genuine oddities, like the American flag and cutlery shop. I spent a while in the angel store, mesmerized by the wall full of angel-embossed Post-it note prayers. It was amazing how many people had sons in jail.

Erle Stanley Gardner, however, was the growth industry around here. If I had deeper pockets, I could have stocked a library full of first edition Perry Masons in five minutes flat. Storefronts were plastered with posters advertising Erle Stanley Gardner walking tours and Erle Stanley Gardner guidebooks, and if you were so inclined you could even buy something called "Podunk" candy at the local chocolatier, made from Erle Stanley Gardner's very own recipe. It stuck to your teeth, just like honeycomb.

As important as ESG was to Ventura, Ventura had been to ESG. Though he'd lived there for only fifteen years (from 1915 to 1917, and again from 1921 to 1933), it was in Ventura that he'd established his law practice and encountered many of the offbeat characters and bizarre situations that had worked their way into his mysteries. It was in Ventura that he'd developed the talent for cross-examination for which Perry Mason would become famous. And it was in Ventura that he'd written his first stories for the pulps, pounding them out with two fingers in a back room at his house on Buena Vista Street.

In Ventura, too, Gardner had met Jean Bethell, his second wife, the original Della Street. According to the story, he used to like to go to the Pierpont Inn, on Sanjon, to celebrate his courtroom victories. Jean had been working as the dining room hostess when he'd come in with a crook he was defending. Immediately smitten, he'd asked her if she'd like to be his secretary. She'd said she already had a job, but that her sister, Peggy, needed one. Peggy wound up going to work for Gardner, and so did another sister, Ruth. Jean eventually followed family tradition. Later, she broke it by marrying her boss.

I pulled out my steno pad. I'd arrived at my destination, the gray Renaissance Revival building located at the corner of Main and California. According to the brass plaque affixed to its exterior, this was HISTORICAL POINT OF INTEREST #86. Constructed in 1926 at the height of the Ventura oil boom, it was the tallest building in town and had the first elevator in the entire county. It was also the birthplace of Perry Mason. Well, just about. The first draft of the first Perry Mason book, *The Case of the Velvet Claws,* was narrated into a dictaphone at Gardner's house, but it was here, in the third-floor law offices of Orr, Gardner, Drapeau, and Sheridan, that it was actually typed up. It was important I get things like that right. One slip could mean dozens of letters. Hundreds, if I was lucky enough.

I decided to go in and snoop around. My trusty editor, Sally, kept insisting the book needed more "picturesque details." Fine.

The foyer was short on charm. There was dust everywhere and piped-in Muzak, but the walls boasted some choice memorabilia: a Xerox of a 1961 issue of *Look* magazine, promising to "spill all" about TV's Perry Mason, and a framed photograph of ESG himself, looking remarkably like a bespectacled Raymond Burr.

Burr had originally been asked to read for the part of the district attorney. But Gardner, who happened to be on the set the day of Burr's audition, had taken one look at him and gasped, "That's Perry Mason!" Gardner later complained that Burr was "cow-eyed" instead of "granite-hard," which I thought was tremendously unfair. Cows have nice eyes. And there was no getting around the fact that it was Raymond Burr who made the show a megahit. Like no one before or since, he embodied the notion that there were jobs worth doing and doing well. Plus, he drove the newest, shiniest cars, thanks to the succession of Detroit automakers who sponsored the series during the course of its nine-season run.

I scanned the building directory. These days, the offices in question were occupied by a La-Z-Boy rep and a multimedia company. Sounded like picturesque detail to me. I made my way up the narrow, twisting wooden staircase, admiring the pebbled-glass doors framed in wood, with their old-time transoms above. The third floor appeared deserted. And dustier than the foyer.

I started scribbling. This was unmistakably the template for Perry Mason's legendary setup: the corner of a suite of rooms that included two reception areas, a law library, a stenographic area, and a pair of private offices. The only difference was that first thing in the morning Perry would toss his fedora onto a bust of Blackstone, while ESG was said to have settled for an ordinary hatrack.

"Hello," I called out. "Anybody here?" No answer.

There wasn't much in the main reception area except a scratched wooden desk and a swivel chair with a stack of Ventura phonebooks piled on its torn leather seat. I put them on the floor and sat down.

"Oh, Perry," I said, channeling Della. "Another courtroom

triumph! Let's go out for dinner and drinks, shall we? I'll just straighten the seams on my stockings, and we'll be off. Oh, Paul Drake? Your unrivaled man on the ground? I'm afraid he won't be able to join us. He's got a headache."

I was blushing, in character, when all of a sudden I heard a crash. I leapt up, sending my steno pad flying. Then I heard a scream. I ran for the stairs like the coward I was.

"Dear me, I didn't mean to scare you," said a voice from out of nowhere.

I turned around. An older gentleman had poked his nose out of one of the back rooms.

"Those La-Z-Boy catalogs get heavier every year. Dropped one on my toe just now. Didn't mean to be yelping like a pup."

That was my cue to go. It was seven P.M., getting dark, and I was exhausted. Nobody was expecting me back home, so I decided to find a cute little inn, the kind you read about in the Sunday travel section. I'd have a glass of white wine, snuggle under the down comforter, and watch a cable movie. And no one would be around to chasten me about raiding the minibar. To hear my ex tell it, my minibar proclivities were more deleterious to our marriage than his sexual infidelity and emotional abuse combined. Go figure.

As luck would have it, there was a room with a courtyard view at the Beau Rivage, a small, European-style hotel tucked around the corner from ESG's office building. The clerk was a sweet kid who couldn't wrap his head around the fact that I didn't have a suitcase. Spontaneity was apparently dead in Ventura.

As soon as I got up to the room, I threw my clothes on the floor and flopped onto the bed naked, but only after having stripped off the attractive floral coverlet. My mother had once told me that hotel cleaning people took special glee in wiping their dirty shoes on the bedspreads, which they never washed. My mother was full of urban legends that, sadly, I seemed unable to expunge from my consciousness.

Buster and Mimi. I almost forgot about those guys. A quick call to the ladies would take care of that. They knew I hid a key in a flowerpot in my front garden. "They" being the ladies, not the pets.

"Where exactly are you, dear?" asked Marlene, who had been known professionally as Hibiscus. Her voice sounded shaky. I suspected that cocktail hour had begun.

"In Ventura, doing some research on the book."

"Oh, Ventura. How I adore the sea air. Now, don't you worry a thing about your babies. Lois and I will take care of them."

"Thanks so much, Marlene. See you tomorrow." Hibiscus and her sister, Lois, a.k.a. Jasmine, were on the job. Now for the minibar.

With visions of Toblerone dancing in my head, I got up, idly took a look out the window, locked eyes with a little boy in a dark suit, and dropped to the floor. A mere twenty feet below, in the bougainvillea-draped courtyard, a wedding party was under way—ring bearer, bride, groom, string quartet, the whole shebang. Why hadn't that front-desk kid warned me?

Slowly, I rose to my knees and peeked out the window. I was clobbered by pink. Pink roses, pink tablecloths, a towering pink cake. The ring bearer was whispering something to a mother-of-the-bride type clad in pink brocade. She looked up to my second-floor window and saw me. I gave her a sheepish little wave, but she was not amused. The wedding planner had not prepared her for the naked woman. That was supposed to happen at the bachelor party.

Time to learn that things don't always work out.

At my wedding I was supposed to wear a sarong and carry fuschia orchids tied with raffia. There was going to be tiki music and torches and a suckling pig with an apple in his mouth. It may have been a bit fey for Asbury Park, I can see that now. In any case, I was vetoed. I carried a tight ball of white roses and wore a white gown that poufed in every conceivable direction. White represents purity, and the mothers had a point to make.

I sank back down to the floor, crawled the rest of the way to the minibar, and opened it. God help me, it was filled with healthy snacks: protein bars, electrolyte-enhanced H_2O, gorp sorts of things, the stuff you put in backpacks when you're hiking and swear never to touch once you're back within spitting range of a 7-Eleven. Catching sight of my thirty-nine-year-old body in the mirror, I decided I needed nourishment of any kind like I needed a hole in the head. I crawled back to the bed, slid between the sheets, and fell fast asleep. I dreamed I married Perry Mason.

9

The morning sun hit me square in the face. Bad Cece wanted to hit it back. But good Cece got up, made a pot of scary hotel-room coffee, and scrounged around under the night table for the yellow pages. Gilbert, Finster, and Johnson, Licensed Insurance Brokers, lower State Street. There it was. Unbelievable. The company where Jean Albacco and Maddy Seaton had worked was still open for business. And times must've been good—they'd taken out a full-page ad, which included a picture of their award-winning sales team, smiling their guts out.

I checked out and headed over to State Street. The roads were full of potholes. I sloshed coffee from my travel mug down the front of my wilted blue halter dress, but given that every day was now casual Friday, I figured I wouldn't look any worse than anybody else.

There were WET PAINT signs all over the front of the building. With my track record, I made sure to be extra careful when I swung open the mint-green double doors. I walked across a plush but ugly rug to a long, low desk. Sitting behind it was a large middle-aged woman, flanked on the right by a younger version of herself and on the left by an older version of the same. All three wore stonewashed jeans, pink Lacoste shirts, and glasses with shiny gold frames. They were deep in conversation. The young one was furiously taking notes. She seemed to be serving her apprenticeship.

The trio looked up and flashed those award-winning smiles. "May we help you?" asked the middle one, clearly their leader.

"Yes," I said. "I'm trying to find someone who worked here some time ago, a Madeleine Seaton. I'm wondering if she's still here, by any chance, or if you could tell me how I might locate her."

A conference ensued. The old one spoke up.

"I knew Maddy Seaton quite well. She worked here forever, nice lady and all, but"—she blushed furiously—"well, I'm afraid she died last year."

Shoot.

"Are you a friend? Or is it business? Might I answer a question for you?" The middle one reestablished control.

"Well," I said, thinking fast, "I'm investigating a crime involving another person who worked here in the fifties, a Jean Albacco, and I thought Miss Seaton could help me out. Nothing to do with company business, of course," I said quickly, sensing their alarm. "Is there possibly someone else who might've worked with them back then whom you could help me contact?"

"Is it an official investigation?" the young one piped up. The older women stared at her, nonplussed.

"Well, yes," I blustered. It was official, sort of. Biographies are official. I had a publisher. I had gotten an advance.

Thinking it over, the old one said, "I was going to suggest

Mr. Gilbert, but he's so busy with his retirement party. Maybe the Johnsons? No, not the Johnsons. Try Jean's sister, Theresa Flynn. She lives on Chase and Centennial, over by the high school."

"Yoo-hoo, over here!" said the middle one, peeved at having lost the spotlight. "I'll jot down her number and address for you." She presided over the biggest card file I had ever seen. Must have been a custom job.

"And please remind her we've still got Jean's lockbox in our safe," she added. "We must insist she come pick it up. She's responsible for it, and we've sent her so many letters on the matter. For years now."

The old one giggled nervously at this. Then they all did.

Did Perry Mason ever have it this easy?

The eye that studied me through the peephole was green and very large. Jean Albacco's sister. I guess I passed muster because she opened the door—halfway. She had lots of fair hair and just enough of a smile. I liked her on sight.

"Yes?" she queried, patting her Gibson girl puff into place for the visitor.

Unfortunately, I didn't have any subterfuges planned, so I proceeded with the truth.

"Mrs. Flynn," I said, "we haven't met, but I'm Cece Caruso and—"

"Cece who?" she asked.

"Caruso!" I bellowed. "Like the opera singer!" Too bad I was tone-deaf.

As Mrs. Flynn took that in, I continued, more soberly, "I'm doing some research on a book of local interest, and I'd be really interested in chatting with you for a few minutes, if you have the time." I handed her my robin's-egg blue card, which I had designed myself to resemble a Tiffany's box. I found it sort of embarrassing now, but I'd made the horrible mistake of ordering a thousand.

"Oh, please come in, Miss Caruso," she said, smiling broadly. "I'm a widow. I've got lots of time. I'm an author, too," she said. "A short book on Wordsworth, long ago. I used to teach English literature. I don't miss grading papers, not one whit, but I do miss the conversations. Sit down, dear," she said, gesturing toward the sofa. "I've just made a pot of tea."

The living room was small but graciously appointed—an upright piano with yellowed keys, a well-worn Victorian settee covered in burgundy sateen, a needlepoint pillow, an etched-glass vase, a framed print of some boaters, one good side chair. There seemed to be just one of everything, in fact, as if anything more would be somehow profligate.

I admired the roll-top desk in the corner.

"It was my sister Jean's desk," Mrs. Flynn explained, emerging from the kitchen with our tea and a plate of butter cookies. "Actually, she inherited it from our grandmother, and I inherited it from her. It was a wedding gift from my grandfather's employer. Extravagant, don't you think? But my grandfather was an excellent worker. Forty-five years at the same job."

I took a sip of tea. Then a bite of cookie. Then I cleared my throat. "Actually, Mrs. Flynn, it's your sister I'd like to talk about."

Her puff drooped. She batted at it nervously. She was wearing a pretty ruby ring.

"Let me explain," I persisted—cruelly, I suppose. "I'm writing a book about the crime writer Erle Stanley Gardner. You know, the one who wrote all the Perry Mason books?"

"Yes, I know. He's our local celebrity."

"Anyway, my research put me in touch with your sister's husband, Joe, who once knew him. I'm trying to find out more about their relationship—Gardner and your brother-in-law's—and why Gardner would have tried to help him."

"Help him? Why on earth would Joe have needed help? He killed a young woman with her whole life ahead of her! My sister was the one who needed help."

"But that's just it. Can we be sure Joe was responsible for her death? I don't think Erle Stanley Gardner was convinced."

"Miss Caruso, let me tell you something before you get in over your head. You've been fooled by that man. Don't feel too bad about it. It's not entirely your fault. He took us all in. He could charm a snake, my dear, always could. Tell me, does he still have that smile?"

I could feel my cheeks redden. But this wasn't about me. I couldn't let it be.

"Did he charm your sister, Mrs. Flynn?"

"Oh, that smile, those beautiful eyes, those beautiful words. He swept her right off her feet. She wasn't easy, my sister. She had a difficult childhood. Our father drank too much. And our mother looked the other way. Lace-curtain Irish. We had to be perfect little ladies. Jean couldn't stand that. She went through some rough patches."

I sipped tea, and she talked about her dead sister.

"Jean was a good girl. She really was. But she always felt she was a disappointment to everyone, making one mistake after another, never living up to her potential."

"That must have been difficult."

"It was. For me, too. She used to see everything I accomplished as an attack on her, as part of some grand plan to humiliate her. But it wasn't like that. Not at all. I loved my sister dearly."

"I can see that."

"Joe changed everything. He worked some kind of magic on her. He made her feel special. And she *became* special. She truly did. She turned herself around. We didn't understand at first, how it all happened. It was right after his mother died that they got serious. Maybe he was vulnerable, maybe he saw something in her the rest of us didn't. Oh, she was pretty, Jean was, and smart as can be. But unpolished, not the kind everybody thought he'd wind up with."

"From what I understand, Joe wasn't exactly born with a silver spoon in his mouth."

"True. But he was on his way up, and everyone knew it. Jean knew it, too. She was sure they could make something of their lives, if only they stuck together. She wanted to be someone, you see. To show everyone. But it was all for nothing," Mrs. Flynn said, her smile dissolving.

"Didn't you ever question his guilt?" I asked, hoping she'd throw me a crumb.

She looked away, as if to even acknowledge the question would be a betrayal.

Finally, she said in a low voice, "I did, at first. I didn't want to believe it. It hardly seemed possible that such a thing could happen, that this boy we all admired so much could be responsible for something so awful." She grabbed hold of the arm of the sofa, as if she needed to steady herself.

I should have stopped her from going on, but I had to know.

"I went to see him in jail that first night, Miss Caruso," she said, her eyes looking into mine now. "He was devastated. It was as if his soul had up and left his body. I was frightened—he wasn't moving, wasn't speaking. I worried about him, I did, but the evidence just seemed to mount." Her voice rose. "And who else could have done it? Tell me. Who could have wanted to harm her? It was the only explanation. The police insisted. It's always the husband."

I wasn't about to convince her that there were dozens of other scenarios that could have played out that night. This was the story she'd chosen to believe. I was ready to give up when she caught me off guard.

"Then I found the scrap of paper. It changed everything. Any doubts I may have harbored about Joe's guilt were gone forever."

Mrs. Flynn was a refined woman, but not one to equivocate. She walked over to the roll-top desk, opened the bottom drawer, and took out a very small, very yellowed piece of paper. It was crumbling at the edges.

"Read what it says."

" 'Meredith Allan. MI6-7979.' " I looked up. "I'm afraid I don't understand."

She sighed. "Maddy Seaton, Jean's best friend, told me Jean suspected Joe of having an affair. The police as much as guessed that anyway. That's usually how it goes. But they couldn't find any proof. That was only because they didn't look hard enough. I found that scrap of paper stuck to the bottom drawer of Jean's desk a few years ago, when I was cleaning it out. The police must've missed it all those years ago when they searched the house after she'd been killed. I had to peel it off the wood. It's Joe's handwriting, you see. And Meredith Allan was the richest, most beautiful girl in town. Joe fell in love with her—how could he help it?—and murdered my sister to be with her."

10

I am a biographer. I understand people the way secretaries understand file folders and doctors understand femurs. Okay, that's ludicrous. A file folder is a file folder any way you look at it, and ditto for a femur, but you'd have to be deluded, really gone, to think a person, any person, could ever really understand another. About as likely as turning base metals into gold.

Still, it's what I do. Given which you'd think I'd have some kind of feel for human nature. Woman's intuition, at least. It *is* my birthright. But as I drove away from Theresa Flynn's house, I had to wonder. Had I been dead wrong? What kind of man was Joseph Albacco, really? Had he been so in love with this Meredith Allan that he'd kill his wife for her?

That name, Meredith Allan. It sounded so familiar. It was an ordinary kind of name. Meredith Allan could've been somebody I went to school with back in Jersey, somebody who'd blackballed me from the cheerleading squad. Or a bank manager who'd denied me a loan. There'd been a lot of those. Had that name come up in the transcript? I didn't think so. Something was nagging at me. And I couldn't help feeling that someone was playing me for a fool. What about Vincent—Vincent, the soul of kindness? Was it possible I had misjudged him, too?

As I merged onto the 101, I pulled out my phone book and dialed Annie at work, almost plowing into a tour bus in the process. Well, Gardner had been a bad driver, too. Worse than me. He'd smashed a brand-new Model T Ford right through the garage of his first Ventura house. I'd visited the spot on a previous trip. There hadn't been all that much to see. It'd been turned into a Mexican restaurant. Killer margaritas, though.

Unfortunately, Annie wasn't at work, though they had expected her that morning and had left dozens of messages because—hello!—they were shooting tomorrow, and the gold facade of the alien ziggurat was hideous, and if I got ahold of her, would I tell her to please, please, call Vanessa? I tried her at Lael's, but there was no answer. Then I called her at home and got the machine. I waited for the beep.

"Annie, it's Mom. Vincent stopped by yesterday. I'm trying to mind my own business, but I think we need to talk, sweetie—"

"Mom, don't hang up!"

"I'm here."

"Sorry, I was out in the garden, weeding."

Annie's garden meant everything to her. It always had. When she was in kindergarten, her class did a unit on plants. Most of the other kids could barely manage to send up a pea shoot. She grew peas galore, plus two twelve-foot sunflowers she decided were husband and wife. We documented them with Polaroids. Annie's tastes were simpler now. A thriving bean tepee was cause for celebration. A patch of mutant, colorless watermelons, equally thrilling. She got it from me, though I've always been more interested in aesthetics than organics. To which end I've learned, under Javier's expert tutelage, to love and respect pesticides. I could never admit this to Annie. Watering, mulching, fertilizing, composting, harvesting, battling pests via alternative means—all were religious sacraments to her.

Before she could get a word in edgewise, I told her I'd be there in an hour with a quart of her favorite veggie chili and hung up. She and Vincent had discovered a rickety stand deep in Topanga Canyon run by an old hippie who claimed that Jim Morrison was one of her customers (still) and that she had invented scented candles. Her chili was delicious, so who was I to argue?

Then I remembered something I'd forgotten to mention to Theresa Flynn. I was on Pacific Coast Highway, waiting for a green light, and ostensibly less of a threat. I dialed the number and she answered with a wan hello. After thanking her again for the tea and cookies, I told her that the secretaries at the insurance company had made me promise to remind her about her sister's lockbox. Sighing audibly, she told me that on innumerable occasions she had explained to them and their myriad predecessors that she had no key and therefore no use for the thing, not to mention no place to put anything so heavy. But she promised to look into it and apologized for troubling me.

I hit the gas. How odd. Your sister is murdered, all that's left of her is one lousy lockbox, and you don't move heaven and earth to get it? You just let it sit around for almost half a century, collecting dust? Maybe Mrs. Flynn didn't want to know what was inside. Maybe she'd had enough surprises. Suddenly I felt very sorry for her. She'd sounded weak and tired. I planned right then not to get old. Older.

By the time I got to Annie's, the Kombucha mushroom tea was ready. Lucky me. I called her place Tarzan's Treehouse because it was smack in the middle of what felt like a jungle, swinging vines and all. We sat outside under a canopy of Chusan palms with yellow flowers that tickled my nose, at least partially distracting me from the poisonous taste of the tea.

"It's also know as 'Miracle Fungus,'" Annie said.

"It's a miracle I'm drinking it," I said under my breath.

"I heard that. It's brewed from a symbiotic culture of bacteria and yeast. If you say 'SCOBY,' everyone knows what you mean."

"Rikes, Shaggy! It's a rhost!"

Annie always ignored my pop-culture references. She had no use for such things.

"Mom, I've never seen you look so wrinkled."

"That's not a very nice thing to say. I thought dappled sunlight was supposed to be flattering."

"No, I mean your dress."

"I've grown very attached to this dress. It may well become my new uniform. No more fuss. You just pull out the blue halter dress, and you're set. And on chilly mornings, you accessorize with the duck sweatshirt."

"What are you talking about?"

"Never mind, sweetie. Have you called back the people at work? They're frantic. The alien ziggurat looks hideous."

"Thanks for the update."

"Annie."

"I'll deal with them later."

"Fine."

"So Vincent told you everything."

"Not exactly."

She picked up her garden shears and started to pace.

"It all started two Saturdays ago. Remember, that day it was so hot? I decided to stay in and organize the filing cabinet. Little Miss Perfect."

She lopped the heads off two perfectly acceptable daylilies.

"There were tons of papers and old bills and stuff, and I was being ruthless about throwing it all away. I filled up every trash can in the house. And then I came across this letter, tucked way in the back, near the deed to the house and the pink slips for the cars. A letter addressed to Vincent."

Two more daylilies down.

"I had no idea what it was doing there, so I read it, thinking nothing of it, that it was probably just more junk."

"And it wasn't."

"It was from this woman, Roxana. Vincent had had an affair with her before he met me. I knew all about her—she was an artist, she left town abruptly, a real flake. Never took her responsibilities seriously, that kind of thing. It was no big deal, their romance, or so I had always thought. As it turned out, after they split up, she found out she was pregnant. She had a son."

"I can't believe this."

"She never told Vincent. Not a word. She was already out of his life, they had never been in love, she thought it would be better to raise the boy on her own. She went down to Mexico, tried some different things, and then she changed her mind. She said her son had a right to know his father. She had been wrong to keep something like this to herself. So she tracked Vincent down, wrote him this letter, and asked him to call or write so they could figure out what to do."

"Well, what happened?"

"That's the thing, Mom," Annie said, starting to cry. "I could have handled this. I could have loved Vincent's son. He could've been a part of our family."

"He still can, Annie."

"I don't think so."

"But why?"

"The letter was dated a year ago. It sat in our house for one entire year, and Vincent never called this woman. He was afraid."

"Afraid of what? Of being a father? Vincent is great with kids."

"Afraid of *me*. Of what I'd say. What kind of monster does he think I am? How could he know me, really know me, and think abandoning his son would be something I'd expect him to do?"

"Did you talk to him about it?"

"I don't need to. I'm done with him, Mom. There's no excuse for this. I wish him well, I really do, but he doesn't know me like I thought he did. And I don't know him anymore."

"So you're auditioning replacements?"

"It wasn't like that."

"Oh, no? It sounds like you gave up on him as much as he gave up on you."

Ignoring that last comment, she gave me an empty smile and headed back into the house, calling over her shoulder, "Let yourself out, okay?"

I did, realizing only when I was halfway home that I had never even bothered to ask the name of Vincent's little boy.

11

$\mathcal{I}$t had been four whole days since I'd had my last Gelson's fix, so I stopped in on my way home from Annie's to pick up a Chinese chicken salad to go. It was only a quarter past four, but I was projecting ahead to dinner and the sorry state of my larder. Somehow, I never seemed to have any of the staples you're supposed to have on hand to whip up a fabulous impromptu meal. My pantry featured various dusty cans, jars, and bottles of things that must have seemed like a good idea at one time or another, but never should've have made the cut: pureed cannellini beans, diet cauliflower bisque, unsweetened cranberry juice. Fodder for the earthquake kit, I suppose.

The minute I walked into the house, I pulled my now-oppressive blue dress over my head and fantasized about burning it. But I was loath to do so. It was by Claire McCardell, who had singlehandedly founded American ready-to-wear fashion in the forties. And in a size ten, with those oversize patch pockets, it was a rare find.

As far as I know, no one except yours truly has advanced a

theory as to why vintage clothing tends to be found only in fours and sixes. At five-eleven and 144 pounds (naked, first thing in the morning, and definitely not between Thanksgiving and New Year's), the only thing about me that's a size six is two-thirds of one foot. I like to think it's because throughout history, voluptuous girls like myself tended to be ravished by impatient mates, their dresses shed in the heat of passion, while our petite counterparts, being inherently less desirable, had ample time to hang up their garments neatly, thus preserving them for posterity on eBay.

A crock of shit, I know. Nevertheless, it does explain why, after checking my messages ("Cece, get your butt over here. Someone your size has died!"), I abandoned my salad and hightailed it over to Bridget's. Like the Duchess of Windsor, I'd rather shop than eat. But it was a tough call.

I considered myself lucky to call Bridget Sugarhill a friend. The sole proprietor of On the Bias, the premier vintage clothing shop in Los Angeles, Bridget wielded power equivalent to (and during Oscar season greater than) that of your average studio head. Bridget knew everything about clothes, and everything about everyone who liked them. Who makes no career move before consulting her Chinese herbalist? Who is really the boss at Sony Pictures Classics? Who ran over her agent's dog? Oh, if the tabloids only knew.

The bell tinkled as I opened the celadon and gold door of the otherwise ordinary brick building located on a small stretch of Burton Way in Beverly Hills. Bridget appeared instantly, a tall African-American woman wearing a swath of kente cloth cut with the precision of a Balenciaga frock.

"Hello, Cece, come in and join me," she said grandly.

Bridget was not exactly old Hollywood royalty, but she was

definitely old Hollywood. Her grandmother, Jeanie Sugarhill, had been a seamstress at MGM in its glory days, renowned both for her moxie and way with a needle. Every good fashionista knows that padded shoulders came into vogue in the 1940s because the great costume designer Adrian decided they offset Joan Crawford's hips. But Jeanie Sugarhill was famed on the MGM lot for even greater subtlety. She could trim fat off your thighs in half-inch increments, deflate your dowager's hump, or give you a D-cup overnight, as the occasion warranted.

Bridget's mom, who was born quoting Voltaire, couldn't be bothered with such frivolities. So Bridget got Grandma's full attention. The girl may have grown up in a cramped apartment in Culver City, but she always looked divine. The night of her senior prom, she was outfitted in a pitch-perfect copy of Rita Hayworth's strapless *Gilda* gown. The year before, it had been Marlene Dietrich's muted yellow satin sheath from *Morocco*. No wonder the woman put on airs.

The bell on the front door tinkled again. A young matron in a red coat walked in. Without missing a beat, Bridget's dachshund made a beeline for her crotch. As the poor woman looked around for help, Bridget told me to hold on for a minute and sashayed over.

"I see you've met Helmut," she said, pleasantly enough.

Now for the rap. I'd heard it maybe a thousand times.

"You've never been here before, have you? Well, we carry only vintage designer pieces. Some of them are very fragile." Bridget turned toward a rack filled with silky tops and soft sweaters spangled with beads. "We do not handle the clothes like this," she demonstrated, yanking a peasant blouse from Yves St. Laurent's Ballet Russes collection by its ultra-puffy sleeve. "We touch only the hangers. Thank you so much for your attention. Do let me know if I can be of futher assistance."

Bridget returned to her reproduction Louis XVI desk and seated herself noisily in her not-reproduction Louis XVI chair.

"You are such a bitch," I said.

"Don't I know it," she replied. "But god save me from the amateurs. Do you know what happened yesterday? Some skinny-assed starlet came in looking for something to wear to a premiere. She grabbed my favorite Schiaparelli gown, the one with the square neckline and floral appliques, hustled into a dressing room, and came out scrunching the waistline between her fists, whining about how big it was. Scrunching that fabric, can you imagine? You can't iron it, for heaven's sake! Anyway, I would've thrown her out if her stylist didn't bring me so much business."

I made sympathetic noises.

"Oh, cut it out. So, you want to see this dead woman's clothes?"

"I'm ready," I said, salivating.

The next forty minutes were bliss. I stripped plastic bags off dresses like there was no tomorrow, and Bridget knew enough to stay out of my way. Of course, there were a few corkers: a peasant/wench gown in transparent floral chiffon with a foot-wide elasticized waistband, perfect for going-a-milkin' at Studio 54; a Rudi Gernreich trompe l'oeil woolen suit that made me resemble a human checkerboard; and the requisite half-dozen Halston Ultrasuede coatdresses, in shades as mystifyingly popular as mushroom and burnt orange.

But I forgot about those fashion faux pas as I luxuriated in a 1930s bias-cut gown in fuschia rayon crepe with a thick velvet belt in a slightly contrasting shade of raspberry; an Oscar de la Renta silk sari printed with a pattern of periwinkle, sage, and gold; a 1960s Nina Ricci empire-waisted gown with the thinnest shoulder straps (more cappellini than spaghetti), constructed out of a single piece of accordion-pleated chiffon dyed into stripes of chartreuse, tangerine, hot pink, and lime.

And then there was the masterpiece, the dress to end all dresses. It was by Ossie Clark, the guru of rock-star girlfriends, the king of King's Road, the designer who could make a woman feel like an angel while she was inspiring wanton lust. It was a cherry-red silk chiffon A-line from the seventies with signature Ossie bell sleeves and a keyhole neckline that plunged from the nape of the neck to the waist. I would need an engineer to construct a bra I could wear under it, but what the hell. When I put it on, I made myself swoon. After recovering, I told Bridget to wrap it up.

While I was seated at Bridget's desk, waiting for my package, I flipped through one of her books on fashion history. Oh, what I would do to own a Claire McCardell Popover. These were wraparound, unstructured denim dresses to be worn over more elegant clothes, you know, while you whipped up cherries jubilee for your husband's boss and his wife. Popovers were produced in response to a request by *Harper's Bazaar* for appropriate clothing for women whose maids had selfishly abandoned them for wartime factory work. For some odd reason, they loomed large in my fantasy life.

I picked up another book on style icons. Talitha Getty, sprawled on a Moroccan rooftop in a floaty caftan. Slim Keith, the ultimate cool blonde. Coco Chanel, the crimson-lipped revolutionary. And Meredith Allan. Ohmigod, Meredith Allan. I *knew* I recognized her name.

"Bridget," I demanded, "what do you know about this woman?"

"Meredith Allan? Why? Did she finally die? Oh, please say yes. I'd give anything to get a crack at her closet."

"I don't think she's dead. Well, she might be. I think I might know someone who knows her. Or knew her. Actually, two people who know her. Or knew her. This is *so* strange."

"Meredith Allan is a legend, darling. You've seen pictures of her, Cece. The cascading ringlets? The kohl-rimmed eyes? The jewel-tipped cigarette holders? She invented the whole gypsy patrician thing, an armful of huge Navajo bracelets, rugged leather sandals, and an haute couture gown. A sleek Chanel suit and an embroidered peasant blouse, topped by a real Tyrolean hat. That was when she lived in Austria. And London, she took that town by storm. Oh, honey, she loved Ossie Clark. Just like you. Would wear one of his butterfly-sleeve things with a gargantuan gold necklace she'd designed herself. Looked like a torture device, studded with lapis as big as your fist. And she'd go out barefoot. Wearing patchouli. She married young, I think, divorced, and took oodles of lovers. Her father was a famous tyrant. Rich as Croesus. Oil."

"What happened to her?"

"Last thing I remember hearing she was in Ojai. Meditating. Throwing pots. Wearing Indian skirts with petticoats, her arms covered with that massive turquoise jewelry. She was sick as a child, you see. Heart trouble. Those bracelets were therapeutic. They were her weights. She wore them to strengthen her weak arms."

As the celadon and gold door slammed shut behind me, I had a thought.

Maybe Meredith Allan was still in Ojai. Ojai was not so very far away, just half an hour inland from Ventura. Maybe the woman was lonely. Maybe she'd like a visitor. Named Cece Caruso.

It should be noted that I've always believed that under the right circumstances pigs could fly.

12

As it turned out, Meredith Allan had left Ojai more than twenty years ago, on the death of her guru, Jiddhu Krishnamurti, to whom she was apparently devoted. And generous. She had finally figured her life out. Ojai was a place for people who had not.

For more than a century, the whole Ojai Valley had been home to a hodgepodge of religious, spiritual, metaphysical, occult, and self-help groups. The Ojai Hot Springs opened in 1887, promising to cure everything from rheumatism to tummy aches. David C. Cook built his "Second Garden of Eden" in Piru around the same time, with the express intention of saving souls. In the early 1920s, the Krotona Institute was established under the leadership of Albert P. Warrington, who moved his followers from the Hollywood Hills to a tranquil 115-acre hilltop in Ojai, where you could smell the orange blossoms from dawn to dusk. Theosophist Annie Besant, who spent time in India studying Hinduism, purchased several hundred acres near the Krotona Institute soon afterward and brought Krishnamurti with her there to serve as in-house prophet. He eventually broke with the theosophists and cultivated his own band of acolytes, among whom could be counted Miss Meredith Allan.

But she was done with all that. She had lived longer than anyone thought she had a right to. She had sown her oats, conquered her demons, and found her way. Ready to attend to her responsibilities, she'd bid a fond adieu to her fellow seekers, left her thriving citrus farm, returned to her ancestral home in Ventura, packed up everything that wasn't nailed down, and bought a mansion in Montecito, just south of Santa Barbara. As it turned out, she hadn't really had that many responsibilities.

All this I learned from Miss Allan's longtime secretary, a lovely man named Mr. Wingate. About whom I learned from a librarian at the Ventura County Historical Society, another lovely man named Mr. Grandy. Both of whom were tickled pink with the idea they were helping me with deep background for my book. That was how I'd put it. They thought it sounded very cloak-and-dagger.

Miss Allan would grant me an hour, Mr. Wingate announced giddily. I was to meet her at her Montecito estate first thing Wednesday morning, and I was to be prompt.

I'd decided right away on an Eve Arden look—you know, the wisecracking sidekick, the one who doesn't get the guy but can expertly dissect his inadequacies. Eve Arden always had great clothes. And bags. I had no intention of competing with the leading lady, of course, but wanted her to know I appreciated her obsessions, and maybe shared one or two.

I put on a crisp white blouse, high-heeled black pumps, and a pink wool Pucci circle skirt I'd bought at Bridget's, covered with a politically incorrect pattern of African masks, totems, and grass huts shaded by palm trees. I would not be accepting food or beverages in this particular garment. First of all, the waistband was so tight it precluded breathing, much less eating. And second of all, the skirt's yellowed label informed me it had to be commercially dry-cleaned with "cold perchloroethylene," whatever the hell that was, and I hardly thought the professionals at Klean-E! Cleaners were up for the challenge.

Into my purse went my steno pad and the directions Mr. Wingate had faxed me, along with my cat's-eye glasses, should they be needed to accessorize my look. Buster tried to sneak into the car, poor thing, but I deposited him on the living room couch, which had become his bed when I banished him from mine due to his accelerating old-age stink. I tossed the new cashmere throw in the closet, just in case.

The drive felt long. I zoned out listening to reggae, then tuned in to talk radio around Oxnard when I needed to perk up. My favorite call of the afternoon was from a woman who was feeling guilty because her ex-father-in-law had left the bulk of his estate to her instead of his wife of forty years. It didn't stop her, though, from rushing right out and buying herself a diamond tennis bracelet and a sterling silver service for twenty-four.

My ex-father-in-law was a whole other can of worms. He taught his son everything he knew, which meant he was a miser and a cheat. Plus, he hated me, the big-haired girl from the wrong side of the tracks. Who has twenty-four people to dinner, anyway? Lael, I suppose. By the time you counted her kids and all their half brothers and sisters, you were up to a couple dozen easy.

Before I could start reproaching myself for having had

only one child, Montecito appeared, a mirage shimmering in the desert. Not exactly, I know, but it felt that way. Maybe it was all that hard money sparkling off the blue ocean.

Montecito means "little mountain" in Spanish. But you didn't need cat's-eye glasses to see that "little" never went over big around here. Pleasure-seekers with names like Pillsbury, Fleischman, and du Pont came to Montecito in the early part of the twentieth century and built themselves a slew of mansions—big ones behind big gates. I followed the palm trees to Miss Allan's, a Mediterranean Revival number with Byzantine, Renaissance, and Moorish accents. In blush pink. I traipsed across the automobile entry court, through the terraced courtyard with its fountain dribbling turquoise beads of water, and rang the bell.

The rich don't open their own doors. Especially ones hewn out of solid mahogany and inlaid with hand-painted Turkish tiles. They have butlers who sneer and make you wait in musty drawing rooms. When Philip Marlowe went calling on four million bucks, it happened to him. But I was not calling on your typical millionairess. And she had a lot more millions than four.

No butler. No drawing room. And no dramatic entrance, though the sweeping staircase was made for it. I was greeted by the lady of the house herself, Meredith Allan, and she looked a lot like Cinderella, before the Fairy Godmother got to her.

She had kept her figure, but the rest was mystifying. She was wearing dungarees, with smudges of what looked to be paint on her chin. There was hair everywhere, tangled ropes of it, silvery gray and auburn, spilling onto a torn flannel shirt. And wrinkles, not that they detracted from her beauty.

Even at sea level, the woman's cheekbones were high enough to give a person altitude sickness.

"Ms. Caruso?" she asked, a pleasing lilt in her voice. "Please come in, and excuse the mess, will you? I've been doing a little redecorating."

I hoped she was kidding. This was a house William Randolph Hearst would have approved of. The foyer was close to thirty feet high, with a crystal chandelier, a rococo dome fresco ceiling, stained-glass windows, and a terrazzo floor. And that was just for starters. She led me through an arched doorway flanked by gold-leaf fluted columns and a wraparound terra-cotta frieze depicting a vulture enjoying his evening meal. We stepped down into the sunken living room. Among its marvels were four gigantic fireplaces, each guarded by a trio of marble phoenixes, and overhead, hand-stenciled wooden beams embellished with dozens of carvings of owls.

"I call this room the aviary," she said, laughing.

"Of course," I replied, not getting it.

"You know, the birds," she explained.

All I could think of at that moment was the Hitchcock movie. And the time in junior high when a pigeon relieved himself on my head.

"Would you like to see what I've been working on? It's this way, in the powder room. By the way, your skirt, Ms. Caruso, it's wonderful. I love that it's Pucci, but not jersey."

That was exactly what I loved about it, too.

The powder room could have accommodated at least thirty-five women with shiny noses. Stained dropcloths covered the floor, along with squeezed tubes of oil paint in various hues, brushes of all sizes, smeared palettes, and dozens of preparatory sketches, lined up with near-military precision.

"I'm just finishing a mural. I've been at it for months now. It's a reproduction of one of my favorite Victorian fairy paintings, Richard Dadd's *The Fairy Feller's Master Stroke*. Do you know it?"

As a matter of fact, I did not.

"It depicts a fairy feller, he's the archmagician of the clan, splitting a hazelnut with his axe. All the fairies come out for the show. Fairy dandies making passes at nymphs, the keeper of the fairy inn, a dwarf fairy monk, a fairy dairymaid, Queen Mab riding in a car of state drawn by female centaurs and a gnat as coachman."

Whimsy, I have to say, usually makes me gag. The minute I found out the British designer Zandra Rhodes spent her formative years poring over Cicely Mary Barker's Flower Fairy books, I swore I'd never wear one of her dressses, perpendicular pleating or no. But this was something else. I had never seen anything like it. I walked up close to take in the details, the sharp folds of taffeta on a flower fairy's bronze skirt, the iridescent wing of a trumpeting dragonfly. The surface of the mural had been covered with a scrim of twisted grasses, as if the scene were somehow forbidden. I felt like a voyeur. It was perfect. But who could possibly pee in this room?

"I didn't realize you were an artist," I said.

"Oh, hardly," she demurred. "I was hopeless in art school. I lack the requisite imagination. I can copy anything, though. I'm good at getting inside other people's heads, figuring out how they see the world. Dadd, you know, had been a promising student at the Royal Academy. But he lost an important competition for the decoration of the Houses of Parliament. He submitted a picture of St. George, but the dragon's tail was too long. He went a little crazy, murdered his father, and wound up at Bedlam. That's where his talents really flowered. He painted this work a short while later, while he was incarcerated at the asylum at Broadmoor."

Just a little crazy. She said it with that lilt. What would it be like, I wondered, to live in a world where the roses are always red and the sea is always warm and no one minds when you go just a little crazy?

"But where are my manners? Let's sit down and I'll get you something cool to drink."

My resolution abandoned, I said, "That would be lovely, thank you." Off in the distance, a bell rang. I wondered how she did that.

As we made our way back into the living room, I watched her snaky curls. The silver strands sparkled in the dim light. Had Mrs. Flynn been right? Had Joe been in love with this woman? And if so, could she have been his alibi for that night, the person he swore he'd never betray? Maybe.

Maybe he had fallen under the spell of her honeyed lilt and was powerless to reveal her name, even to save himself.

Maybe he was the last good man, protecting the woman he loved from the indignity of testifying in open court. God knows the state prosecutor Hamilton Burger, Perry Mason's nemesis, would have made mincemeat of a witness like her. Destroyed her reputation. Painted her as a fallen woman.

But there was no Hamilton Burger. This was real life. And real people had scruples. If Meredith Allan had been with Joe the night Jean was killed, she would have stepped forward.

What could have stopped her? Only someone without a heart could allow an innocent person to rot in jail.

Then, speaking of fairies, I remembered J. M. Barrie's description of Tinker Bell. She was a creature not wholly heartless, but so small she had room for only one feeling at a time.

13

$\mathcal{M}$y hostess gestured toward a plush red couch. Just as I was sinking into it, I caught sight of one of those owls glaring down at me. I felt like Snow White wandering alone through the dark forest. Disney had obviously hijacked my imagination.

Salvation took unexpected form. He was carrying two tall glasses of something pink, but he was no butler. Tall, dark, and handsome—I believe that's how it's usually put. He was wearing sleek Italian boots, narrow black pants, and a gray silk shirt cut close to his body. And what a body.

"How sweet of you to bring us our drinks, dear. Raspberry iced tea, lovely. Ms. Caruso, may I introduce you to my son, Burnett Fowlkes? Burnett, this is Cece Caruso. She's here to interview me for a book she's writing on old Ventura."

His hair was curly, and his gaze was steely. In fact, the look he gave me was so intense I felt like I was being x-rayed. The sensation was not altogether unpleasant. I decided to look back and was pleased to see his color rise.

"Nice to meet you, Ms. Caruso."

"Call me Cece." I couldn't remember if I had invited her to do the same. I didn't think so. How humiliating. There was no way I was asking these people for sweetener.

"Burnett is a restoration architect in L.A. He's here helping me with some detail work upstairs."

"I could really use you in my bedroom," I said. Idiot. "What I mean is, the molding is in shambles, and the fireplace has only one andiron and I've been looking for a good match for years." Oh, man.

"There are lots of antique shops in the area. I'd try along Main," he said graciously. "For a good match."

Miss Allan was having a rollicking good time now. "Dear, tell Ms. Caruso something about this wonderful house."

"It was built in the 1920s, for the film star Norma Talmadge. It's a replica of a seventeenth-century villa belonging to a duke in Florence. There's only one false note in the whole of it. Miss Talmadge was out to impress Irving Thalberg, the head of the studio, so she had the fireplace in her bedroom decorated with marble reliefs resembling the MGM lion. At parties," he said, laughing, "she would hire bit players to growl from the closets."

People growled at my parties without being asked. But I didn't have to advertise this.

I cleared my throat. "The lion is actually a well-known symbol of the Medici. Maybe your movie star knew more than you're giving her credit for."

"I hadn't considered that. You're very astute, Ms. Caruso— Cece."

"Oh, I don't know about that. It's just that I don't like

being underestimated, so I try never to underestimate others."

"I'll remember that—the part about never underestimating you."

I blushed.

"Mother, I've got to run some errands. I'll be back in a few hours. Cece, I hope we have the opportunity to meet again."

A look passed between them as he leaned down to peck her cheek. She wanted him to stay, but he left without so much as a backward glance.

"Ms. Caruso," she said, the lilt now gone, "about your book."

This was the part I'd been dreading. I didn't have any legitimate reason to be there except to find out what she did or didn't know about the murder of her maybe-lover's wife.

"Yes, well, I think Mr. Wingate might have misunderstood me a little when we set up the appointment," I said, which was not a total lie, but about as close as you can get. "My book isn't about old Ventura, not per se."

She looked at me curiously. I smiled, trying not to show too much gum. Too much gum makes you look insincere. I learned that on the pageant circuit.

"What I'm actually researching," I continued, "is the author Erle Stanley Gardner. He spent fifteen years in Ventura, back in the teens and twenties, and wrote the first Perry Mason books here."

"Mr. Wingate doesn't make errors."

"No, of course not."

"He didn't believe in fairies."

"Mr. Wingate?"

"Erle Stanley Gardner. He was a plodder. Some people

are. They play by the rules. The shortest distance between two points is a straight line. You know what I'm talking about."

You know what I'm talking about. That was exactly what Joseph Albacco had said to me.

"Sir Arthur Conan Doyle believed in fairies. He took up the cause of two young English girls in Yorkshire who claimed to have met a pair of pixies, seen them riding snails and jumping off toadstools and such. The girls had photographs to prove it. I'd love to own those. But I suppose I'm digressing."

She waited for me to contradict her. She was obviously used to having her every stray thought celebrated.

"Oh, no," I intoned dutifully. It was for the cause.

She looked satisfied.

"Shall we get on with it then, Ms. Caruso? What exactly might Erle Stanley Gardner have to do with me?"

"Well," I said, talking as fast as I could, "you're really the only other well-known person to come out of Ventura. I know what Ventura meant to Gardner. I want to find out about its impact on you. I suppose I'm trying to think through the significance of people's hometowns, you know, how they figure into their accomplishments. Sense of place, that sort of thing. What I'm looking for is another perspective on Ventura, a feeling for what this particular town offered to a young person with talent and energy."

That was pathetic. Still, I kept going.

"Let's go back to your teenage years in Ventura, Miss Allan. Were you already interested in fashion then? Where did you buy your clothes? Were there other girls with similar tastes you spent time with? What was it like at Ventura City High for someone like you?"

"I loathed Ventura," she said. "Every single thing about it. But what I hated most of all was the smell of it, the stink of oil on my father's fingers. As soon I was old enough, I went as far away from Ventura as I could, away from the derricks and the oil fields, somewhere I could breathe. Is that what you're looking for, Ms. Caruso?"

"Oh, that would certainly do it," I answered. Had no one ever told this woman that discretion is the better part of valor? Not that I was complaining.

"No one thought I would live past the age of ten, you realize." She took a sip of iced tea, wrinkled her nose, and poured the rest into a nearby potted palm. "I had suffered a serious bout of rheumatic fever. When I recovered, everyone treated me like I was made of glass. It drove me mad. I became a ragamuffin. I refused to wash or comb my hair. I ran the hillsides with the butterflies. I swam with the toads. I was a freak, an untouchable with a rich daddy who stank of petroleum."

We were on her favorite subject now: the life and lore of Meredith Allan.

"When I was fourteen, my mother died and my father began taking me places with him. London. Paris. Rome. My brothers were useless. They stayed home and ran wild while I became a lady. I brushed my hair. I put on perfume. I paid attention. I came home with getups nobody around here understood. Vionnet. Givenchy. Antique jewels worn by the daughters of maharajahs. Around here they thought everything you could ever want was in the Sears catalog. My father understood, though. He was only too happy to foot the bill. At school, the other girls were a little afraid of me. And the more outlandish my outfits, the more scared they were. I liked it. That's how I developed my sense of style, Ms. Caruso. I wanted to scare people."

It was definitely working. She was the Colossus of Rhodes of scary. But I wasn't a psychoanalyst. I had a mystery to solve. But before I could get a word in edgewise she rose from her chair.

"You'll have to go now. I'm very busy today."

I had only one chance left.

I followed her to the door.

"It was kind of you to see me," I said, hoisting my purse on my shoulder. "You've been so generous with your time."

"Not at all."

"There is one last question I wanted to ask, though."

"Yes?" she asked distractedly. She'd turned her attention to something far more interesting than I'd turned out to be—a loose door hinge.

"One of the things I've stumbled upon in the course of my research is an old Ventura murder case, one that Gardner took quite an interest in. You know what a plodder he was." I had her attention now. "Well, he was going over the evidence and something just didn't seem right to him. What's curious is that the case involved a young couple that you must have known, Joseph Albacco and his wife, Jean. You went to high school with them, didn't you?"

It was as if I had clipped her wings. Her eyes filled with panic as she spiraled down to earth. She was quiet for a minute. Then she threw back her shoulders and wrapped her hauteur around her. Back where it belonged.

"That was a long time ago," she said. "Another life. But yes, I knew them both well. A dreadful story."

"Indeed. Two such wonderful young people, their lives destroyed."

"Wonderful people?" she repeated, trying to appear unmoved. But there were beads of sweat on her exquisite nose. "I won't speak about Joe. But Jean Albacco—let me clear something up, Ms. Caruso. She was a nasty bit of goods. Don't be so foolish as to romanticize her just because she was murdered."

"Well, her sister did say she had a difficult upbringing."

"You've spoken to Theresa? Oh, she has plenty of stories to tell. Ask her about Lisette Johnson, Ms. Caruso, and watch her blanch. And don't blame their childhood. Jean was never a child. Children don't—"

"Don't what?"

"You know about Jean's little sideline, of course?"

"Actually, no."

That may have been one digression too many.

"Never mind. It's just that my dearest friend was hurt. Ellie thought Jean could be trusted, so she confided in her about an affair with the gym teacher at the high school. And what a mistake that turned out to be."

"What else can you tell me about Jean?"

"There isn't enough time. All I'll say is I think you're writing the wrong book. Good day."

Her voice was honey all over again.

14

I heaved a sigh of relief to be out of there, and promptly popped the snap right off my Pucci skirt. It served me right for drinking that woman's tea.

I found a safety pin in the glove compartment and fixed myself up, without drawing blood. A good sign, I thought. Of what, harder to say. That success comes to those who don't self-mutilate? That she who does not expose her ratty undies to strangers will be lucky in love? Though I'm loath to admit it, I believe in all that stuff—signs, omens, astrology. Where I draw the line, though, is fairies.

Fairies. The stink of oil. And blackmail? Was that what Meredith Allan had meant by Jean's little sideline? I wasn't prepared to make sense of what had just happened. Not until I got home and had a pen in one hand and a glass of Pinot Noir in the other. I pulled onto the 101 and tried to empty my mind. But Scorpios are notoriously uncooperative. I focused on a splat on the windshield that used to be a bug. I opened the window a smidge, then closed it, diverted by the staccato blast of air. All right, that was it. Plus, I was hungry.

I dug around in my purse for something to eat and found a Snickers bar that was only slightly mashed. I washed it down with the remains of a bottle of Diet Coke that had been rolling around the floor of my car for a week or so. It was warm and flat, but at least it wasn't raspberry iced tea.

Working the caramel out of my molars took a while. Start with the little things and the big things will follow. I think it was Perry Mason who said that. Ellie and the gym teacher. It sounded like the name of a Sandra Dee movie. Only Sandra Dee never got mixed up in anything as sordid as blackmail. The worst it ever got for her was probably a tardy slip. Then I had a great idea. But I had to get off the freeway that second or I'd blow it. Honking the horn like a she-devil, I maneuvered my Camry across three lanes to exit.

Schools often look like prisons, but Ventura City High looked like a mausoleum. I parked outside the front entrance, which had the monumental geometry of a Pharaonic tomb. The graffiti on the facade heightened the effect; like hieroglyphics, it anointed a doomed power elite. Even the GO COUGARS banner draped across the chain-link fence seemed vaguely funereal. Maybe it was the missing exclamation point.

The student stationed at the front desk couldn't be bothered to look up. She jerked a beautifully manicured thumb in the direction of the library. As I walked down the hall, my eyes darted nervously about. I felt like I was about to be busted. High school will do that to you. The air reeked of french fries, B.O., and benzoyl peroxide.

The librarian was absorbed in a book. I couldn't make out the title, just the chapter heading "Retribution as Ritual." She didn't seem to like being interrupted and was discombobulated by my request. Her tiny, wizened head alternated between bobbing up and down and shaking back and forth—yes, no, yes, no. I thought she was going to pass out or, worse yet, put a hex on me, but she disappeared into the back and tottered out with a foot-high stack of dusty yearbooks.

I promised to be careful with them and settled down at a desk in the back. There was a kid behind me, smoking. Though it was a fire hazard, I decided not to turn him in.

I opened the 1954–55 volume. That year's theme, printed in florid, Old English letters at the top of the first page, was *"Quo Vadis?"* Talk about lofty. That was just the question to ponder if you were eighteen, unqualified for everything, and staggering around under the weight of postadolescent hormones. I would've killed myself. When I graduated from high school in 1981, the yearbook editors picked the rainbow as our theme. Very profound. You can be blinded by its colors or confront the spectrum.

Now I smelled Cheetos.

I flipped to the index and found Joseph Albacco. Pages 49, 65, 67, 69, 101, and 111. Football team, debating society, yearbook staff. Voted Best-Looking and Most Likely to Succeed. I studied the boy in the picture. There was nothing left of him except maybe the smile. "What we seek we shall find." That was his class quote. You couldn't even call it ironic. It was bigger and sadder than that.

I picked up the next book in the stack. The theme for the class of 1956 was "Seize the Day." Jean Albacco had graduated that year. Jean Logan had been her maiden name. I knew that from the transcript. And there she was, looking exactly like every other girl on the page. Short dark hair, neat white blouse, a string of pearls around her neck. Jean's quote was also from Emerson: "I hate quotations. Tell me what you know." What cheek.

The Fairy Queen had graduated the same year as Jean. I looked her up in the index. Absent on picture day. And she'd missed the make-up day, too. Why did that not surprise me? But she was listed on page 107. Father-Daughter Night, 1956. A local band named the Whirly Birds sang doo-wop, and the guests drank cherry Cokes until they were fit to burst. I scanned the happy faces. The dads were spinning their little girls around, skirts flying. Awards were bestowed—Best Father? Best Daughter? I saw a beautiful girl I thought might be Meredith wearing a dark dress with a Peter Pan collar. Her father was nowhere in sight. My father had never been around, either. There was police business to take care of, leads to follow up, reports to file, double-shifts around the holidays. And I was just a girl anyway.

Back to the little things. The bit players. Ellie. She was the one I came here to find. I turned back to the index. Could she have been Eleanor? No, no Eleanors in that class. What about Ellen? One listed. I turned to her picture. Ellen Sammler wore glasses and looked like the sort of girl who would have been forced by her mother to take her cousin to the prom. She was going to get contacts, move to New York City, start a literary salon, and live happily ever after. You could just tell. Wrong girl. What about Elspeth? Here was an Elspeth Galloway. Oh, she had to be Ellie. Long wavy hair, dreamy expression, a soft chin. She had delusional written all over her.

Phys ed, phys ed. Page 38. Now for Ellie's lover. Well, it couldn't have been Logan Hiney, who had no hair at all and must've been close to a hundred years old. Here he was. Oh, yes. This had to have been him. Bill Winters. A mountain-climber type with a devilish grin and a Kirk Douglas cleft. Just the type to make a sixteen-year-old's heart flutter. A long time ago Jean Albacco had made his life miserable. Maybe she had. And maybe he had been angry enough to put a stop to it.

On my way out, I stopped at the front office. I needed Ellie's phone number and address. Did they give out information like that?

A matchstick-thin woman pretending to speak no English refused to meet my gaze.

"My mother went to school here," I said, enunciating as clearly as I could. "She graduated in 1956. Ellen Sammler, that was her maiden name."

The woman was extremely busy, paper-clipping pieces of paper to other pieces of paper-clipped paper.

"We're visiting from New York," I continued, my voice getting louder, "and we wanted to get in touch with an old friend of my mother's from high school."

Now she was slitting envelopes with a daggerlike letter opener.

"Shall I spell my name? S-A-M-M-L-E-R."

A humongous woman sitting in the way back near a bank of copy machines bellowed up to her colleague, "Lee, we talked about this, remember? You agreed, Lee. Public relations, remember?"

"I do not understand."

"Yes, you do, Lee. Give the lady an alumni directory right this minute."

She didn't budge.

"Take two steps forward, reach down, and pass it on. Do not, I repeat, DO NOT make me get up from my seat!"

It was a thankless task, restoring dignity to the term "civil servant." Muttering to herself, an irked Lee fumbled around behind the counter and eventually produced the goods.

"Ten dollars. Exact change required."

I didn't sense much of an attitude adjustment, but at least she hadn't asked for ID.

By the time I made it back to the car, I'd found her. Elspeth Day, née Galloway. She was a furniture designer who lived in La Jolla. Oh, god, I didn't want to drive down there. Maybe I could do it by cell phone.

I let it ring five times. Finally, someone answered.

"Mrs. Day?"

"You people!" She slammed down the phone. Probably thought I was selling something. I hit redial.

"Mrs. Day, please don't hang up. I got your name from Meredith Allan—"

"Meredith? I haven't heard from her in years. Is she in trouble?"

Interesting. "She's fine. I saw her earlier today."

"To whom am I speaking? What is this about?"

Might as well spit it out. "It's about Bill Winters."

"Why are you harassing me? I don't have to talk to you. That whole business was resolved years ago. Are you a lawyer?"

"No, I'm not a lawyer. I'm a writer from Los Angeles. My name is Cece Caruso."

"And?"

"And I'm researching an old crime. A murder. Jean Albacco. Do you remember her? From high school?"

"Of course I do. Where is this conversation going?"

"I'm not sure. I guess I want to find out about Bill and Jean. For my research."

"Listen, I don't want to get into all of that again. Bill's been dead for years. What good can it do to dredge it all up again?"

"When did Bill die?"

"Just after we graduated from high school. It must have been 1958. No, 1957."

What year was Jean killed? Suddenly I couldn't remember.

"They shipped Billy home in a box," she said softly. "There was a big memorial service. Everyone in town showed up. It was awful."

"In a box? I don't understand."

"Bill had been a big deal in Korea, special forces, I mean. When things started up in Vietnam, they sent him to Saigon to work with the CIA. But the Viet Cong got ahold of him soon after he got there, not that the government ever wanted to acknowledge it."

This wasn't making sense. "I thought Bill was a gym teacher."

"He was, in between stints of killing people. Why is any of it your business? What do you want with us?"

"Listen, I'm not trying to hurt anyone, Mrs. Day."

"I'm divorced. You can call me Ellie."

"Cece. I'm divorced, too."

"Tough luck. Was he a bastard?"

"Do you have to ask?"

That got her.

"Everything was so different then, Cece. Men were so different. Bill was really something," she said wistfully. "He belonged to an important Ventura family. His grandfather was a state legislator and his father was prominent in local government. The grandfather helped clear the way for the oil business to really take off in Ventura. But Bill didn't have a head for politics. Sexy, but no brains at all."

She knew she was talking too much, I could feel it, but she needed to know how her life sounded, and I was as good an audience as any.

"After Korea Bill just sat around, not knowing what to do with himself. So his dad got him a job coaching at the high school. That's when I fell for him. I guess Meredith told you about that."

"She mentioned it."

"I was young, and he was handsome. Oh, we made fools of ourselves."

"Did Jean blackmail Bill about your affair?"

"Yes."

Unbelievable.

"Could he have hated her enough to kill her?"

"Yes."

I held my breath. "Did he?"

"No."

"How do you know?"

"Her husband did it."

"Let's say he didn't."

"Somebody far away killed Billy first."

Damn it.

"Jean was there. At Billy's memorial service. I remember perfectly. Decked out in a brand-new black suit. Probably laughing her head off. You never knew her, but, believe me, Jean Albacco deserved everything she got."

Apparently there was a growing consensus on that.

15

I hated driving on the freeway at night. The glare made my head spin. But I made it home safely by keeping two hands on the wheel at all times and turning off the part of my brain consecrated to the Albaccos. The remainder of the evening was spent with *The Case of the Sunbather's Diary*, which turned out to have a surprise ending I loved. Energized, I tromped outside for a late-night session with my flashlight, handpicking snails off the last of my tomato plants. Javier had instructed me to crunch them under my heel, but I took pity and tossed them over the fence. They made a nice gift for my neighbor, who had recently complained to Animal Control about Buster's "obsessive" barking.

I woke up late the next morning, around eleven. Breakfast consisted of leftover ahi tuna with a tapenade crust (one of my specialties, though very pricey), washed down with black coffee since I was out of half-and-half. Following the meal, I returned queasily to bed.

I left a message for Annie, who seemed to have gone AWOL. I resisted my god-given right to worry and flipped

back and forth for a while between a *Perry Mason* rerun and
All My Children (the yin and yang of duty and pleasure).
Then the phone rang. It was Meredith Allan's son, Burnett
Fowlkes, asking me out on a date. At least I think it was a
date. The man had to be five years younger than I was, at
least. He was working on a house in my neighborhood and
thought I might like to see it. He'd be over in half an hour.

I snapped out of my lassitude. A choice had to be made:
my house, or me. Piece of cake. But I had to do something
about the living room. I surveyed the carnage. There were bits
of paper everywhere. In a fury, I had cut up a stack of index
cards last week while agonizing over the sociosexual implica-
tions of Della Street's seamed stockings. The broom was god
knows where, so I picked up the offending pieces by hand.
As is their wont, the dust bunnies had congregated under
the stained-glass window, which offered a view to the great
green beyond. I returned those guys to their friends and rel-
atives under the couch. Then I grabbed the carry-on bag
that had taken up residence in the entry hall after my trip to
New York six months ago, shooed Mimi out, and crammed
today's dismembered newspaper in and threw the thing into
the powder room, which I prayed Burnett would not need
to visit.

While the hot water warmed up, I flung open my closet
door. Mimi knew it was showtime and settled herself on the
bed.

I could go for something very un-me, like blue jeans,
maybe with my embroidered top from Mexico and my
beaded Filipino slides with the high wooden heels. I get the
latter in bulk for $16.99 a pair from one of my favorite
stores. It's in Los Feliz, next door to the Joe Blasco Makeup

Academy, and filled to bursting with wildly colored plastic icons and sheer white baptismal shirts just right for the tropics. And they always throw in a complimentary Imelda Marcos doll. But who was I kidding? I didn't want to look like one of those forty-year-olds who reads *Seventeen*. I like my crow's-feet. Well, I don't hate them. Did Burnett even have any? Mimi purred with satisfaction when I pulled out my favorite old Agnès B. black dress, the one with the cap sleeves and full skirt. It was ladylike with a twist. The twist was the zipper that ran all the way down the front and said, "Maybe, maybe not." It had worked before.

I had just decided on a pale mouth and dark eyes when the doorbell rang.

Burnett was holding a bouquet of tiny, velvety-looking flowers. They were a deep shade of brown.

It was definitely a date.

"Smell them," he said, smiling.

"Chicken mole?"

He laughed. His eyes were the crinkly kind. "Close. They're chocolate cosmos. I thought you'd like them."

"I love them. I'll put them in water, and we can go."

"Absolutely." He followed me in and, gentleman that he was, fixed his gaze somewhere above my waist. You can feel those things, even when your back is turned.

"Great moldings," he said. I put the flowers in a small glass vase and stepped into the dining room, nodding. "Great everything, actually." I think he was nervous, too.

"Yeah, looking for this place was heart-wrenching. Sort of like looking for love in the personals. Then I found it: 'New X. Spanish charmer. Emotional.' I fell hard."

"Isn't that the way. Then you've got to pick up the pieces."

"Which is where you come in—professionally, I mean."

"I got that."

"Oh."

"Shall we?"

He opened the front door, and the knob pulled off in his hand.

"Whoops," he said.

I laughed. "It looks like you're holding a disembodied limb."

"Aunt Martha!"

"You're gruesome."

"Takes one to know one. I'd suggest a trip to Liz's Antique Hardware on La Brea."

"I know the place. The guy who installed my French doors was in love with Liz."

"It's a rite of passage."

We hopped into his dented white Range Rover. He had just washed it. I knew because the front bumper was still a little wet.

"The house is just a few blocks from here, but since this is L.A., I thought we'd drive."

"This is L.A. Don't think so much."

Sitting that close to someone that handsome was disturbing. He was freshly shaven and smelled like pine trees. I'm not sure what possessed me. I leaned over and kissed him on the lips. He took my chin in his hand and looked into my eyes for a good, long while. Then he kissed me back for a good, long while, and that was that, for the moment.

We pulled up in front of a house that was demented. Well, that wasn't fair. It was magnificently demented. The lot was small, maybe the size of mine. I could make out a perfectly nice stucco box a reasonable person could have loved, hidden in there behind the latticed facade with its towering double doors soaring heavenward. These were topped by a pediment with a niche holding a plaster bust of Apollo. There were finials, too, at the edges of the stucco. Did I mention the row of eugenia shrubs trimmed in the shape of perfume bottles?

"Wow," I said.

"It gets better inside."

The ceiling was low, and the chandelier in the entry hall dripped crystals on my head. There was a trip of a wet bar, decorated with small Doric pilasters, and the most enormous Lucite coffee table I'd ever seen, resting on a zebra-skin rug. Curved glass walls wrapped around a kidney-shaped swimming pool in the back. Behind the pool was a draped pavilion, perfect for a bored housewife nursing a tumbler of vodka.

"It's a Home Depot take on the Hollywood Regency style," he said. "Amazing."

"The Hollywood what style?"

"You've seen them all over West Hollywood. Sloping mansard roofs, false fronts like stage sets, oversize carriage lamps? With a little know-how, you, too, could've transformed your Spanish Colonial Revival into a Second Empire townhouse."

"If only I'd thought of it."

"Dozens were done in the fifties and sixties. This remodel was a strictly DIY affair. The son inherited it last year and has a thing for camp. He wants to use the place as a backdrop for photo shoots, that kind of thing."

Said son appeared. He had a goatee and was chewing green apple bubble gum. He ushered Burnett into the pavilion to take some measurements.

"I'll just be a second."

"Great."

I took the opportunity to fix my lipstick. Luckily, there were mirrors everwhere. I sat down on the sofa, which was hard as a rock, and found myself face-to-face with a gold Buddha. Under its watchful gaze, I thumbed through an old copy of *Beverly Hills People*.

I looked up when I heard the swoosh of the sliding glass doors. Burnett introduced us. The guy's name seemed to be Barry White. I assumed that was some sort of joke. Barry said hello, and that he liked my dress.

"You know, architecture is just like fashion. Both are species of sexual fetishism. All buildings have erogenous zones, zones of pleasure. Burnett can tell you all about it," he said with a wink. Or a tic. It was hard to tell.

Burnett looked embarassed, but a client is a client.

"In my fantabulous house, for example, all the orifices—the windows, doors, chimneys, mail slots—are overarticulated. Also the protuberances, you know, the things that can be fondled—door knockers, handles, balustrades, carriage lamps. Please touch, I always tell my guests!"

We decided to go out for a coffee after that. Burnett had a headache. He put four packets of sugar into his tiny espresso.

"I would've asked for sugar for my raspberry iced tea yesterday, but your mother intimidated me."

"The woman has a gift. So tell me more about your work."

We talked for a long time. He ordered another espresso, and I had another cappuccino. His head felt better. Memories of Barry White receded into the distance. I told him about my writing, about how much I loved it, puzzling over people, finding them in their books, finding myself in them, too.

"Did you ever want to write a mystery yourself?"

"No, not really. I've thought about it, of course, but I'm more of a forensic pathologist than a killer. I mean, I don't want to do the deed, I want to pick apart the corpse. Does that make sense?"

"Even your metaphors are morbid," he said jokingly. "But I get it. It's sort of the same reason I became a restoration architect."

"How so?"

"Well, I was always the kid who wouldn't let the other kids knock down the tower of blocks. I didn't build the tower of blocks, I just protected it."

I laughed.

"I remember my mother taking me to Venice when I was about thirteen or fourteen. The most romantic city in the world. She wanted to show me the Doge's Palace and St. Mark's Cathedral. The poor woman was devastated to discover they were covered in scaffolding, part of a restoration effort that was going to take years. But I was thrilled. I spent days watching the guys working up there. I sketched the metal framework, the jacks, poles, and brackets, the geometric patterns they formed. Everyone thought I was nuts."

"No, just perverse."

"Is that wishful thinking?"

"Don't get fresh with me, Burnett."

"Give me a reason."

It was quiet for a moment.

"So, why'd you kiss me like that?" he asked.

"Why'd you kiss me back?"

"Because you're beautiful."

"I thought I was morbid."

"Speaking of morbid, what's up with that old murder case you talked to my mother about?"

I told him about finding Joseph Albacco's letter to ESG, and about my visit to Tehachapi. I told him about Theresa Flynn, leaving out the part about the scrap of paper with his mother's name on it. That seemed the politic thing to do. Mostly, though, I found myself talking about Jean. A girl who had gotten in over her head. What exactly had happened to her that night in that small Ventura bungalow?

It was her first wedding anniversary, hers and Joe's. She was peeling potatoes. Everything had to be perfect. It was mid-December and strangely hot. The sweat dripped down her forehead and stung her eyes. She walked into the living room and wiped her hands onto her apron. She cracked open a window. She studied her neighbor's wilted pansies. She watched a cat scurry by, looking for a bird to kill. She had a roast to kill. But Joe was late. Again. She went back into the kitchen and turned on the oven. Then she heard the screen door slam. It didn't take long after that. Did she even have time to scream?

"Whoa! Are you sure you don't want to be a mystery writer?" Burnett asked.

Red as a beet, I shook my head. For heaven's sake, who did I think I was, Erle Stanley Gardner? More like Daphne du Maurier. Talk about your gothic romances. Someone save me from my lurid imagination. I finished my cappuccino and tried to change the subject. Back to Burnett, Burnett and his mother, Burnett and architecture, anything. But he kept turning the conversation back to me—my family, my daughter, even my divorce. Not many men are willing to hear you complain about old mistakes. Or are sweet and sexy enough to make you want to forget about them. I thought I could get used to that.

Later, when he kissed me good-bye, I thought I could get used to that, too.

16

*B*urnett called the next day just to say hello, and the day after that, he left a bouquet of dahlias on my front step, along with a first edition of *The Case of the Daring Divor-cée*. It had a great cover. The vixen in the shiny cocktail dress even looked a little like me. I had planned to spend the rest of the afternoon with Lael, analyzing these developments, but I was interrupted by a call from Mr. Grandy at the Ventura County Historical Society. He had received some interesting ESG material and thought it would be worth my while to make the quick trip. At that point, I'd have done anything to revive my moribund book. So off I went.

"Cece! Cece! Right this way!"

Mr. Grandy was all smiles, his hands tightly clasped in anticipation. We bounded upstairs and he pulled me into the back.

"Look, look! Twenty boxes of Gardner's legal files, dating back to the teens. The estate has donated them to us. So much one could learn about old Ventura, don't you think?

And Gardner! All his old cases! Can you even conceive of what you might find in there, Cece?"

No way. Absolutely not. First of all, I was no legal scholar. And second of all, I had more Erle Stanley Gardner material than I could use in twenty lifetimes. Given my lack of focus, not to mention my looming deadline, I knew better than to start going through those boxes. That way lay ruination. Well, that would be four and a half hours wasted, counting the round-trip drive time, thank you very much. I said good-bye to Mr. Grandy, who looked like a wilted lily. I wish I could say it was the first time I had offended a librarian.

I needed candy. The convenience store on the way back to the 101 would be good for a Hershey bar, but I was partial to the stronger stuff.

I headed over to the candy store on Main. The good news was I found a spot right away. The bad news was I didn't have any change for the meter, but that wasn't critical. I'd just add the ticket to the pile accumulating on my desk. Those things catch up to you only if you commit a felony. Or a misdemeanor—I can't remember exactly. Not that I had plans along either of those lines.

Stash in hand, I walked back to the car, past the Busy Bee, formerly the Townsend Café, where Gardner used to take his morning coffee breaks. Past the shoe store next door, which didn't seem to have changed its décor since the twenties. I could picture old Erle stomping in there for a new pair of brogues, nothing too fancy. I stopped to admire the weathered signage in front of C&M Locksmiths, a flickering neon key decked out in a top hat and tails. I bet Burnett looked amazing in black tie. He hadn't been wearing a wedding ring, but I knew from experience that didn't mean a thing. I stopped short. C&M Locksmiths. Why did I know that name? I thought for a minute. I had seen that name in the court transcript. Yes, C&M Locksmiths was the place Jean Albacco had gone the afternoon she died—to pick up some keys, a couple of which hadn't been ready. Who had just been talking to me about missing keys? Mrs. Flynn. Mrs. Flynn had never picked up her sister's lockbox from the insurance office because she had never found the keys. Slowly, it sank in. Mrs. Flynn had never found the keys because Jean had never claimed them. On the last day of her life, they still hadn't been ready.

The front door creaked open. It needed oiling, unlike the hair of the clerk stationed behind the counter. I could count the strands, each one jet black and meticulously waved à la Rudy Valentino. Pinned to his neatly pressed Oxford cloth shirt was a button that read, IF THE SHOE FITS, YOU MUST BE CINDERELLA! A regular ladies' man.

My mother's words rang in my ears: "Butter 'em up before you hit 'em up."

"Hello there!" I gave him my most dazzling smile.

He looked me up and down from behind thick-framed black glasses selected, I surmised, to complement the hairdo. "Are you from the Publishers Clearing House?"

"No, no, nothing like that. I have a dreadful problem. A locksmith problem," I said. "You see, I live in an old Spanish house with the original front doorknob, which keeps coming off from the inside. Plus, the key sticks in the lock. Half the time I have to climb in the window!"

He shook his head, aghast.

"Anyway, I know of your reputation, of course, and that

you people are experts with antique hardware. Just brilliant. Is that true?"

"Well, we're a family business, been in the game for some seventy-five years," he boasted. "I'm sure we can solve your problem, ma'am. Shall I page my father?"

"By all means, yes. But before you do, just out of curiosity, my mother, God rest her soul, had some keys made here ages ago, and never did get around to picking them up. Jean Albacco was her name. I'd like to see if they're still here. Sentimental value, you know."

"When did she place the order?"

"1957."

He chortled unbecomingly. "Do you see the sign, ma'am?" He pointed over his left shoulder to a faded placard reading, WE ARE NOT RESPONSIBLE FOR GOODS LEFT OVER 60 DAYS.

Wasn't he just the type to go and get his panties in a twist. "Yes, I see it, and I do understand it's been . . . a while."

"Forty-five years, ma'am? That's not just 'a while.'" He slid his glasses back up the bridge of his nose.

"All I'm asking is if you have the keys or not."

"Oh, they're here, all right. Guaranteed. I learned a couple of things from my dad, who learned them from my granddad. One is, keys are private business. You don't ask questions and you don't offer information. And two is, you never, ever, throw anything away. We have over three hundred thousand keys in this building, ma'am!"

My heart pounding, I said, "In that case, I'd like to collect my mother's property. I'll just get out my wallet, and—"

He pointed over his right shoulder to another faded placard, this one reading, NO GOODS DELIVERED WITHOUT CLAIM CHECK.

I should have seen that coming.

"What an excellent rule," I said, nodding. "We wouldn't want anybody to get anybody else's keys, would we? You could be held liable for all sorts of nasty turns of events."

His eyes brightened at the word *nasty*.

"Listen, I respect your rules. I like rules, discipline, that sort of thing."

Now his eyes were incandescent.

"But," I said, a becoming catch in my throat, "we're talking about my mother here. The keys are all I have left of her. She had nothing else. Not even a watch. Not even a family Bible. So let me dig down in here . . ." I said, diving into the recesses of my purse. "Ah, yes, do you think fifty dollars will cover your trouble?"

I had exhausted young Valentino. The recalcitrant glasses went back up the nose. He disappeared into the storeroom and returned with two small keys, tagged "Albacco." Those he put into a small manila envelope; my fifty dollars, into his pocket.

"I'll page my dad now. About your front door."

"You know, that won't be necessary. My husband suggested Liz's Antique Hardware in Los Angeles. I'll try there first. Thanks again for the keys."

He looked crestfallen, but I sailed out of there, elated. No wonder so many crooks are recidivists. Who knew scamming one's fellow human beings could be so exhilarating? My first misdemeanor! Or was it a felony? I was going to have to pay those tickets right away.

I was dying to try the keys. I was certain they'd fit the lockbox. It was possible—more than possible. Mrs. Flynn had gone through all her sister's effects and never found any keys. And these babies had never been picked up. Maybe there'd be something in that lockbox that could make sense of things. Maybe something that would clear Joe's name. Better yet, something that would implicate someone else. I hadn't forgotten Perry Mason's Rule #1: If the client is innocent, someone else is guilty. Find the guilty party, and the client goes free. It seemed simple enough.

As I hurried back to the car, I punched in the number of the insurance office. I got a cheery greeting from the Queen Bee herself, who was pleased to inform me that because of my efforts, Mrs. Flynn had come in the day before and picked up the lockbox. Bingo.

Traffic notwithstanding, I made it to Mrs. Flynn's in a couple of minutes. I tore out of the car and bolted up the steps.

I rang the doorbell, waiting for that green eye to appear in the peephole. Nothing. There was no way I was giving up now. I rang again. Maybe she was taking a nap or a bath or something. When I tried knocking, the door pushed right open. Somebody else needed a locksmith.

"Mrs. Flynn? Are you there? Do you know your front door is open? Hello, Mrs. Flynn?"

The late-afternoon sun was blinding. I blinked a few times, then gasped. The living room was in shambles. It was as if a tornado had struck. The pictures were torn off the wall, the books ripped from their shelves, the chair overturned, the vase broken to bits. There seemed to be nothing left of the couch but stuffing, gray and swollen like storm clouds.

And where the hell was Mrs. Flynn? I tiptoed inside, trying not to breathe.

"Mrs. Flynn," I whispered, "it's Cece Caruso. You can

come out now. Are you all right?" The kitchen was a sea of broken dishes. There were pots and pans everywhere. The only thing that appeared untouched was a shiny set of knives poised on the counter: a steak knife, a paring knife, a serrated knife perfect for cutting grapefruit. I always wanted a set like that, but they were so expensive. I started to reach for one, then drew back with a shudder. What was I, crazy? I didn't have to do this. I could call for help. I pawed wildly through my bag, but I had left my cell phone in the car. Shit.

The hallway was narrow and dark. I moved toward the back, treading as lightly as possible over the clothes and papers strewn across the rug. I almost tripped over Mrs. Flynn's sewing kit, a tiny wicker basket with a wooden handle. I picked it up and tucked the pincushion back inside. It was one of those red ones with the little strawberry hanging by a thread. My grandmother used to have the very same one.

Clutching the basket to my chest, I crept past the tiny bathroom. The white tile floor was littered with a rainbow-colored assortment of pills, and the empty containers had been tossed in the tub. At the end of the hall was the door to what I guessed was the bedroom. I approached it slowly, reaching out for the knob. Suddenly impatient, I gave the door a good push and it swung open, hitting the wall with an unceremonious thump.

I don't know what I expected to see. Or whom. I called out for Mrs. Flynn once more, but it was obvious the house was empty. Even the burglars had gone home. Not before stripping the bed and flipping it on its side, though. What got me were Mrs. Flynn's cleaning skills. Not a dust bunny in sight. I got ahold of myself. I'd master the rudiments of housekeeping later. Right now, I had to leave. No, I had to call the police, then leave. But something caught my eye. There, on top of the dresser, twinkling in the sunlight, was a small ruby ring, the one I had seen on Mrs. Flynn's hand the other day. Why would the burglars have left it behind? I put it in my pocket, thinking I'd keep it safe for Mrs. Flynn.

As it turned out, she wouldn't be needing it. I tripped over the woman's dead body on the way out the front door.

17

$\mathcal{I}$'m useless with dead people. When I was sixteen, my father had a sudden heart attack. I fainted just before the funeral and wasn't permitted to attend. Since then, I've made an art form out of avoiding open caskets. My mother insists I have a nervous condition, inherited from my father's mother, whom she detested. Maybe so, but I doubt it. The truth is I'm afraid of ghosts.

But it was too late this time. She was under all that stuffing, covered in blood. I don't know how I missed her the first time. I bent down to feel for a pulse. Nothing. I could see her green eyes, but they couldn't see me.

Sangfroid eluded me. I felt the bile rise to my throat. Clutching my hand to my mouth, I stumbled out to the car and grabbed the phone but could barely hold it, I was trembling so badly. I dialed 911 and told them what I'd found. Then I sat down on the curb and gulped fresh air. I wasn't sure I could stand up again until I heard the sirens wail around the corner.

The cops were kind. They brought me coffee and someone

draped a blanket around my shoulders. I watched the coroner's truck pull into the driveway and the medical examiner go inside. Through the front window I could see flashbulbs popping. The neighbors came out and were standing around, pretending to turn on their sprinklers and look through their mail. A tall woman with a phone clipped to her belt affixed yellow tape around the perimeter of Mrs. Flynn's front lawn. It was a crime scene now.

After a while, two men came over and sat down on the curb next to me. They introduced themselves as Detectives Moriarty and Lewis. They inquired as to how long I had known the victim, and the nature of our relationship. I said five days, and that we had no relationship. We were acquaintances, that was it.

We talked for another half hour or so. They asked all the right questions but didn't seem very interested in my answers.

"That about wraps it up," Detective Lewis said, stretching out his long legs. He rose and a shower of crumbs hit the ground. Doughnuts. The blanket lady had brought them. "I have to ask you, Ms. Caruso, to let us know if you're planning to leave the area. This case will probably go to trial fairly quickly, and you'll be needed to testify."

"Excuse me, Detective, are you saying you know who's responsible?" Forensics had come a long way, but things were moving pretty fast for me.

"We've got a good idea. We've visited Mrs. Flynn before. She had a complicated life. Do you know her sons?"

"I didn't even know she had children."

"Well, you wouldn't want to boast about these two. Twins, but they don't look anything alike. One uglier than the other. They've been on our radar for years. Damon runs a crystal meth lab. Gil just beats people up. A couple of months ago, Gil showed up on his mom's doorstep with a forty-five, demanding money. Roughed her up pretty bad. Mrs. Flynn called us but decided not to press charges. We told her that was a bad idea, but mothers get kind of sentimental."

"So that's it?" I asked. "The investigation is over?"

"Well, she took a couple of bullets to the gut," Lewis said. "You figure it out."

Detective Moriarty finally spoke up. He was older, and had a Southern drawl. "No offense, ma'am, but we've been in the business for a while. Used to be we'd take our time, mull things over. We don't operate that way anymore. After all these years, Lewis and I, we can read a crime scene at a glance. The thing is, you don't want to throw too wide a loop. You don't want to look for something that isn't there."

I remembered a riddle I'd once heard:

Q: What's the difference between the cops and everyone else standing around at a murder scene?

A: The cops are the only ones who don't know who did it.

I decided to keep it to myself.

Moriarty and Lewis walked me to my car. I gave them back their blanket. That meant it was time to drive home. So I did.

I didn't sleep well that night. It was hot. I was sweaty. My hair stuck to my neck like flies to flypaper. I got up to pour myself a glass of water at four A.M. and sat at the kitchen table until I heard the thwack of the newspaper a few hours later.

I waited until seven to call Lael. She sounded sleepy and

pissed off. Baby August had been up all night with a fever, which had broken at six, and she had finally gotten him to sleep when I called. I apologized for my timing, explaining that I had just found a dead body and needed to talk.

She arrived an hour later, after arranging various play dates and baby-sitters. It was Sunday, so we headed over to the Hollywood Farmer's Market. Lael patted my back as I wept into my blue corn tamale.

"I just don't understand," I said, sniffling. "All I want to do is finish my book. That's not too much to ask, is it? Just some peace and quiet so I can work. But all of a sudden everything's gone to hell in a handbasket. Poor Mrs. Flynn. To be murdered by your own children. And I'm a witness, a witness in a hideous murder case! And I get to meet this fabulous, legendary clotheshorse, and she turns out to be a lunatic, and I wind up with a crush on the lunatic's son, who's too young for me. And Joseph Albacco, somehow I have to find out who really killed his wife since the prison chaplain thinks I'm a good Catholic, and—"

"Stop right there, missy," Lael said. "Let's go over this. First of all, the police are going to find that woman's sons and they're going to go to jail. You stumbled upon an ugly domestic drama, that's all. But Joseph Albacco, he needs a lawyer, Cece, or an investigator—a real one. You're not the person to handle something like this. C'mon."

"What do you mean by that?"

"Oh, don't get touchy, please. You know exactly what I mean. You're a writer, for Christ's sake. You write about this stuff—you don't get involved with it. You're not a cop. It's too late to impress your father."

"That was unkind."

"I'm sorry, but you can't let these people insinuate themselves into your life. You've got enough on your plate right now with Annie and Vincent."

"I know, I know. You're right. But Annie doesn't even want to talk to me. I suppose I've been obsessing about this whole Joseph Albacco thing because I was flattered to be needed."

"Well, maybe that's so, but don't let your weaknesses get you in more trouble than you're already in."

"Excuse me, aren't you supposed to be comforting me?"

"I'm supposed to be shopping."

Lael bought two dozen ears of corn, a dozen avocados, and a bagful of artichokes. Plus some gorgeous boysenberries. I bought candy-striped beets and tiger-striped tomatoes, some arugula, a pound of mountain-grown cherries, and cat grass for Mimi.

We stopped to listen to a Caribbean steel drum band. The front man was wearing an American flag top hat. I began to cheer up. We wandered past the incense and aromatherapy candles, past the yeast-free muffins and the flavored honeys. While we sampled white nectarines, a bald guy holding a bunch of kohlrabi sidled up to Lael.

"I don't know why I bought this stuff except I know it's supposed to be good for you. Do you have any idea how to cook it?"

Lael looked like a cross between Barbie and Strawberry Shortcake. Men adored her and she adored them. "Steaming is always nice," she said. "Or you could sauté it with a little garlic and white wine."

Soy and ginger would be better, I thought. But I kept quiet.

The tamale stand was on our way back to the car, and we decided on two more for the road.

"Have you tried the turkey, cranberry, and chipotle one? It's awesome. Would you like a bite?" It was an agent type, in horn-rims and a baseball cap, trying his luck like the rest of them.

"I don't eat meat, actually, but thanks," Lael said, with a smile that could've melted steel.

How did she do it? I suppose niceness is genetic. Lael's kids were nice, too, especially Tommy. Annie was nicer than I was, so maybe it skipped a generation in our family. Well, my mother wasn't actually that nice—maybe it skipped two generations.

While Lael paid for our tamales (I got another blue corn and she tried the lox, cream cheese, and onion), I inventoried hat styles. Everyone in L.A. lives in fear of carcinoma. Lots of hats in L.A. A tall, dark-haired woman in a floppy number caught my eye. She was wearing a cropped black T-shirt and had the flattest stomach I had ever seen. Lots of flat stomachs, too. Then I noticed the man she was with. It was Vincent. And in between them, holding their hands and laughing, was a little boy. I caught my breath. Vincent's little boy. He had his father's curly hair and his mother's dark skin and was holding a red balloon as big as he was. I stopped and watched, and wondered as I watched how I would tell Annie what a beautiful family they made.

18

*I*t's a sign of how well Lael knows me that she didn't seem at all surprised when I called her at two A.M. the following morning and asked her to help me break in to Mrs. Flynn's.

"I love you, Cece, but I think you've lost it," she said. I heard the rustle of sheets. Lael was reaching around for her reading glasses, which she had dropped on the floor late last night just before falling asleep with a book, most likely a cook-book, on her stomach. I knew her as well as she knew me.

"I also think you're searching for excuses not to work on your book. And that you don't want to accept what's going on with your daughter and son-in-law. And that you're afraid of a real relationship. And that you've been watching too much TV, reading too much crime fiction, and fantasiz-ing about how great you'd look in a black catsuit, scaling a wall. Am I right or wrong?"

"When did you become such a know-it-all? I need you, Lael. I can't do this alone."

"And why exactly do you want to do this at all?"

I had sat bolt upright in bed when I remembered. The

lockbox was in that house, and I needed to find out what was in it. The shock of seeing Mrs. Flynn dead had knocked clear out of my head my reason for being there in the first place. I had the keys, but she had the goods, and I had to find out if I could help Joseph Albacco or not.

Time was running out.

The parole hearing was in a week. And Father Herlihy had as much as told me that Joe wouldn't live to see another one. That he was on the verge of committing a mortal sin. I couldn't let that happen. There was no way the police were going to hand over that box so I could check its contents. Not right away, at least, and probably not ever. And it wasn't like I could explain how I came to be in possession of a dead woman's keys anyway.

I went through all of this calmly and rationally with Lael, but she wasn't buying. So I reverted to bribery.

"Will you do it for a Scooby snack?"

"Cece," she said, laughing.

"How about two Scooby snacks?"

Like the pooch in question, Lael was true blue. And she tolerated my obsessions, unlike certain daughters I could name. I heard the water go on, then a jacket being zipped up.

"I'll be waiting outside."

"With a flashlight and a nail file?"

"Check."

At that hour, there was no one on the road, and I broke the speed limit without even trying. You might think it would've dawned on me that I'd been breaking a lot of laws lately, but that realization came when it was already too late. At three-thirty A.M. that Monday morning, as we cut the motor and got out of the car in front of Mrs. Flynn's, I was still caught up in the fantasy not only of me in a catsuit, but of fixing something that had been broken beyond repair.

"Put on your gloves. And don't forget the stuff," I whispered. "What's that thing?"

"It's Tupperware."

"You brought food? We don't have time to eat right now," I said, frowning.

"No, it's for peeing into."

"What?"

"You know, for the stakeout."

"Lael. We're not waiting for anyone. We doing a quick B and E. In and out, you know the drill."

"I don't, I'm pleased to say."

I gave her a look. "Leave it in the car."

"It was a good idea. You're just annoyed you didn't think of it. Maybe we'll have to flee the house and hide in the car for hours. Maybe the killer is in there right now, or on his way back."

"Why'd you have to say that?"

"I'm sorry," she said, not meaning it, and unzipped her windbreaker.

"Sssh—are you trying to wake the neighbors?"

"I said I was sorry."

Looking around to make sure no one was watching, I lifted up the tape in front of the house, and we ducked underneath. When we got to the front door, I started fumbling around with the nail file. I had seen people pick locks millions of times on TV, and though I had never been stupid enough before to believe anything I'd seen on TV, at that moment I was operating on full loco mode. But the door pushed right open.

"That's what happened the last time I was here," I said.

"It is strange the police didn't lock up."

"Let's not get spooked here. We're going to get this over with and that'll be that. Lael, you search the back part of the house. I'll start up here."

"No way."

"Oh, fine."

Lael stuck to me like glue, which made it hard to maneuver in the dark. Plus, the place was the same mess it had been the day before. Lael held the flashlight, I did most of the poking, and we tried hard not to trip over anything or each other.

It took a solid forty-five minutes to make it through the house. With every "ouch" and "oof" and "sorry," I watched for the neighbors' lights, but they appeared to be heavy sleepers, thank goodness. We searched every cupboard, every drawer, every closet. The worst part was seeing Mrs. Flynn's clothes. They looked so frail on their hangers, like phantoms. We looked behind the armoire, in the hampers, in the shoeboxes. I even checked the freezer. Nothing. The lockbox was not in the house. It was gone.

"It's gone," I said to Lael.

"Gone," she echoed.

Of course it was gone. What a fool I'd been. Whoever had broken in to Mrs. Flynn's house that night hadn't been looking for money, or jewelry, or anything like that. He had been looking for Jean's lockbox. And he'd found it. Mrs. Flynn had been killed because she'd gotten in the way.

"Lael, we need to get out of here right now."

Lael turned off the flashlight and opened the front door.

"Wait, I hear something."

"Stop playing around, Cece. Let's go."

"No, I'm serious. Something in the backyard."

"It's probably crickets."

"I don't think so. It sounded like crackling leaves. I'm going to check."

"Oh, no, you're not. We're leaving this second."

"Sssh. Go outside and call Detective Lewis. Tell him what's going on."

"Where's his number?"

"Damn. It's at home."

"I'm going back there with you."

"Be quiet, then."

We tiptoed to the back door and opened it very slowly. Outside, it was pitch black. I couldn't see a thing. Lael was breathing down my neck.

"There! Did you hear that?"

But before Lael could answer, someone whipped past us at lightning speed, knocked me down onto the wet grass, and shot through the house and into the night.

"Cece, are you all right?" Lael gasped. "Who was that?"

"I'm fine. I didn't see him. Did you?" I picked myself up. I was shaking only a little bit. Less than the other morning when that Camaro guy had followed me. Maybe I was getting used to it. Big trouble, I mean.

"No. It was too dark."

"You're telling me," I said, peeling off my gloves.

"This isn't funny."

"Do you see me laughing?"

"We're going now."

"Wait."

"No!"

"But do you think he's still out there?"

We made our way to the front window and peeked through the curtains. They were beautiful, ivory lace. The street was deserted except for a pair of crows in Mrs. Flynn's jacaranda tree. They sounded like they were arguing.

"The coast is clear."

"I'll be right there."

I fished Mrs. Flynn's ruby ring out of my pocket. I hadn't meant to take it with me yesterday. I hadn't meant any of it. But having my heart in the right place wasn't something I had a right to be proud of. Not anymore. Facts were facts. I had put Lael in danger. I had put myself in danger. Worst of all, I had put Mrs. Flynn in danger, and I'd have to live with the consequences forever. Disgusted with myself, and more scared than I was willing to admit, I put the ring back on the dresser, where Mrs. Flynn had left it on the last day of her life, and went outside to ask my best friend if she would take my keys and drive us home.

19

$\mathcal{I}$t was close to seven A.M. when we got back to Lael's. She needed to get everyone up and ready for camp, so I went out to breakfast alone. At that hour, there weren't many choices. I picked Norm's on La Cienega, where it's Day of the Dead every day. Somehow, it seemed appropriate. Norm's was the sort of place where the vinyl seats were never wiped down between customers, and chances were good you'd sit in someone else's syrup, or worse. I attracted a bit of attention in my cat burglar ensemble, and I suppose it didn't help that I ordered bacon, sausage, and a Denver omelet. I was hungry. The slack-jawed patrons were electrified, the waitress was impressed, and the cook, well, he was bowled over and threw in a complimentary side of home fries, with lots of fresh onions and peppers. I would have liked to have reported that it was delicious, but I couldn't taste a thing. By the time I'd finished my third cup of coffee, it was the respectable hour of nine A.M. I went home and pulled Detective Lewis's card out of my desk drawer.

Unfortunately, he was out sick, so they connected me to

his partner, Detective Moriarty, the smug one with the drawl. Actually, they were both kind of smug. I asked him how Mrs. Flynn's case was progressing.

"Nothing's changed. We're still looking for the boys."

"I thought you were keeping tabs on them."

"We were, but they're smart for a pair of dummies. They knew we'd come looking so they flew the coop, both of 'em."

"How is that possible?"

"Damon's stuff is still at his apartment. He left in such a hurry he didn't even bother to take his favorite cowboy boots. That's what the building manager said. And Gil, well, that son of a bitch—excuse my French—ripped off his girlfriend to the tune of five hundred dollars and hasn't been seen or heard from since early Saturday morning."

I wasn't sure how to broach it. I was scared of getting sucked in deeper than I was. But I had to try.

"Do you think, Detective, that there's a possibility someone else could have been responsible? I mean, isn't it kind of strange that the boys would have trashed the house like that? Wouldn't they have known where their mother kept her money?"

"I told you they were dummies."

"But it doesn't exactly make sense."

"How's that, Ms. Caruso?"

"Well, for heaven's sake, why would they have left their mother's ruby ring behind?"

"What ruby ring?" he asked sharply.

Me and my big mouth.

"Didn't you see it, Detective? It was on Mrs. Flynn's dresser, in plain view. You must have missed it in all the hubbub."

"Suppose so."

"Check again."

"Thanks for the advice."

I ignored the sarcasm. "Listen, could there have been some other motive, some other person you might consider? Like maybe Lisette Johnson—have you come across that name?" She was the person Meredith Allan had mentioned. "I think she might've been an old enemy of Mrs. Flynn's or something—"

He cut me off. "Lisette Johnson?"

"You know her?" I asked, surprised.

"Of course I do. This is a small town, lady."

"Well, excuse me."

"Lisette Johnson is a Christian Coalition type running for the school board. She of all people isn't running around with a gun in her handbag. And besides, it's not your job to think about the murder of a woman you met only once. That's my job. And I know what I'm doing. You just go about your business, and Lewis and I will call you when you're needed. I appreciate your concern, but let the professionals handle it."

He hung up abruptly. I was annoyed. I remembered what Joseph Albacco had said about the police investigating his wife's murder. He had said they decided right from the beginning that he was guilty and never considered anyone else. And now it was happening all over again.

I lay on the floor and sulked a little, not sure what to do next. I wanted to talk to Annie. I dialed her number but hung up before it started ringing. I could wait until our date later this afternoon to drive the poor girl crazy. I ate some Moroccan olives and some dry roasted peanuts and watched Mimi play jump rope with Buster's tail. They were pretty good buddies, those two, except for Mimi's eating disorder. She was always sneaking Buster's diet kibble. She preferred it to tuna. He took his revenge by raiding her litter box, which I found most unappetizing. My train of thought was interrupted by the man of the house, who sprinted to the front door, tail wagging. He always beat the bell by a couple of seconds.

It was the cute UPS guy, struggling with a package. I signed that queer computery thing you sign and told him to dump it in the entry hall. It slid off the dolly and hit the floor with impunity.

It was my order from the Mystery Manor. I had to hand it to them. The bozo over there had found something incredible—a complete set of Gardner's "Speed Dash" adventures, which had appeared in one of the big-time pulps, *Top Notch,* in the twenties and thirties. I loved Speed Dash. Perry Mason was invincible, sure, but Sidney "Speed" Dash was a superhero. He could climb anything, plus he had a photographic memory, plus he didn't smoke or drink or harbor at any time or under any circumstances an impure thought. His virtue gave him that little something extra a person needed to vanquish evil.

Gardner had been inspired by something he came across one day in Ventura. It was 1927, and he was walking from the county courthouse back to work when he saw a crowd gathered outside his office building. They were watching Mr. "Babe" White, a human fly, scale the building's four stories without a net. One false move, and good-bye Babe. Luckily, he made it. The crowd went wild. Gardner jogged upstairs full of ideas. Some wonderful stories came out of that experience.

One of the best things about this project was getting to look through old issues of *Top Notch, Black Mask,* and *Best Detective.* They were called "pulps" because they were printed on cheap wood-pulp paper, unlike the higher-toned and more expensive "slicks." I loved the gaudy illustrations, full of blood and cleavage, the advertisements for things like mustache wax, and the sheer pleasure of stumbling across a story by somebody like Raymond Chandler, who'd claimed, somewhat improbably in my opinion, that he'd learned to write by dissecting one of Erle Stanley Gardner's Ed Jenkins novelettes.

There were sports pulps, Western pulps, adventure pulps, fantasy pulps, science-fiction pulps, and sexy pulps (the *Spicy* series is one of my favorites). At their height, the two hundred pulps that were published once or twice a month needed hundreds of millions of words' worth of stories a year. Eager to get in on it, Gardner had tried his hand. The first story he submitted to *Black Mask* was "The Shrieking Skeleton." It was a dog. One of the big muckety-mucks at the magazine read the story and sent a note around the office saying the characters talked like dictionaries and the plot had whiskers on it like Spanish moss hanging from a live oak in a Louisiana bayou—obviously a frustrated writer himself. They sent the story back, but someone had inadvertently left the note between the second and third pages of the story, and Gardner read it. Instead of falling into a depression, as I would have, he stayed up for three nights rewriting the story. He typed with two fingers, and when he pounded his skin off, he just kept hammering away on the blood-spattered keys. He was that kind of tough guy. Finally, he sent the story back and it was accepted, mostly, he suspected, because the editors at *Black Mask* were so disconcerted by the whole incident.

My book was going to be good. This guy was great material. I was going to figure everything out. And I couldn't wait to get my hands on my newest acquisition. Only I couldn't lift the box. I got a knife from the kitchen and sliced through the tape right there in the entry hall. The box was full of those styrofoam peanuts, which I tossed on the ground to Buster's and Mimi's delight. But what I found underneath was not a collection of *Top Notch* magazines. It was Jean Albacco's lockbox, and it seemed to be made of solid steel.

20

*I*f I had bothered to look at the return address, I would have seen right away that the package had been sent to me by Mrs. Flynn. There was a note inside:

> *Dear Miss Caruso,*
>   *I'm leaving this in your care. I don't think it's safe to keep here. I've been hearing noises. I think you may be right about everything. You will know what to do.*
>   *Best,*
>   *Theresa Flynn*

The stationery had a row of teacups on it, with a fluffy kitten right in the middle. This was a horror show. What had I done? How could I be right about everything when I obviously knew nothing? Mrs. Flynn had been hearing noises. That had to have been the killer. But how did he know she'd had that lockbox in her possession? She hadn't claimed it for forty-odd years. He must've known she'd gone to that insurance office. He must've been watching her.

He must have followed her there. But why? What had triggered his interest? My stomach gave a sudden lurch. It wasn't her he'd been watching. It was me. Was he watching me right now?

I leapt up and yanked the living room curtains closed. The sound of the iron rings skittering across the rod was worse than nails on a chalkboard. I picked up the knife I'd dropped on the floor and ran to the phone table in the hallway. I got my hammer out of the drawer. Holding one weapon in each hand like a lunatic, I ran around the house, searching every corner and throwing open every closet door until I was satisfied there was no one hiding anywhere. Only after turning on the burglar alarm was I ready to retrieve the keys I'd scammed out of the locksmith. They were hidden in the butter dish.

I sat down on the floor of the entry hall and tried them, half expecting the lock not to turn. But it did. Slowly, I lifted the lid of Jean Albacco's lockbox. It felt heavy, like your limbs as you're falling asleep.

Then the doorbell rang. It was Javier. He wanted to talk about my black mondo grass, which I already knew was failing. I told him I had laryngitis and we'd work it out on Thursday. I slammed the peephole shut.

I sat back down on the floor and closed the box. Did I really want to do this? Wasn't I taking this method-acting thing a little too far? I was no Erle Stanley Gardner, much less Perry Mason. Wouldn't it be better to get out of these people's lives and hand the whole thing over to the police, who knew what they were doing? Well, yes, that would've been fine in principle. But the police didn't know what they were doing, and even if they did, they didn't care— about any of it. Joseph Albacco was being punished for a crime he didn't commit, and Mrs. Flynn had gotten in the way. I'd put her there. Looking inside that box was the least I could do. I lifted the lid again. It smelled like the past, like ashes.

There were pictures on the very top. Jean and her sister as children, at the beach in 1947. Jean's parents at their wedding, the bride and groom looking terrified. Joe in high school, handsome in his football jersey. A stained photo of a small child wearing a frilly white dress. There was Jean's social security card, and Joe's life insurance policy, which would pay out five thousand dollars to his survivors. Then some receipts, one for a watch purchased in New York City at Promenade Jewelers in 1933, another for a stove, dating from 1956. A warranty for a camera. A letter from Joe to Jean, written while he was working on an oil rig the summer after high school. Sweet.

Underneath the photos I found two slim bankbooks held together by a rubber band. I peeled off the rubber band and put it around my wrist. Then I studied the book on top. It was navy blue, with embossed gold letters that read "Ventura Savings and Loan." I turned to the first page. The Albaccos' joint checking account. They'd opened it in 1956, the year they were married. I scanned the pages, a little surprised at how easily snooping came to me. But then again, I'm the sort of person who looks inside people's medicine cabinets at parties. It's horrible, I know.

Jean, or Joe, one of them, was frighteningly organized. Every entry was annotated with a red pencil. There were regular deposits made every two weeks. One set was marked "JLA," the other "JA." Jean Logan Albacco and Joseph

Albacco. Paychecks, I assumed, from Gilbert, Finster, and Johnson, the insurance company where Jean had worked, and the *Ventura Press,* where Joe had been employed. Jean earned more than Joe did. He would've hated that. He seemed the type. Had she rubbed his nose in it? Probably. The withdrawals were all for small amounts—twenty-five, thirty, one hundred dollars. Household expenses, rent maybe. Nothing unusual. The second bankbook was more curious.

It was for a savings account at the Bank of Santa Barbara. And it was held in the name of Jean Logan. It seemed to have been opened while Jean was still in high school. I didn't have a bank account of my own until I got divorced. I guess I lacked Jean's ambition.

There were no withdrawals made. None whatsoever. I looked over the deposits. There were a hell of a lot of those. There was a series in the amount of $35 that were made every two weeks for a year starting in July of 1953. These were marked "LP." Then a series of deposits of $150 that were marked "BW." They came every three weeks for six months in 1955, then stopped. There was a group from 1956 marked "DG," and these were in the amount of $200. They appeared at irregular intervals, a couple a month, nothing for two months, then deposits for three days in a row. The last group was from 1957. Every week like clockwork, in the amount of $400. They were marked "MA," and the last one was made a week before Jean's death, on December 6, 1957.

Now my head was swimming.

Any way you did the math, it came out the same. Jean had accumulated a small fortune. The conclusion was inescapable. She was a teenage blackmailer, just like Meredith

Allan had said, and making a pretty good go of it up until
the moment she went and got herself killed.

Yeah, up until that moment Jean had done everything
right. She was a real pro. She'd even stashed her loot out of
town, in Santa Barbara, where nobody knew her. Where
nobody would've paid a lick of attention to a dark-haired
girl looking for someplace to hide a whole lot of dollar bills.

But who were these people lining up to make her rich—
"LP," "BW," "DG," and "MA"? "BW" had to have been Bill
Winters, the infamous gym teacher. Ellie had confirmed
that. "LP" was a mystery, as was "DG." And then there was
"MA." It couldn't be a coincidence that those were Meredith
Allan's initials. That woman was in this mess up to her eye-
balls, I just knew it. But it didn't make sense. If she had been
one of Jean's victims, why would she have breathed a word
about it to me? Even implied anything of the sort? Sheer
perversity, maybe. But why would Jean have been blackmailing her husband's mistress to begin with? Isn't the cheating husband the one who gets blackmailed? Perhaps Jean
had something on Meredith Allan that was entirely unrelated to the woman's affair with her husband. It wouldn't
surprise me one bit. I'd bet the farm Meredith Allan had
skeletons in every one of her overstuffed closets.

At the bottom of the box there was a manila envelope
marked PERSONAL. I hesitated for a second, but who was I
kidding? I had gone too far already. I opened the envelope
carefully and pulled out a sheet of paper with a California
State Legislature letterhead. It was dated May 17, 1928. It
was a carbon copy, but it was here, in Jean's lockbox, so
clearly it had meant something to someone. I had to read it

a couple of times, but it still didn't exactly make sense. Somebody was advising a Mr. Allan (Meredith's father?) to dispose of his tidelands holdings immediately. Besides that, there was a lot of mumbo-jumbo, business-type stuff, and I didn't speak that language. So how come Jean did? Who taught her? What was she doing with this letter? How badly had someone wanted it back?

21

*C*all me crazy, but I had a feeling Jean's lockbox should not remain on the premises if I wanted to keep breathing, which I did. But I needed help. The thing was small but heavy. I called Yellow Cab and asked them to send some muscle. I had a safe-deposit box at the Bank of America on Santa Monica Boulevard near Crescent Heights that was empty except for the deed to my house and some floppy disks so old they should probably go to the Smithsonian. It was the perfect hiding place. Public and inviolable. I'd tip the cab-driver, and he'd haul it in.

Ahmed was a peach, and no one said boo. I raced home. I had to change and meet Annie in less than an hour, and the setting warranted a hat.

The Huntington Library, Art Collections, and Botanical Gardens is located in Pasadena, the oldest of Los Angeles's old-money enclaves. It's a stone's throw from Caltech (home of the Mars Rover and many bespectacled earthquake pun-dits) but immune to the siren call of intellectual panic that echoes there. At the Huntington, the air is warm, but not thin. At the Huntington, all is *luxe, calme, et volupté*.

It's not often that a railroad magnate decides he has to have 150 acres of gardens, filled with the world's rarest and most beautiful blooms. And grottoes and *tempiettos* and a Zen rock garden and a Gutenberg Bible and Gainsborough's *Blue Boy* and Lawrence's *Pinky* and an English tearoom that serves scones with real clotted cream. The old guy wasn't responsible for the scones, of course. But back in 1903, Henry Edwards Huntington had had the vision to buy a working ranch in San Marino (it came with a dairy herd, a bunch of chickens, orange and avocado groves) and turn it into a landmark. Inside the museum was a portrait of Henry's wife, Arabella, which I studied every time I visited. Arabella wore dark-rimmed glasses and looked fierce. I suspected she provided Henry with additional impetus.

The last time Annie and I had been at the Huntington was back in May, for their annual plant sale. The theme was "Weird and Wonderful Magical and Mystical Plants," and we went determined to put together a black garden. Burnett was right. I was morbid, and I'd infected my only child early on. But what was I supposed to do? Was it my fault she found Miss Marple more compelling than Winnie the Pooh? Her kindergarten teacher certainly thought so.

Anyway, we'd had Lael's red Radio Flyer wagon that day, and we'd piled a fabulous assortment of plants into it, plants that were not truly black but superdark shades of purple and maroon: black-flowered hollyhock, a dark ajuga called "Chocolate Chip," a dianthus named "Sooty," a cordalis with dark purple leaves, a strange columbine named "Chocolate

Soldier," the camellia "Midnight Magic," and the doomed
black mondo grass I'd have to deal with on Thursday with
Javier.

"There's nothing like the enthusiasm of a new convert,"
the smiling docent had said to me at the checkout area,
cracking my hard-won veneer of sophistication with a single
blow. You can take the girl out of New Jersey, blah, blah,
blah. My whole problem was I didn't want to accept that.
That wasn't my whole problem, actually.

Today, Annie was waiting for me in front of the galleries.
Arm in arm, we walked inside. We ogled a Hepplewhite
desk with turquoise tile inlays that I'm sure would have
helped me write my book faster. We marveled over the
shelves and shelves of first editions under glass, like pheas-
ants, and the miniatures in pearl- or diamond-encrusted
frames. Anything except talk to each other. In a dimly lit
room we stopped in front of a seventeenth-century painting that depicted a little girl reading the palm of a boy
about her age. He was looking out at the viewer as if to
confide that he knew he was being scammed but didn't
mind. The painting was a perfect metaphor for the way
men patronize women, which made it all the more alarm-
ing that I found it so cute.

"I don't like it, Mom," Annie said.

"Good for you. It sends a bad message."

"I'm not talking about the painting, Mom. I'm talking
about the creepy stuff you're into lately. It's like you think
you're in one of your Perry Mason mysteries. It's not healthy."

"Annie, you don't need to worry about me. Let me worry
about you. That's how it's supposed to go."

"Everything's fine with me," Annie said as we stepped

outside into the sunlight. It was quiet except for the steady hum of lawn mowers.

"That's what I wanted to talk about. Annie, there's something about Vincent I need to tell you."

"Well, don't be so melodramatic. I said I was fine with all of it."

"I saw Vincent at the farmer's market on Sunday, with Lael."

"What was he doing with Lael?"

"No, I was with Lael. He was with somebody else."

"With Alexander, his son? And Roxana?"

I was taken aback. "How did you know?"

"I've spoken to Vincent, Mom. He told me he had gotten in touch with them. It's wonderful, don't you think?"

"Well, yes, of course. But how do you really feel?"

Annie laughed. She seemed to have not a care in the world. It was unnatural.

"Look at all these heat lamps, Mom. In the middle of a desert garden. It's so funny."

We sat down on a bench in front of a field of small cacti as round and white as snowballs. They were surrounded by some orange plants that resembled huge pumpkins. I was riveted by the six-foot phallic plumes. They were pointy all over and reminded me of Annie's father. A lot of sound and fury, signifying nada.

"Well, San Marino isn't Madagascar, sweetie. That's where these babies came from."

"I guess it can get cold here in winter."

"What are you going to do?"

"I'm going to help Vincent do what's right."

"But what about what you want?"

"That doesn't matter anymore, Mom."

"Are you saying that you want him back? Because he wants you back."

"He needs to be with his son. And if he can make it work with Roxana, that's how it should be. Do you really expect me to get in the way? It would be selfish."

Annie was anything but selfish. And I was as proud of her as I was devastated for her.

We strolled past the towering stalks of bamboo and the lily ponds stuffed with carp, past the herb garden, where the docents ordered us to pinch and sniff. By that time the sweat was pooling under the brim of my hat and I'd had enough. Even the lemon verbena couldn't tempt me.

On my way out to the car, I noticed the morning-glory vines trailing across the tops of some Italian cypresses. It made me feel better that the Huntington had morning-glory troubles, too. Bloodsuckers, Javier called them. Got to pull them up the minute you see them, or they'll take over and eventually everything will die. It was hard. They were so pretty.

We said good-bye in the parking lot, and I gave Annie an extra hug.

"Mom, don't freak out on me," she called out of her car window, waving.

"Do I ever?" I called back. She didn't reply. She must've been too far away to hear me.

So I had a little problem on the 134 going home. Someone was following me. Again. It was when I peered into the rearview mirror to check my makeup that I first noticed the car. Also, that the Mango-a-Go-Go had bled into the little bitty lines around my mouth. I reapplied my lipstick and forgot about the whole thing, but there it was, fifteen minutes later, that same car, a dark SUV, right behind me. I sped up and changed lanes a couple of times, but there seemed to be no getting away.

I tried to remember the tricks of the trade, how to lose a tail and all, but since investigating murders past and present wasn't really my trade, I found myself at a loss. But I didn't fall apart. In fact, I was surprised at how calm I was. And why shouldn't I be? It was still light out, I was in a Camry that had seen me through worse days, and I'd suddenly remembered that the best thing to do when you thought you were being followed was to drive straight to the police station. So I got off the freeway at the Forest Lawn Cemetery exit, which I hoped wasn't prophetic, and headed straight to the only precinct house in L.A. whose address and phone number I knew by heart.

I met Detective Peter Gambino (no relation to the crime family) one night about three years ago when, following a lovely Placido Domingo concert at the Hollywood Bowl, I discovered my car had been stolen. At the police station the booking sergeant listened to my tale of woe, nodded sagely, and told me to wait while he called for Detective Gambino.

I remember being a little surprised they'd put a detective on a run-of-the-mill car theft, especially once I told them I owned a 1983 Camry, which in Los Angeles is roughly equivalent to being invisible. Perhaps there was a car-theft ring operating in the area or something. And it wasn't as if I'd never owned a sexy car. There was a Karmann Ghia one of my ex's ex-students needed to sell in a hurry because he was moving to London. He was the spoiled type who couldn't be bothered, so I got a great deal. And I lost my head. Just sitting in that beautiful thing made my heart beat faster. But I learned my lesson after the top wouldn't open and the privilege of fixing it set me back $1,700.

Anyway, that evening had been full of revelations. I found out my theory about the stolen-car ring was beside the point because my car had not been stolen, merely towed away for blocking someone's driveway. I also found out that Sergeant Owens had taken one look at me and decided Gambino and I would make a nice couple. Owens had a good eye. We did make a nice couple. But that was a long time ago, and this was now. I burst through the double doors, dragging my hat behind me.

Apparently, Sergeant Owens hadn't budged in three years.

"Cece Caruso? I'm having déjà vu. But I'm fresh out of Italian cops, sorry to say."

"Owens, I think I'm being followed. That's why I came here," I gasped. "It's a dark SUV. Black, I think. It followed me all the way from Pasadena."

"Jesus Christ. Calloway," he bellowed at a kid in uniform who was just coming on duty, "get out there and see if you see the car."

Without a word Calloway sprinted outside, his hand poised on his gun. I was sobered by the fuss I had generated without exactly meaning to. I wanted to scream "No guns!" but doubted Calloway had been trained to take orders from a civilian trailing a picture hat.

Owens came out from behind the desk and put his arm around me while we waited for the kid to return.

"Did you get the license plate?" he queried.

I hadn't.

"Forget about it," he said, all avuncular. "Your hair is different. I like it."

Calloway came back, panting. "No one out there, Sarge. I went around both corners, but didn't see anything out of the ordinary. No SUVs at all. I'm really sorry, ma'am," he added politely.

"Oh, don't be sorry," I said, wondering if I had imagined the whole thing. "Can I just sit down here for a minute?"

"Of course. Calloway, get her some water. Caruso, you want water? Or coffee? Coffee would be better. Calloway, get her some coffee."

While I sipped the coffee, which was suprisingly good, I thought about it. I liked excitement. I tended toward hyperbole. I was making something out of nothing, as usual. That was all it was. The black SUV was one of the thousands, tens of thousands, hundreds of thousands, probably, going from Pasadena to Hollywood at the same time I had been.

Feeling sheepish, I got up to leave. Then I heard a familiar voice.

"Caruso, you in trouble again?"

"Don't you have work to do, Gambino?"

"Still got a mouth on you. And as gorgeous as ever."

Gambino wrapped me up in a bear hug. I closed my eyes and felt the warmth of his body. Then I pulled away, suddenly shy.

"How've you been, Peter?" I managed. At that moment, I had no memory of why we'd broken up. None whatsoever. Well, maybe a glimmer. Something about oil and water.

"Getting by. How about you? God, it's been a long time."

"Everything's good."

"Then what are you doing here?"

I was about to answer when there was a ruckus at the door. Three ladies, actually three gentlemen decked out as ladies, were being dragged in, boas flying.

"How come you never dressed cute and sexy like that for me?" Gambino cracked.

I burst into tears.

"Aw, jeez. I guess it's been that kind of day. Me, too. Let's go back here."

I followed him into the interrogation room.

"You must have a guilty conscience," he said, laughing. "Don't look so worried. This is the only place we can have any privacy, that's all."

"I'm not worried about that," I said, drying my eyes.

"What's going on, Caruso?"

I looked up into his intelligent brown eyes, framed by a pair of worn-out wire-rimmed glasses, and told him everything.

I told him how I'd been blocked with my book, and how I'd thought meeting Joseph Albacco would give me some insight into ESG. I told him about Jean and her penchant for blackmail, and about Meredith Allan, whom I could swear was hiding things, and about stumbling over Mrs. Flynn's body. I was about to get into the stranger who had plowed into me in the middle of the night but thought better of it. Ditto the lockbox. I didn't want to have to admit I'd violated a crime scene. And impersonated a dead woman's daughter. Actually, more than one person's daughter, if you were counting Ellen Sammler. And I told him about Annie.

He listened intently. I remembered what a good listener he was. And that he didn't like watching sports on television. That he had a million good stories about Buffalo, where he grew up, like the one about his neighbor, who started a fish hatchery in his basement, forgetting that water freezes in Buffalo starting in October. That he hated capers. That he had a soft spot for so many things it couldn't really be called a spot. It was kind of a general condition.

At the end of my story, he shook his head in disbelief.

"Look, Cece, do you realize what you're doing? Let me put it clearly so you can understand. You are not a police officer. You are not a prosecutor. And lord knows, you are not a defense attorney. Even assuming this guy is innocent, which I highly doubt, you do not have the slightest idea of what has to be done to get him out. Do you think you're going to walk up to the warden and bat your eyes and they're going to apologize for everything? Your dad was a cop. You should know better."

"You don't have to be so condescending. I'm not an idiot."

"I'm sorry. I didn't mean it like that. But this guy's dangerous, Cece. There's more here than meets the eye."

"I know. That's my point."

"That's not what I'm talking about. Listen, Cece, you don't sit in prison for forty-plus years for killing someone, not unless you're Charlie Manson. It just doesn't work that way. This guy's been up for parole before, guaranteed, many times, and the reason he's still in Tehachapi——Jesus, fucking Tehachapi——is he's been denied."

"So?"

"Prisoners are denied parole when they're considered a threat."

That hadn't been Father Herlihy's interpretation.

"Albacco's probably caused all kinds of trouble since he's been inside. I'm telling you, the guy is violent."

"He certainly didn't seem that way."

"They never do."

"Are you seeing anyone?" I asked, less casually than I'd meant to.

"Sort of," he answered. "You?"

"Sort of," I said. "And what about Mrs. Flynn?"

"What about her?" he asked, all flustered. I'd remembered how it used to bug him when I would switch gears all of a sudden. That's why I did it just then.

"The police think her sons killed her, but I'm not so sure."

"What were the names of the detectives on the Flynn case?"

"Moriarty and Lewis."

"Look, I am willing to call them and talk to them about it, see what's going on. But these are completely unrelated matters, Cece. You can't take on other people's problems."

But they weren't unrelated, and they were my problems.

"Just promise me you won't do anything foolish. Wait until you hear from me." He reached out to stroke my cheek. "I care about what happens to you," he said softly. "And Annie."

But I couldn't wait. So I went ahead and did exactly what Gambino told me not to.

23

I headed back to Tehachapi first thing the next morning. And after the long ride out there, I was impatient. So when Joe sat down, looking paler than I'd remembered, I got right to the point.

"What's your blood type?"

"AB positive," he answered, knowing exactly what I was asking him. "Same as Jean's."

The same as Jean's. Of course. The police had just assumed the blood on Joe's sleeve was his wife's. And that he had gotten it on his shirt when he killed her. But he hadn't killed her, I knew that now—I believed it absolutely. It was his blood on that shirt. I don't know how it got there, but it was his blood nonetheless. But why bother with the facts? They were inconvenient. They clogged the works. The husband was going to take the fall, the truth be damned.

Sometimes things come to you in dreams, things that elude you by day. It makes getting up a hell of a bummer. But if you trick yourself a little, ease into consciousness, you can keep hold of what's been revealed to you. You can grab on to the truth while letting your dreams slip away.

The night before, I had seen it. Like a jigsaw puzzle with a thousand pieces you despair of ever finishing, and anyway, you've lost so many of the pieces it doesn't matter, but you keep going, you keep trying, and you finish, only to realize you had the pieces all along, not a single one was missing. In my dreams, it made sense, just like that. I couldn't put it into words yet, but it was only a matter of time. Too bad time was what I didn't have.

"So where is that shirt now?" I asked, my thoughts racing. "We have to get the DNA analyzed."

"It's in an evidence locker somewhere, but even if we could prove the blood on it was mine, it wouldn't change things."

"It would change everything. It would destroy the case against you."

"No, it wouldn't, Ms. Caruso."

"Why, because you still don't have an alibi?" I snapped.

He didn't answer me.

"You have an alibi, Mr. Albacco. We both know you do. I'm through pretending."

He called for the guard. He was through, too. "Get out of here," he said coldly. "I'm hanging up the phone."

"What's wrong with you?" I shouted. "You're a fool! Do you realize you've wasted your life for nothing? She wasn't worth it."

"Shut up," he said in a voice that frightened me. "You don't know anything."

"Yes, I do. I've seen her. I've seen Meredith Allan."

Everything stopped. The clock stopped ticking. The molecules in the air stopped circulating.

"Do I have your attention now?"

He didn't answer, but I needn't have asked.

"I went to her house. I met her son. She told me things about Jean."

He was breathing hard now. He wanted to leave the room, to go back to his cell, back under the covers, back in time. But he wasn't strong enough. He never had been. That was why he kept choosing the wrong woman.

His blue eyes were red. I owed him something, so I didn't look. I stared at the wallpaper instead. It looked dirty and wrinkled, like used paper towels.

He cleared his throat. "Ms. Caruso?"

I turned to him.

"Did she ask about me?"

I wanted to lie but couldn't.

He swallowed hard, accustomed to disappointment. I had misread him so badly the first time we met I had to laugh.

"Is something funny?"

"I'm sorry. I didn't mean to make light of this. I'm just nervous."

"My father killed himself when I was just a kid," he said, apropos of nothing.

"I didn't know that."

"It was horrible for my mother. He betrayed her, left us with nothing. So what did I do? I was no better than my old man. I betrayed my wife. I cheated on her. She trusted me and built a life for me and I betrayed her. I couldn't do it again. Not twice. Not to Meredith. I can't even now. Don't you understand?"

"No, I don't."

"It doesn't matter. So what did Meredith say about Jean? That she knew about us." It was more of a statement than a question.

"No. That she blackmailed people."

He was stunned, and I mean like he'd been hit in the gut. He accused me of lying to him, he accused me of everything in the book, but I couldn't back down, not now.

"Your wife socked away a lot of money, ruining people's lives. Meredith's life, for example."

"Meredith's life?" He looked more puzzled than ever.

"Tell me something. Why would your wife have black-mailed your mistress?"

"You're out of your mind."

"I don't think I am. Maybe Jean did know about your affair. Maybe she knew and didn't care. You never consid-ered that, did you? But someone else might have cared. Meredith's father, maybe? Maybe he didn't want his daugh-ter wasting her life on someone like you. Or a boyfriend? Did Meredith have a boyfriend, someone who couldn't find out she was sleeping with a married man?"

He wouldn't look at me. That was fine. I didn't need him to.

"Maybe Jean knew something else about Meredith. That she went a little crazy sometimes? Like that night, maybe? Did she hurt you that night, Joe? Is that why your shirt was covered with your blood?"

Still no answer.

"Or maybe it was something else entirely. Did your wife know something about Meredith's father's business dealings, something that wasn't right, that could ruin him? Like about some tidelands holdings? Does that sound familiar? Meredith would've paid Jean to keep something like that silent. She would have, wouldn't she?"

"I don't know anything about Morgan Allan. This is ridiculous."

"How long could Meredith keep it going? Forever, I suppose, a rich girl like her. But it must've stung, having to keep her lover's wife quiet with her father's money."

"What are you asking me?" he demanded.

"I'm not asking you anything. I'm telling you something. I'm telling you Meredith got sick of paying off your wife, so she killed her."

"That's impossible, and you know it."

"So now you admit it. You were with her."

"I'm not admitting anything."

"She still could've done it, Mr. Albacco. Don't you get it? She has that black magic. If anybody could, that woman could have been two places at once."

"Why don't you stop this?"

"And the thing is, that wasn't the end of it, oh, no. She killed Jean's sister, too."

"Theresa?" he asked weakly. "What happened to her?"

"She was killed on Saturday."

"That isn't true."

"I'm sorry, but it is. And I think that the person who killed your wife killed her, too."

"It wasn't Meredith, I'm telling you. She could never do anything like that. Not to Jean, not to Theresa, not to anyone. I know that. She's a good person. Beautiful and good. And I loved her."

He was a wounded animal who needed to be put out of his misery. But I wasn't the one who could do it.

"Has she had a good life, Ms. Caruso?" He was pleading with me now. "Has it been a good life?"

It was my turn not to answer. I just left, feeling sick at heart.

24

$\mathcal{I}$ knew I'd have to see Meredith Allan again, but the very thought of her turned my stomach. I called her secretary, Mr. Wingate, from the car. I had interrupted his lunch. Tarragon chicken salad. His mouth was full and he was vague. She had gone away for a few days; oh, he didn't exactly know where, just that she was taking a leisurely drive up the coast and she'd be back over the weekend. I wondered if Meredith Allan could have been the one who'd followed me. And who'd mowed me down at Mrs. Flynn's. But she didn't seem like someone who'd do her own dirty work. She'd hire out. Mr. Wingate suggested I call him back on Monday afternoon, after he'd had a chance to confer with the Fairy Queen about her plans for the following week. I supposed it could wait that long.

When I got home, Buster was hiding under the bed. This meant only one thing. I sniffed around. It was never the obvious places. Aha. He'd tried to hide the evidence under the bedspread, but it isn't hard to spot a torn bag of La Brea Bakery rolls. Not given its distinctive shade of burnt sienna.

I loved reading the advice on the back of the bag about how to make a good egg salad sandwich, but it was about time they came up with something new. One roll had been left on my pillow, like an offering. At least I still merited some respect. I walked back to the kitchen and plugged in the Dustbuster, then wandered over to the answering machine.

There was a message from Lael reminding me about her annual Labor Day barbecue on Saturday afternoon. How could I forget? Every year something cataclysmic happened at Lael's Labor Day barbecue. Also, a message from my editor. I erased it. And a call from Burnett. His birthday was this weekend, and his mother was throwing a party on Sunday at the Oviatt Building. It would have a 1940s theme. Would I consider going as his date?

Wow. It was great for my ego, this being pursued by a gorgeous, younger man thing. But given my suspicions about his mother, I felt strange about accepting the invitation. But then again, maybe that was all the more reason to stay close. And his voice was so sexy. And those kisses. And I loved dress-up. I listened to the message two more times, twirling the phone cord around my fingers. What about Gambino? We were history. Oil and water, I reminded myself. I called Burnett back and got his machine. I waited for the beep then told it, him, whomever, that I'd be there. Did I dare don a snood?

Then I dialed Annie's number, but hung up after it had rung only once because I was getting another call. I hoped it was Burnett. I wanted to hear his voice again.

"Hello?"

"Yes, hello, is this Cece Caruso?" It was an old man's voice.

"It is. Who's calling, please?"

"Don't concern yourself with trivialities," he said portentously. "May I suggest you stay out of other people's business? I'm sure you're aware that curiosity killed the cat."

"You must be kidding," I said. "Who is this?"

"A friend. I can't say any more. Well, maybe one more thing, and that concerns—"

"Oh, can you hold on a minute? I have another call."

"Very well."

It was Annie, wanting to know if I'd just called.

"How'd you know?"

"I star-sixty-nined you. I thought it might've been Vincent."

"Did you have something you wanted to say to him?"

"Mom."

"Listen, I'm in the middle of an anonymous call. Can I call you back?"

"Sure."

"I'm back," I announced.

"Fine. As I was saying, let sleeping dogs lie."

"Could you be more specific, please?"

"I have to go now. Someone's here. Good-bye."

My mystery caller hung up, so I star-sixty-nined him.

"Good afternoon, Gilbert, Finster, and Johnson, licensed insurance brokers. May I help you?"

I hung up instantly. I needed to think.

The phone rang.

"Gilbert, Finster, and Johnson, licensed insurance brokers here," said the same sugarcoated voice. "I must have lost you. May I be of service?"

Damn that star sixty-nine. Now what? I could hardly ask to be connected to the old man with the quavering voice. Could I?

"This is Cece Caruso, do you remember me?"

"Yes, we do." I think it was the young one, the rebel. Were they wearing their blue Lacoste shirts today? "Oh, Ms. Caruso, isn't it just terrible about Mrs. Flynn?"

"It is."

"And to think, you were probably one of the last people to see her alive."

"Listen, I have a quick question for you. Do you happen to know who else besides you ladies might have been aware of the fact that I was going to pay a call to Mrs. Flynn? And that she came in to pick up her sister's lockbox?"

"Might I ask how that would be relevant?"

"It's just that I thought I could send a condolence card." Well, that made about as much sense as starting a fish hatchery in Buffalo.

"Old Mr. Gilbert, the one who was Mrs. Flynn's sister's boss. He knew. We told him. And he was around the day Mrs. Flynn stopped by."

Old Mr. Gilbert. "Is he in? I'd like to say hello."

"Well, you're in luck. He is, and he'll be delighted to chat. Not too many people call him these days. He usually just sits around, reading the papers. Just a moment, please."

She put me through.

"Hello?"

"Hello, Mr. Gilbert. It's Cece Caruso. You just called to threaten me? We must have gotten disconnected."

Now he had nothing to say. I almost felt sorry for the man. But not that sorry.

"What kind of car do you drive, Mr. Gilbert? A black SUV, by any chance?"

"I don't drive any longer, I'm afraid. My license was taken away after a few unfortunate incidents."

That'd happened to my grandmother recently. She was ninety-two years old. Something about her bifocals and a rude crossing guard.

"Why did you call me, Mr. Gilbert? Are you aware that stalking is a federal offense?"

"Oh, please, Ms. Caruso, I wasn't stalking you. Dear me, I suppose I've gotten myself into another pickle."

"What are you worried about, Mr. Gilbert?"

"Well, I just didn't want anyone digging into that Jean Albacco business, that's all. I wanted things to be left as they were."

Old Mr. Gilbert. Jean's boss was Douglas Gilbert. D.G. Oh, ho. So that was it.

"Mr. Gilbert, I know Jean was blackmailing you. I found her bankbook, and I know all about the payments you made to her."

"Yes," he said. "That's what I was afraid of. Will you be making the information public?"

"Well, I don't know. That depends."

"On what?"

"On what you can tell me. I want to know who killed Jean."

"Her husband did. He's in jail, as you must know."

"Yes, but I don't think he killed her. I think you did, Mr. Gilbert."

No one who had been able to conceal a murder for forty-five years would be dumb enough to make threatening phone calls from his office. Not with that trio in the next room. But I wanted to see how he'd react.

"That's nonsense," he said, bristling. "I have an alibi for the night in question."

"How organized you are. Tell me about it."

"I was miles away on a fishing trip. I'm a bass fisherman. Well, I used to be, a very good one, I might add."

"Well, that's convenient. But where were you this Saturday?"

"I did not kill Jean's sister!" He was outraged. "Who do you think you are, young lady? How dare you?"

"You knew Mrs. Flynn picked up the lockbox and you wanted it back. You were afraid of what might be inside it. You knew it could ruin you."

"Nonsense. It would take a lot more than that to ruin me. So I cooked the books a million years ago, so what? Who cares now? Nobody, that's who!"

"It might be hard to celebrate your retirement from a jail cell."

He mumbled something I couldn't understand. I tried a different tack.

"Who else was Jean blackmailing?"

"Get yourself a yellow pages, Ms. Caruso."

"Help me out here, Mr. Gilbert. I don't want to have to call your wife and tell her you've been stalking me."

"Oh, all right," he said, sputtering. "Well, Jean's sister was involved in some . . . funny business, you could call it, back when she was in high school."

"Jean's sister? Mrs. Flynn? Jean blackmailed her own sister?"

"I'm not saying that. Not exactly. All I know is that Theresa Flynn was involved with another girl, and in the fifties that just didn't happen. The families would've died of shame. And Jean wasn't one to let a lucrative opportunity slip through her fingers."

"How do you know what Jean would or wouldn't let slip through her fingers?"

"She talked to the girls around the office."

"And?"

"Ms. Caruso, you can't run a successful business and not have spies."

"Was Maddy Seaton your spy?" She was supposed to be Jean's best friend.

No answer.

"So who was this other girl Mrs. Flynn was involved with?"

"I have no idea."

Meredith Allan had told me to ask Theresa Flynn about Lisette Johnson. I'd thought she'd been some kind of enemy. Could she have been Theresa's lover?

"Lisette Johnson? Was that her, Mr. Gilbert?"

"What on earth? Lisette Peterson Johnson is a fine woman. She's married to my colleague, Avery Johnson, for heaven's sakes. That's utter nonsense."

Lisette *Peterson* Johnson. Who would be the former Lisette Peterson. Well, well, well. Looked like the Bible-thumper was our very own L.P.

Interesting. Jean had drawn the line at blackmailing her own sister. How thoughtful. But her sister's lover had apparently been fair game. Maybe it was just that Lisette was the better victim. More vulnerable. With greater cash reserves. A prime investor in Jean Albacco's private hedge fund. What exactly had Detective Moriarty said about her? She was running for office. Talk about your perfect motive to kill Jean. And Theresa, for that matter. Lisette Peterson Johnson's past was unlikely to look good on a family values platform.

Oh, great. I had another call.

"I have to call you back, Mr. Gilbert."

"Not a word to my wife?"

"Fine, but eighty-six the crank calls, you got me? Hello?"

"This is Father Herlihy, from Tehachapi."

"Father." The last person I wanted to talk to. "How are you?"

"I'm fine, but Joseph is not. His hearing is on Monday, six days from today. How are you faring?"

"I've encountered a few roadblocks, but I think I'm getting somewhere, I really do. I just need a little more time." I paused. "I went to see Joseph this morning."

"I'm aware of that."

"It didn't go well."

"No, it didn't."

"Father, I don't know what the right thing is anymore."

"I have no answer."

"Joseph thinks he's done the right thing. He's given up everything for love. But the woman he loved, the *women* he loved, they weren't whom they pretended to be. And I don't know if I was right in forcing him to confront the truth. He was happy with his illusions."

"That has hardly been the case, Ms. Caruso."

"That's not what I meant to say. It's just that before, he could make it through the day convinced he had suffered for a reason, that he'd done the best thing in a bad situation. Now I don't know. I'm afraid for him."

"Believe in him. He believes in you. And so do I."

But we were going in circles. I didn't want them to believe in me. Wasn't this whole thing a story about what happens when you put your faith in the wrong person?

25

$\mathcal{W}$ednesday morning. Another day in paradise. The birds were singing, the lilies were blooming, the squirrels were stealing my nectarines. After coffee and Advil, I flew out the door. I had things to do, places to go, people to see. I filled up the gas tank, pointed the car north, and lo and behold, there I was at the campaign headquarters of Lisette Peterson Johnson. And I had every right to be there. Goodness knows, if I'm a believer in anything, I'm a believer in the sanctity of church and family.

Lisette Peterson Johnson. Married to Avery Johnson of Gilbert, Finster, and Johnson. Motive, means, and opportunity. She could very well have gotten wind of my visit to the insurance offices from the Powerpuff Girls running the show over there. She could have followed me to Mrs. Flynn's, figured out what was going on, and come back later to finish the poor woman off. Her ex-lover. What kind of stomach would it take?

Located just around the corner from the Busy Bee, where all paths in Ventura seemed to converge, the tiny storefront was plastered with color photographs of the lady in question. She was plump and grandmotherly, with white hair that looked like thousands of minimarshmallows conspiring to create a halo effect. There were notices posted advertising a rally the following night at which Mrs. Johnson was to be the featured speaker. Her topic would be creation science in the classroom—i.e., Charles Darwin was a bum.

Inside, all was hustle and bustle. Never in my life had I beheld so many rosy-cheeked young people so hard at work. Scurrying this way and that, typing up flyers, poised at the copy machine, manning the phones, organizing the filing cabinet, and not a piercing or a tattoo or even a pimple in sight. It was August, but I swore I heard Bing Crosby singing "White Christmas."

"Lisette Peterson Johnson! Making the world a more virtuous place one step at a time!" a girl chanted into a megaphone from the back of the room. "Could you hear me up there?"

"All hail!" I shouted.

An older woman finishing up what looked like a grilled cheese sandwich stepped forward, wiped her hands on her jeans, and stuck one in my direction.

"I'm Martha," she said, smiling. "Sorry. We're a little unorganized. We're just getting ready for tomorrow's rally. It should be great. We've got lots of news coverage lined up. And you are?"

"Cece," I said, since we were going by first names.

"Cece, nice to meet you. What can we do for you today?"

"Well, I love what the candidate stands for, and I'd like to help, maybe with publicity?"

"Is that your field?"

"Sure is. I publicize things. In L.A.," I said, gaining confidence as I went along. "I'm here for a while because of a family emergency."

"Oh, my," she sympathized.

"It'll be fine," I said cheerfully.

"Well, great, we can use all the help we can get. Even from somebody from Sin City." She chuckled.

"Isn't Las Vegas Sin City?"

"They all are," Martha explained. "Vegas, L.A., New York. So what were you thinking about for the campaign?"

Hell if I knew.

"Well, maybe a chat with the candidate would be good," I said, "just to get the ball rolling. Is she expected in today?"

"Actually, she's over at the Busy Bee, having coffee, I think. You might be able to catch her."

"Did she drive? What kind of car does she have, out of curiosity? Just so I can watch out for her."

Martha wrinkled her brow. "I think she drives a Toyota 4-Runner."

"What color?"

"I can't say I know," she said, eyeing me coolly.

"Well, I'm on my way," I said. "Making the world a safer place, one day at a time!"

"It's a virtuous place, one step at a time," Martha corrected me.

"Don't forget to drop your business card in the bowl," said the girl in the back. "You can win a free lunch at Tony's Steak and Seafood. The popcorn shrimp are to die for."

I wasn't about to do that, but I didn't want to arouse anybody's suspicions, either. So I reached into my purse and grabbed the locksmith's card and slipped it in the bowl instead. That's when I noticed the card lying on top. It had an official-looking emblem on it. "Detective Thomas Moriarty, Ventura Police Department." How amusing. Either Moriarty was a popcorn shrimp fan or he'd followed up on my lead. Given the size of his gut, probably both.

There was a line in the front of the Busy Bee, but I walked straight to the back, where the puffy-haired candidate was huddled over a pile of papers. She was wearing a flowered cotton shift that redefined the word *bland*. I suppose that was the point. She was supposed to be unthreatening. A mullet cut, lumberjack shirt, and Dickies work pants would've probably alienated her constituents.

I got a smile a mile wide, so I slid into the booth.

"Martha sent me over."

"That's just fine," she said, turning over the sheet of paper she'd been studying. The other side was blank. "And what is your name?"

"I'm Cece, and I do publicity. Martha thought I should have a chat with you, to get some ideas. I'm here to help raise awareness of your good works."

"How wonderful!" She laughed merrily and started rolling up her sleeves, like we were going to bake a pie.

Now I had a problem. First of all, I don't bake. That's Lael's thing. I cook. And second of all, here I was, face-to-face with a double-murderer, well, maybe a double-murderer. What was I supposed to do? I'm not a cop, as Gambino had so delighted in reminding me. Confront her? That seemed a bit rash. Trap her into admitting something? I wasn't wearing a wire, for god's sake. Process of elimination? That's good. Eliminate her as a suspect. Excellent.

"Just a couple questions. Have you seen Theresa Flynn lately? Did you visit her, say, last Saturday?"

"Excuse me?"

"Theresa Flynn. You went to high school with her. Don't you remember?"

"Of course I remember. What is this, young lady? Who sent you? You're with Frank Shattuck's camp, aren't you? You people will stoop to anything to win an election. You should be ashamed of yourself."

"What should you be ashamed of?"

"Nothing. I have absolutely nothing to be ashamed of."

"Did you know Theresa's dead?"

"I read about it in the paper," she said quietly. "I was so sorry." Her eyes went squinty. One tear trickled southward. It looked like the genuine article, but nobody runs for office without being a skilled performer.

"You haven't answered me."

"I don't have to answer you," she said, indignant again. She gathered up her things. "Let the past be."

With that, she made her exit. I finished the doughnut she'd left sitting there, thinking that my interrogation technique could definitely use some work.

26

My next stop was Bridget's, back in town. I felt like a yo-yo, going back and forth, back and forth. Yet not a word of complaint out of my Camry. That Japanese engineering really is something. I don't think I've ever even checked the oil. You just fill the tank with gas, and away you go! Miraculous. As for my destination, well, I had sworn restraint, it's true. But this time I had an occasion—no money, but an actual occasion. Surely that counted for something. It wasn't like I was being frivolous. Or some kind of shopaholic. Not at all. I was there to secure a loan, not to make a purchase. It was very simple. No involvement of credit cards. Nevertheless, the beads of sweat began forming on my brow the minute the bell on the door tinkled.

Bridget was at her desk, bellowing at a young man in an acid-green frock coat.

"Are you listening, Justin? Let's go over it again. I am not in for that woman, ever. I'm in New York or Paris, I don't care, anywhere but here. In fact, next time she calls, tell her

I had a stroke! Went to Cedars Sinai in an ambulance, oh, that's good! Cece!" She'd deigned to notice me. "Come in, don't be shy. We're just practicing our phone etiquette."

Every summer, a different intern was indoctrinated into the cult of Bridget. This involved mastering mysterious rites (i.e., operating the steam iron and the espresso machine) and memorizing bizarre arcana (Helmut the dog's food allergies and the color preferences of various Hollywood starlets). Justin had proved an able initiate. A graduate student at NYU's Institute of Fine Arts, he was working on a dissertation entitled, "The Drape in/and/of/ Madame Grès." But he needed to get his hands dirty some and, like the best of his predecessors, was willing to play masochist to Bridget's sadist. That made two of us.

I gave Bridget a big hug. I had come on a begging mission and was fully prepared to pay the ritual obeisance. But the woman had a nose on her that knew no rivals.

"Cece, what are you up to?"

She was like a lynx. She could see storm clouds before they rose above the horizon. She could feel the earth vibrate from a hundred miles away.

"I need to borrow a gown," I said. "It's for a party at the Oviatt Building on Sunday night. Forties theme. I wouldn't ask, Bridget, but a handsome man is involved."

"Say no more." She turned to Justin. "Your moment has arrived. You are in charge until I come back. But don't you dare try on a thing. I've seen you eyeing my Azzedine Alaias."

Bridget grabbed her purse and ushered me out the door. "Oh, Cece, the most amazing shipment arrived this morning. Three Christian Dior New Look dresses! One of them is plum wool—plum wool!—with fifteen yards of fabric!

Plus, matching Dior corsets, with taffeta underbodices and ruffles at the breasts and hips!"

"Where are we going, by the way?"

"Aaron Arden's, of course."

On the way over, Bridget filled me in. Aaron Arden had made his name twenty-five years ago as an award-winning costume designer for TV variety shows. A sketch about hayseeds visiting the city? Aaron could whip up a pair of overalls and a red-and-white-checked shirt with shoulder pads that would make a porky guest star look positively soignée. A bit about space aliens confronting a New York City pretzel cart? You needed helmets that could accommodate three-inch false eyelashes, Aaron's specialty. A Versailles parody? Marie Antoinette he could do in his sleep.

Aaron went on to design regrettable evening gowns for the occasional celebrity friend. These betrayed his overweening ambition—asymmetry, beading, starched ruffs, capelets, sometimes all in the same dress—and provided tabloid fodder for years to come. Bruised but undaunted, Aaron used his connections and back stock to open up a costume rental house the likes of which this town had never seen. At Aaron Arden's, you could get everything from a Roman gladiator ensemble, cuffs and all, to an authentic Carnaby Street minidress with matching go-go boots and wig. The smaller studios and TV production companies unable to fund their own costume departments relied heavily on him.

"And so," Bridget concluded, her eyes shining, "the *schmata* business paid off! It's the stuff that dreams are made of!"

The girl at the front desk recognized Bridget and snapped to attention.

"I'll get Mr. Arden right away, Miss Sugarhill."

"Please tell him we're interested in the 1940s. Evening wear."

"Of course."

"Thank you, dear."

When Aaron entered the foyer, the girl pressed a can of Tab into his hand like an operating room nurse handing a scalpel to a surgeon. Bridget pushed me forward. I was her prizewinning cow.

"Cece here has met Meredith Allan!" she proclaimed by way of introduction.

"Get outta town!" Aaron said, leading us into the elevator. He was a short, compactly built man clad in black from head to toe. He had a graying Afro and a goatee.

"It's true! Tell him, Cece."

Knowing I was going to have to pry a gown out of this man, I nodded.

"Well, I'll be. So, dish!"

I knew what he wanted to hear. "She looked like hell."

"Appearances are never deceiving," Aaron said thoughtfully. "Here we are, fourth floor. Everybody out."

"You know, *you* look fabulous, Aaron," Bridget interjected. "You've had work done, haven't you?"

"No knife touches this face, doll. I'm skinny, that's it! Look at these." He ran behind a counter holding the most amazing selection of Bakelite jewelry I'd ever seen, organized by color from the reds, oranges, and ambers to the midnight blues and blacks, and pulled out a pair of wide-wale corduroys. "Look, look! My fatty pants! I use them as a sleeping bag now!" He started to crawl into one leg.

I looked at Bridget, but she shook her head. Aaron was

now lying down in his fatty pants, waiting for us to say something. We nodded approvingly.

"I have something in mind for you, Cece," he said at last, scrambling to his feet, "but, oh dear, you're not exactly Barbara Stanwyck, are you?"

"She was tiny," Bridget whispered.

"I know that," I snarled. I had spent a year on the New Jersey pageant circuit being told how gargantuan I was.

"You're more of a Jane Russell type—oh, don't get me wrong. What a babe! Most people know her from the bra ads, but there was so much more to Jane than that," he said consolingly.

We sauntered past racks and racks of clothes, all of which were sheathed in heavy plastic and labeled. There was a group of young women gathered around a case filled with cloche hats. "A low-budget remake of *The Great Gatsby*," Aaron murmured.

Bridget stopped to study a top hat sitting on a pedestal.

"Marlene Dietrich," said Aaron with pride.

"Erle Stanley Gardner wanted her legs for the cover of *The Case of the Lucky Legs*," I said.

"Good legs," he confirmed, doing a little two-step.

"But too expensive. After discussing it with the people at Paramount, where she was under contract, the publishers decided on a less beautiful pair in their price range."

"Compromise," he proclaimed. "Story of my life. Ah, here we are." He handed me an armful of bags. "Try this, this, this, and this."

While I was in the dressing room, he chattered with Bridget.

"Are you still doing the thing?"

"I am. You?"

"The thing is perfection."

"I'm so glad the guy told us about the thing."

"What's the thing?" I asked, poking my head out of the dressing room. They looked at each other and cracked up.

"I like bad girls. Meredith Allan has always been such a bad girl," Aaron said.

"What do you mean?" I asked, needing help desperately now. I was stuck in the spiraling overskirt of a maroon satin cocktail dress with a nipped-in waist.

"Never mind," he said in a singsong voice.

My curiousity was piqued.

The next dress I tried on had been worn by Ingrid Bergman in a publicity shot for *Notorious*—a black silk skirt and white wraparound top cinched at the waist with a thick suede belt with diamanté clips. It was simple and elegant, but I was going for va-va-voom.

"What about the sarong?" Aaron asked.

"The sarong!" Bridget exclaimed.

"Are sarongs forties?" I asked, slipping into what was perhaps the most divine dress ever.

Bridget launched into lecture mode. "Edith Head designed the first sarong in the movies for Dorothy Lamour in 1936. *Jungle Princess,* a Paramount film. That started a vogue for tropical fabrics and sarong draping that lasted through World War Two."

I came out and there was a collective gasp.

"It's perfect on you," Bridget said.

"Somebody, put out the fire!" Aaron said.

"I can't breathe! My ribs are being compressed into my lungs."

I loved it.

The dress had a sweetheart neckline and a diamond-shaped cut-out over the stomach, and folds and puckers and sarong draping in all the right places.

"Do you think Rita Hayworth could breathe when she sang 'Put the Blame on Mame'?" Aaron chided, patting my stomach meaningfully. "Think again."

I stared at myself in the mirror. I was a sea siren. I was a symphony in fuschia and orange. I was the sun setting over the waves in Trinidad and Tobago, wherever they might be.

"It comes straight from the MGM costume department," Aaron said, with a nod to Bridget. MGM was where her grandmother had worked. "It was worn by the singer in the nightclub scene, but I forget which movie. Nobody would actually wear a midriff-baring top in those days, but it was the movies! Bigger than life! You, Cece, are going to wear it with a hot pink orchid tucked behind one ear, and if your feet aren't too big, I have ankle straps covered in iridescent copper beads, and yes, yes, yes! Carlos the genius is going to do your hair!"

Bridget nodded happily. If there was anyone she'd defer to, it was Aaron Arden.

Back downstairs, Aaron asked, "Do you have silk stockings and a garter belt?"

"I do."

Bridget raised an eyebrow.

"So, Aaron, let me ask you something. What do you think silk stockings signify?" I was thinking of Della Street.

Bridget piped up. "By 1941, they were already the sacrificial lamb of the fashion industry. The war effort, you know. Thick wool legs at cocktail hour! What an affront!"

I looked at Aaron.

"Silk stockings mean you're fuckable."

There was no arguing with that.

27

*A*nd precisely what was I supposed to think when the doorbell rang at eight-thirty P.M., and it was Peter Gambino with a white box from my favorite bakery?

"I was in the neighborhood and remembered how much you loved the berry cake from Sweet Lady Jane." What he didn't mention was that he used to run out and get it for us after we had made love.

I went into the kitchen and came back with two forks. We sat on the couch and ate in silence, neither of us daring to so much as glance at the other. But we were thinking the same thing.

"So," he said.

"So," I said.

"How's tricks?"

"Gambino, you can do better than that."

"You're heartless," he said with a funny look, like maybe he meant it. "I finally got ahold of Detective Moriarty."

"And?"

"The guy's an idiot."

"I told you."

"Well, maybe not an idiot. But I will admit he's not interested in this case."

"How can that be? A woman is dead, for god's sake! And he can't even find her sons!"

"They found one of them, Damon. And he's got an airtight alibi. He was caught robbing a convenience store that Friday and spent the day his mother was killed in county lockup. He's in the clear."

"What about the other one?"

"Don't know. I don't think he's shown up."

"Well, it doesn't matter. He didn't do it."

"Yeah, and who did?"

"I'm not sure yet. There's this woman who was involved with Mrs. Flynn in high school who wants to keep her past quiet."

"Involved how?"

"Involved involved."

"And?"

"And I don't know. I'm working on it."

"You're working on it."

"Don't worry so much about what I'm doing, okay?"

"Detective Moriarty also mentioned that someone was messing up his crime scene."

I picked up the whipped-cream-smeared doily, put it in the box, and walked into the kitchen.

"Caruso." He'd followed me in.

"I'm tidying up."

"I don't remember you being particularly tidy," he said, picking up Mimi, who clawed at his arm. He dropped her like a hot potato.

"Baby," I murmured, bending down to scratch her behind the ears. "Mean old cop hurting you?" She purred contentedly.

"What do you want me to say? Good for you, taking the law into your own hands?"

"Maybe give me a little credit for trying to do the right thing."

"It isn't the right thing if people are getting hurt."

He was thinking of me, but I was thinking of Mrs. Flynn. It was my fault, her dying. I knew that even if no one else did.

He followed me back to the couch and sat directly on top of a heavily beaded Indian pillow. I have no idea why he did that. He was too big for a booster. He looked like Baby Huey. Plus, it couldn't have been too comfortable.

"Gambino, can I ask you a hypothetical question?"

"Shoot." He pulled the pillow out from under him and shoved it behind his back.

I was still working the Meredith Allan angle. "Why would a woman blackmail her husband's mistress?"

"Why do you want to know?"

"C'mon."

"Blackmail usually comes down to money. Defending the bottom line. Man cheats on his wife, he doesn't give a damn if she finds out. Her feelings mean nothing to him, he just doesn't want to pay the piper. Then there's shame. People do things all the time that they don't want to see the light of day. You'd be amazed. And they'll do almost anything to protect themselves and everyone around them from who they really are."

Meredith Allan knew very well who she was. Would she have been ashamed to have been sleeping with a married man? Not a chance. Like Jean, she'd never been innocent. But corruption is measured by degrees. Was she already married when she was sleeping with Joe, for example? I knew she married young, but I didn't have the timing figured out. If she wasn't married, maybe she was engaged at the time of the affair. Was she about to let her fiancé find out who she really was? Maybe, like Joe, he had a vision of her—beautiful, blameless Meredith Allan. That had to have been part of the deal. The guy had wanted an angel, but what he hadn't understood was that angels don't walk on this earth.

Jean. What didn't make sense was Jean. She was supposed to have been crazy about Joe. He changed her life, he was going to be her ticket out. Was it possible that when it came down to it, she cared so little for him that she'd use the dissolution of her marriage as a cash-and-carry opportunity? Why the hell not?

"Cece, I've lost you. Come back."

"Do you want me back?"

"Maybe I do," he said, looking at me. That was the thing about Gambino. It could have been the police training, I don't know, but when he looked at you, you got the feeling he really saw you.

It started to get hot, so I unzipped my sweatshirt jacket. Just because Gambino and I had been a mistake once didn't mean we'd be a mistake now.

"Lael's having her Labor Day barbecue on Saturday," I said.

I exasperated him, that much was obvious. He was chewing his lip. "I remember her Cesar Chavez cake. How's she doing?"

"Good. Her kids are so grown-up, you wouldn't believe it.

Nina gets straight A's. Tommy's an amazing surfer. Zoe can jump rope. And she's got a baby now, little August. He's adorable."

"Nice woman."

"Yeah, well, she always liked you." I shook my head. "I mean, for me."

"I had no idea." He gave me a little smile.

"So," I said, zipping up my jacket, then unzipping it again, "would you like to come with me, to the barbecue?"

"Sure."

"Is that all?"

"What do you mean?"

"Do you want to say anything else to me?"

He had come here with that cake. I wanted him to tell me why.

"That's one silly pillow you got there," he said, getting up. "They're expecting me back at the station house." He stretched his arms over his head. The fabric of his white shirt strained across his broad chest. I took it as a mating signal, but my mind was obviously in the gutter.

"See you Saturday, Caruso."

He opened the front door, and the knob came off in his hand.

"I guess you must want to keep me here," he said.

So maybe I did.

28

$\mathcal{G}$iven my recalcitrant technophobia, my spending the morning on the Internet amounted to a victory of sorts. My search on Lisette Peterson Johnson yielded some interesting results. The woman had run for school board five different times in the last fifteen years, which told me she was either oblivious, a fatalist, or some kind of megalomaniac. She was definitely a press hound. I scrolled through no less than twenty-five interviews she'd done with the local papers over the years, promoting herself and her pet causes, one of which seemed to be something called "reorientation therapy" for unhappy homosexuals. How hideous.

The woman was canny, I'll give her that. All that talking and she never let anything of a personal nature slip out, except for the fact that she'd gone to Hollywood after high school to try to become an actress (!), but had come back home after a couple of depressing years. I was about to launch a search on reorientation therapy when I reminded myself of why I had started all this in the first place, that being the urgent need to resuscitate my dead-in-the-water book on ESG.

I had enough on Perry Mason. I'd done the literary analysis. I'd done the political and social context. I'd even devoted a chapter to the merchandising philosophy, which involved deemphasizing individual books in favor of the lengthy list of titles available through a constant stream of reissues. What I needed was a more extensive discussion of Gardner's travel books, which were not as well known.

Back in his Ventura days, Gardner had joined a sailing party to Cabo San Lucas, a lark that had ended prematurely when the boat tipped over in the shallows off the coast and marooned itself, along with the entire group of revelers. ESG was not one to be discouraged, however. In 1947, he'd made his first trip to the peninsula and on his return began a series of thirteen travel books. These documented his Baja explorations, as well as his adventures in the desert, blimp expeditions, and treacherous journeys deeper into Mexico. What I really wanted to check on, however, was the story Gardner recounted in *The Hidden Heart of Baja* about making a find of prehistoric cave paintings. Even more interesting was that two years afterward he'd been barred from Baja, accused of stealing archeological treasures and taking them back across the border. It was a trumped-up charge, everyone acknowledged, but I wanted the details.

That investigation, however, was on hold while I waited to hear back from the helicopter pilot who'd accompanied Gardner on the trip in question. But I needed to keep busy. I jotted down some inconsequential factoids from the Baja California Tourist Bureau site, knowing full well I'd never use them, and then I sat there for a while. And sat there, thumbing through my books in despair.

Then I started doing crazy things, like counting the number of times the word *diamond* appeared in one of Gardner's titles (five, starting with *The Case of the Candied Diamonds,* a Speed Dash novelette).

I looked up the word *diamond* in the dictionary: "A native carbon crystallized in the isometric system, usually nearly colorless such that when free from flaws is highly valued as a precious stone because when faceted shows a remarkable brilliance, and when flawed is invaluable for industrial purposes because it is the hardest substance known."

Colorless: my prose.

Flawed: my mental processes.

Remarkable brilliance: the thing I lack.

The hardest substance known: material you're trying to shape into a book.

I spun around in my chair until I felt nauseous. I got up to get some Diet Coke, even though I'd sworn I'd no longer touch the stuff before noon. There wasn't any. I checked my messages. There weren't any.

I got Mimi and went back out to my desk. I seated myself with my cat in my lap and got out a fresh yellow legal pad. Nothing like a fresh yellow legal pad.

I wrote *ERLE STANLEY GARDNER* at the top, in capital letters. But I was distracted by the dust on my desk. I got out the Fantastik, which did the trick. No more dust. No more excuses. I looked at *ERLE STANLEY GARDNER* again. I started to count the letters. I shook my head, clearing out the cobwebs. Nothing.

I counted how many times a color appeared in one of ESG's titles (twenty-three, with *crimson* in the lead: *Crimson Jade, The Crimson Mask, The Crimson Scorpion, The Case of the Crimson Kiss*). It was like reading tea leaves. If I could just see the patterns, it would make sense. If it made sense, I'd know what to do.

I turned to a new page and wrote *JOSEPH ALBACCO* on the first line. I looked at it for a while. Then things started to get interesting.

The collect call came from the California Correctional Institution in Tehachapi.

"How are you, Ms. Caruso?"

"I'm fine, Mr. Albacco. I'm glad you called. I was sitting here thinking about you, literally. Listen, I want to apologize for the other day."

"Don't."

"I was awful. Everything you've been through. I was wrong to speak to you like that."

"Stop. I've been thinking about you, too, Ms. Caruso. About the things you said to me. I needed to hear them."

"Not like that."

"Please. I remembered something. I don't know if it's important or not."

"Tell me."

"You mentioned Morgan Allan, Meredith's father. You thought Meredith might have been trying to protect him. You mentioned something about the tidelands."

"Yes, that's right," I said. "Jean had a letter about it. Meredith's father was advised to sell some tidelands holdings he had, way back in the twenties. I don't know why exactly, or what it might have to do with Jean or you, for that matter."

"How did Jean get a letter like that? And what do you know about it?"

"Don't worry about that now."

"Well, I don't know if there's any connection, or what it

could have to do with anything, but my father owned some tidelands, too."

I didn't understand.

"Your father? Are you sure about that? How would your father have gotten his hands on something so valuable? I mean, I don't want to insult your family, but I thought you grew up poor."

"I did. We never had a cent."

"And?"

"And one day, after my father was gone, my mother was going through some papers and found the deed to some tidelands, dating way, way back. There was a lease or something on the land that had expired, an oil lease. My dad had been a roustabout in the oil fields, back when he was a young man. I worked on a rig a couple summers, too. He must've raised some money to buy the land, I don't know. Nothing he ever did worked out right. Turned out what he had wasn't worth much of anything. Big surprise. But my mother found out only after she'd spent our last dime on the lawyers."

"When was this?"

"Must've been, I don't know, when I was twelve, thirteen. Late forties, I'd say."

"Did Jean know anything about this?"

"I never mentioned anything to her."

It seemed like too much of a coincidence.

"Do you have any idea how I could pursue this?"

"Well, the case was handled by an old Ventura law firm."

It couldn't be.

"Was it Benton, Orr, Duval, and Buckingham?"

"That was the name. Erle Stanley Gardner's old law firm. Funny, isn't it?"

29

That was one too many coincidences. I've been around the block enough times to know that if it walks like a duck and talks like a duck, it ain't a ukelele.

My mind went back to Joe's heartbreak file, the one that contained the letter Joe had written to ESG all those years ago. ESG had thought something about the case "rang a bell." Those were his very words. I think I finally understood why. ESG must have remembered the Albacco name from his Ventura days, when he'd represented Joe's grandfather in an assault case. And, remembering the name, he must've followed Joe's trial, at least closely enough so that when he received Joe's letter, it seemed familiar. And that wasn't the end of it. ESG had played a role in Joe's mother's life, too. It made perfect sense when you thought about it. Mrs. Albacco needed an attorney. Who better to turn to than the man who had rescued her family once before?

I was on the road by two-thirty. The sun was still shining through the palm trees lining California Street when I walked through the doors of Benton, Orr, Duval, and Buckingham.

"I love your sunglasses!" said the receptionist, a plump young woman encased in too-tight everything. "Dior, right? I almost got the same ones, pink lenses and everything. But they were priced too high. Not on my salary, no way, José! They're great on you, though."

"Thanks, Ms. . . . ?"

"I'm Allison."

"Cece."

"You're not a client of ours, are you? All we usually get around here are drooling old farts. I'll bet you're an actress or something. Your outfit is so cool. Vintage, right?"

I was wearing a navy-blue Norma Kamali disco dress I'd bought the first time around and had had sense enough not to toss when power suits came along.

"I can't afford what I want most of the time," I said. "But I'm a dedicated shopper."

"I like that. A dedicated shopper. Me, too."

"Listen, Allison, I need some information about a former client of this firm's. About a particular case, actually. I know it's late in the day, but I drove here all the way from L.A. Any chance I could talk to someone this afternoon?"

She gave me a conspiratorial glance.

"Anybody can talk to anybody around here, assuming they're willing to pay the price, and I'm talking, like, five hundred an hour. That's eight twenty-five a minute, if you can believe it. These guys even bill you when they go to the bathroom! I guess they do their best thinking on the john."

"Men," I said superciliously.

She giggled. "So what do you think of this belt? I got it on sale."

"It's very Chanel."

She beamed.

"Listen, the case concerned the sale of some land, back in the forties. Somebody here handled it. The client's name was Albacco. I just need the details."

"I'm going to law school at night, starting next year."

"That's great."

"Yeah. I'm pretty proud of myself. Only thing is, you have to wear such ugly outfits, I'm talking bo-ring! Plus, there's a glass ceiling and that kind of thing. But I'm not too worried. I know how to stick up for myself, you know?"

I could tell.

"Anyway, you don't need a lawyer to tell you that stuff."

"I don't?"

"I'll just look it up." I followed her down the hall to a small room with filing cabinets stacked from floor to ceiling. "This is all the old stuff. Inactive files."

"Listen, I don't want to get you in trouble."

"Forget about it."

Before I could say another word, she started riffling through the A's.

"Cece." She looked up. "Can I try on your sunglasses?"

I handed them over. Allison put them right on, then pulled out a thin file and walked over to the copy machine.

I was pacing. "Shouldn't you be up front, in case somebody comes in?"

"Relax. Nobody's coming. They're all at a retreat at some spa. You know, solving the world's problems with a Shiatsu massage and a round of golf. What a scam. I've got this whole place to myself!"

She stapled the pages together and handed them to me.

"Enjoy!"

So much for client-attorney privilege. "Thank you so much."

She looked at me as if our business wasn't quite done.

"Listen, why don't you keep those sunglasses? They look much better on you."

"No offense," she said, admiring her reflection in a mirrored paperweight, "but I do think you're right."

I walked out into the setting sun. Allison was going to make some lawyer.

ESG had been some lawyer, too. He had honed his skills in the old Ventura County Courthouse, now City Hall, which I could see from where I was standing. There it was, way up at the top of California Street, its facade fronted by the obligatory statue of Father Junípero Serra. A tiny man, no more than about five-three, and crippled because of an untreated bug bite, Father Serra established the first nine of the twenty-one Alta California missions, the last of which was Mission San Buenaventura. He was ubiquitous around these parts.

So here was the dilemma. I was anxious to check in to the hotel and go through the papers I had just misappropriated, but I didn't know how soon I'd have another opportunity to check out ESG's old stomping grounds. I wanted to see if the brass spittoons were still there. I wanted to pace the marble halls Gardner had paced while waiting for the jury to come back with a verdict.

I'd be quick. I started up the hill. The temperature had dropped at least ten degrees in the last twenty minutes. I pulled on my sweater. Even after living in California for eleven years, I hadn't gotten used to the rapid shifts in temperature. Evenings could be chilly here, even in the dog days of summer. The desert ecology and all. Californians were actually meant to live like lizards, hiding in the shade by day and crawling around at night, in search of water. But who wants to be a lizard? Not when you can steal water from places where it rains, or just drain a few lakes.

The California dream was built on such hubris. The courthouse, which dated back to 1913, was symptomatic. Take the exterior, an eighty-foot span of gleaming terra-cotta, flanked by two hundred-foot wings, all of classical Roman proportions. Also, fluted columns, a pedimented entry, a copper dome and cupola. And, between the first- and second-floor windows, a truly mad inspiration: twenty-four happy friars, carved of stone. Architects don't usually have a sense of humor, but this one went on to design Grauman's Chinese Theater in Hollywood, so he obviously did.

The entry was full of telling details, like the medallions on the bronze gates. These displayed bouquets of the humble lima bean, a sly reminder that Ventura County's longtime chief cash crop underwrote the civic fathers' appetite for luxury. The reception desk was unattended. I took a brochure about ESG's Ventura and a map to historic downtown bungalows and started up the marble staircase.

"Excuse me, coming through!" shouted a stern-looking woman in a dark pantsuit, wielding her briefcase like a shield. I leapt out of her way, feeling somewhat conspicuous. Unlike Allison, I had never ascribed to the theory that sexy clothes were anathema to being taken seriously. Then again, I didn't have to spend much time around lawyers. One thing I've noticed about them is that they take things very literally—that is, if you're wearing a tarty dress, you must be a tart. My ex's divorce lawyer had tried to insinuate something to that effect at one of our custody hearings, but the judge had just rolled his eyes and told the guy to move on.

I rounded the corner and there it was, Superior Courtroom #1, the place where the "real" Perry Mason had learned everything he knew. It was city council chambers now. There was no one around, so I walked in and sat down in the first of several rows of mustard-colored chairs. It felt sort of illicit, my taking one of the seats of the aggrieved, irate about zoning ordinances and no smoking policies and the invasive roots of ficus trees. Not particularly aggrieved about anything, I gazed out the arched windows to the Ventura Pier and vast blue ocean beyond. It was a clear day, and I could see all the way to the Santa Cruz and Anacapa Islands.

ESG said he always knew it was time to write another Perry Mason book when he got nostalgic for Superior Courtroom #1. And no wonder. Everywhere you looked there was gleaming cherry. And one, two, no, three large stained-glass domes on the ceiling, depicting three symbols of the Law: a book, a sword, and the scales of justice. And that view! ESG would've been able to see the waves crash when he was up in front of the judge, arguing a case. I wondered if his track record even came close to Perry Mason's. I remember reading somewhere that Perry had lost only once, in *The Case of the Terrified Typist* (I think the client wanted to lose; I'd have to doublecheck).

And right then a chill went up my spine. Superior Courtroom #1 was where all the big cases had been tried in ESG's day. If that was still true in 1958, it meant that Joseph Albacco had stood trial for murder in this very room.

I swallowed hard. It had seemed so abstract, this whole thing—like a book I'd read or a movie I'd seen. But it was real, all of it. Real lives had been changed forever inside these four walls. I tried to imagine what Superior Courtroom #1 would have looked like from the point of view of a man fighting for his life. A book, the scales of justice, a sword. When did Joe realize that the law would fail him? Was it when he saw the faces of the jury returning with the verdict? Or was it during opening arguments, when the D.A. laid out the perfect circumstantial case? Meredith Allan probably sat in the back, watching her lover sink deeper and deeper into the hole she had so ably dug for him. Had Lisette Peterson been there? Or was she already in Hollywood, not making it as an actress? What about Theresa Flynn? She was Jean's next of kin. That would have put her in the front row, maybe in the seat I was sitting in right now.

Unnerved, I got up and went out into the hallway. It was lined with paintings and photographs of Ventura's mayors, past and present, each the picture of municipal pride and responsibility. "I do not know who is responsible," Joe had written in his letter to ESG. Neither did I, and there were only a few days left before his parole hearing. That letter wouldn't go away. I saw it in my dreams. It had been written by a young man with stars in his eyes, a young man who believed the truth would set him free. The day I showed up at Tehachapi, I had brought that young man back from the dead. And if nothing else, this much I understood: when you bring someone back from the dead, he is your responsibility forever.

30

*C*uriouser and curiouser. I tugged off my shoes, collapsed onto the bed with the file Allison had given me, and took another slug of soy milk, the least objectionable of the so-called refreshments available in the hotel minibar. This much I had been able to decipher. On June 17, 1944, Joseph Albacco's mother, Ava Anderson Albacco, sold Parcel 66 of Lots 11 and 13, map of the Buenaventura Palisades Tract, filed September 19, 1905, Map Book C, page 64, Ventura County Hall of Records. She got $2,900 for her trouble, which didn't amount to much these days, but would've meant something in 1944, especially if you were dirt poor like Ava was. I nibbled on an oat-bran cracker. The attorney of record was Julius O'Rourke, Esq., of Benton, Orr, Duval, and Buckingham. By that time, ESG was no longer practicing law, of course. Now here comes the good part. The buyer was Mr. Morgan Allan.

Morgan Allan. He and his ghoulish daughter, Meredith. Talk about the undead. But why would the man have bought tidelands property from Joe's mother, Ava, when he had received a letter twenty years earlier telling him to dump precisely that? And why did Jean have a copy of that letter? And, furthermore, how had Joe's father gotten ahold of that parcel of land to begin with? According to his son, he was a roustabout who had never had a dime, not to mention a good idea, in his life. I sat straight up in bed, threw away the rest of my soy milk and crackers, and pulled out the yellow pages.

I found a dozen listings for title companies. Luckily, there was someone still there at the second place I called. For the modest sum of $125, they could trace the history of any piece of California real estate back to the Spanish land grants. And if I could fax the particulars over tonight, they'd have the information to me by two P.M. tomorrow. It was a place to start.

The fax machine in the lobby was broken, but there was a little copy shop a couple blocks away, on Valdez Alley. I walked out the door and headed down the street. It was six-thirty P.M. according to the digital readout flashing over Tri-County Savings Bank. The moon was out and the air smelled like jasmine, but there wasn't a soul around to enjoy it except me. Pretty much everything seemed to have been nailed shut, except A-Plus Printing, which glowed electric blue.

Fifteen minutes later, I was done. The sky had gone from pink-streaked to black. The wind was picking up. I wrapped my sweater tighter around me, clutching the papers to my chest. Something caught my eye in the window of the used bookstore a few doors down. It was a first edition of *The D.A. Cooks a Goose*, a Doug Selby book by ESG. I had seen one of those at the Mystery Manor. They were charging an arm and a leg for it. I'd have to come back tomorrow and see what it was going for here. I needed more on Doug Selby, but those titles weren't exactly enticing. I'd read *The D.A. Breaks an Egg* a few weeks ago, and, sad to say, it was about as exciting as an omelet.

The used bookstore on Valdez Alley. I knew about this place. Jean Albacco had stopped in the day she was killed, to pick up a book for her husband, a book on California history. Ghosts everywhere, I thought, shivering. A stray cat howled as it skittered across my path. I think it was black. I'll admit to being superstitious, but something wasn't right. I heard footsteps. They were too close. I could feel someone bearing down on me. The guy in the blue Camaro? I remembered his face perfectly. No, he had nothing to do with this. Did he? The person at Mrs. Flynn's? The person in the black SUV? Man, was I in trouble. I picked up the pace. The steps quickened in turn. The cat screeched behind me. Main Street was only thirty yards away. I could see the lights. I could hear the cars. I tried not to go to pieces.

"Stop, miss!"

Do killers yell "Stop, miss"? Slowly, I turned around.

The kid from the copy shop was grinning at me. "You forgot the last page of your fax. Here."

Back in my room, I dumped the complimentary bottle of bath oil into the tub and soaked for a while. I needed to relax. Desperately. I tried to think calming thoughts, but that never did any good, so I gave in and thought hysterical ones. How was Annie? I hadn't spoken to her in a few days and I was worried. I called her from the tub, but got the machine and hung up without leaving a message. It was all my fault, this Vincent thing. That's what my mother had said when I made the colossal error of calling her yesterday for advice. It was my fault because I had gotten a divorce and set a bad example. My mother had stayed married for twenty-five years, though my father, god bless his soul, was no Ward Cleaver.

What about Mrs. Flynn's missing son? Had they found him? Maybe he knew something. Maybe he'd done something. I wondered if Gambino had found out anything else. I wanted Gambino. I was relieved to have at least that much figured out. I ordered a pepperoni and anchovy pizza in the man's honor and ate the entire thing, though I didn't enjoy it as much as I should have. Then I found a Joan Crawford movie on cable. The last thing I remember before falling asleep was her stomping all over her wedding dress. Did anybody ever give that woman a break?

When I woke up in the morning, my jaw ached. I must've been grinding my teeth again. My dentist keeps suggesting a night guard. "Cut the euphemisms," I keep telling him. "You're talking about a retainer."

I performed my morning hair depoufing and pulled on my black capri pants and a skinny white tee, a sensible choice given the powdered-sugar doughnut I planned to eat for breakfast. I needed to erase the memory of that pizza. I slung my purse over my shoulder and headed for the Busy Bee. They know food over there. Doughnuts. Coffee. None of that cappuccino nonsense. I had three cups while I went over the plan for the day.

#1. I scribbled on my legal pad, *Visit to the historical society.* Mr. Grandy was sure to have some ideas about how I could research the history of oil in Ventura. Like Meredith

Allan, I couldn't get away from the stink of oil. It seemed to be everywhere, but I didn't understand why.

#2. Well, maybe I'd just start with #1.

Mr. Grandy was delighted to see me.

"Cece, Cece! I knew you'd reconsider! You made such a hasty decision about those Erle Stanley Gardner files. A treasure trove, I guarantee it! Mrs. Murphy, she's the big kahuna around here, she'll be thrilled! Why, you're better than a cataloger, Cece! And we don't even have to pay you!"

My ex-husband used to say things like that. But I suppose I have his cheapness to thank for my current vocation. Back when he was an assistant professor up for tenure at the University of Chicago, he was given the ignominious task of teaching Genre Fiction, affectionately know as Shit Lit. Too tight to spring for a teaching assistant, and convinced the entire subject was beneath his dignity anyway, he had me do the research for his lecture on police procedurals. I'd had nothing else to do, what with raising our daughter and waitressing thirty hours a week at the faculty club. By the time I'd composed more than a hundred pages on Ed McBain, however, we both understood that something had happened that was going to change our lives forever. My first book was published eighteen months later.

Now I was stalled on my sixth book, ESG was a mystery to me, and the only thing that could fix things, it seemed, was figuring out who killed Jean Albacco and her sister, Theresa Flynn. But, as I said, I have my limits. Mr. Grandy was disappointed I would still have nothing to do with his boxes. Nonetheless, he went into the back and came back with an armful of books he thought would help with my query about oil in Ventura.

"Remember, Cece, pencils only, please!"

Three hours later, I came up for air. My back was sore from sitting in the same position for so long. I stretched my legs, got a drink of water, sharpened my pencil, which I'd worn into a sad nub, then sat back down to try to make sense of the reams of notes I had taken.

Up until 1865, the main oil interest in California had been in whaling. No one had much thought it could be otherwise until a Yale geologist reported that California had more oil in and around its soil than all the whales in the Pacific Ocean. Most everyone thought this guy was out of his mind, except the vice president of the Pennsylvania Railroad. Just after the Civil War, he snapped up seven ranchos in Ventura County for the purpose of constructing shipping facilities for the crude oil he expected to flow. He and his nephews hauled the latest in steam-powered drilling equipment across the country, opened a bank account, and prepared to get richer.

The first California oil boom went bust a few years later. Seventy oil companies had drilled sixty wells, but it had cost them a million bucks to net $10,000. Even I could tell you this was not a good return on your investment. Still, oil had changed the area forever.

The 1870s brought the formation of a new Ventura County, with San Buenaventura as the county seat. Saloons, dance halls, and hookers sprang up to take the money of speculators, tool-dressers, and other susceptible types. In 1885, an oil pipeline was constructed. By 1890, three of the dominant companies merged to form the Union Oil Company of California.

World War I was the first real turning point. Gasoline,

fuel oil, and lubricants were needed in large quantities for tanks, airplanes, and ships. The key technological breakthrough was the development of rotary drills, which replaced the older cable-tool rigs. In 1925, the first major strike was made when Lloyd No. 9A and Lloyd No. 16A in the Ventura Avenue oil field each yielded close to five thousand barrels a day. Within five years, companies like Shell Oil were bringing in fifteen thousand barrels a day. The hills and flatlands of the Ventura River plain, once covered with apricot and walnut trees, were studded with oil derricks, like spines on a porcupine's back.

Okay, this was all very interesting, but what I wanted to know about were the tidelands. I pulled another book from the stack and flipped to the index. Offshore drilling. Here it was.

By the early 1920s, the state of California had begun to grant exploration leases to prospect for oil in the tide- and submerged lands. Less than a decade later, some 350 wells had been drilled under the sea. In 1929, a worried legislature called an emergency moratorium on further leases, and a few months later it repealed the Lease Act of 1921. Hello—this was starting to ring a few bells. The repeal rendered further exploitation of the tidelands unprofitable. Here we go. This was what the letter in Jean's lockbox had been about.

Someone at the state legislature had warned Morgan Allan that the Lease Act was going to be repealed and that if he didn't get rid of his tidelands in a hurry, he'd be stuck. That letter was proof that Morgan Allan had a politician in his pocket. But so what? What businessman didn't? Was it illegal to sell your own property? I didn't see why it would be.

I kept reading. After World War II, new breakthroughs in

petroleum technology encouraged several of the major oil companies to recommence geological exploration of off-shore sites. I slammed the book shut. So Morgan Allan was in on that, too, long before everybody else. He bought a tidelands parcel from Ava Albacco for next to nothing, in 1944, just in time to make a mint. How convenient.

But again, so what? Ava didn't know what she had. And even if she did, she wasn't in a position to do any wildcat drilling, was she? In any case, Jean didn't necessarily know Morgan Allan had been the buyer of the parcel Ava sold. I didn't even know if Jean knew the parcel existed. All I knew that Jean knew of was the existence of a letter written in 1928. And what did that letter really prove?

31

*B*urnett was up on a ladder, painting wings on fallen angels.

"I don't know a thing about you," I said, to get a reaction and also because it was true.

"Sure you do," he said, smiling. God, that smile. "Hand me pale blue, will you? It's over by the closet."

It turned out that our getaways had coincided, Burnett's and mine. I was in Ventura, trying to go in a straight line instead of circles, and he was in Montecito, restoring a fresco in his mother's bedroom.

Painted in the style of François Boucher, the fresco depicted a pair of lascivious rococo cherubs enjoying some *après-midi* delight amongst the sugarplums. I could practically feel the thing rotting my teeth. But it could have been my mood. Or being in that woman's bedroom. At least she was out of town and wouldn't suddenly appear, offering flavored iced teas all around.

"I keep wondering if I should just let the paint peel,"

Burnett said, chewing thoughtfully on the back of his paint-brush. "It works with the theme, don't you think?"

"I suppose it literalizes the notion of striptease."

He turned and gave me a look. *Smoldering* would be the proper adjective. "Could I interest you in literalizing the notion of striptease?"

"Not with those little chubbies watching."

"Paranoid."

"Just because I'm paranoid doesn't mean I'm being watched."

"I don't think that's exactly how it goes."

"Nothing wrong with a malapropism."

"I need eggshell, do you see it over there?"

I picked up a small can. "Number Thirty-three?"

"That's it. Thanks," he said, stretching his arm down to grab it from me.

I picked up an embroidered pillow from the bed and tried pushing some threads back from where they had come loose.

"So," I asked, "is your father coming to your birthday party?"

"My father? Where did that come from?" Burnett looked up from his work. With a few quick strokes of paint, he had made two pairs of angel eyes glisten.

"I told you, I don't know anything about you."

Turning his back to me, Burnett said that his father had come in from England early last week to celebrate the grand event. Those were his words, and they got a little stuck coming out.

"How does your mother feel about that?"

"They're on speaking terms, if that's what you mean. They actually like each other these days."

"Was that not always the case?"

"Not always."

"Why?"

"She'd never admit it, but she grew up pretty rough-and-tumble. My father's family has been rolling in dough for generations. They've got that aristocratic thing going, the cultivated pallor, bad teeth. They never much liked her."

"When did your parents meet? I've never heard that story."

He gave me a hard stare. "Why are you asking so many questions today, Cece?"

"I don't know. You ask me something."

"How's your book coming?"

He knew how to hurt a girl. "Fine, though I've been diverted, as you know."

"I need persimmon. Can you pass it up? Sorry. Go ahead. What's going on with the case?"

"Actually, it's kind of interesting," I said carefully. "Did you know your grandfather was involved?"

He didn't look too surprised. "My grandfather was involved in everything. Tentacles everywhere, like an octopus. What'd he do this time?"

"It's oil. These people owned some tidelands property. Your grandfather bought it."

" 'Yes it's oil, oil, oil / that makes our town boil.' That was an old drinking song." Burnett ran his fingers through his hair even though there was paint all over them. "Oil, oil, oil, that's why I never had to toil."

"Come on," I said.

"Well, it wasn't as if I started from nothing, like my

grandfather did. Man, I need a break," he said, climbing down the ladder. He flopped onto the bed and patted the spot next to him. I lay down.

"So why do I feel like we're in high school?" I asked, staring up at the ceiling.

"Because my mother's not home and we're lying on her bed fully clothed. When's the last time you did something like that?"

"The time I swore I'd never do it again." I sat up and adjusted my T-shirt before I made another big mistake. Still, I had work to do here.

"So tell me about your grandfather."

Now he was staring at the ceiling.

"Old Morgan came from Ohio. Came to Los Angeles in the teens, I guess. Looking for Oil-do-rado." He dragged out the syllables.

"Go on."

"He followed the cries of the pitchmen. They set up circus tents along the highway and promised the world to every sucker who happened by. In L.A., there was an oil derrick for every palm tree. You'd go to the beach and people would be sunbathing next to derricks planted right there in the sand. My grandfather operated a rig for Shell Oil at Signal Hill. I'll never forget something he used to say. When the oil starts to flow, he'd say, you'd hear a growl below like waves roaring through a sea cave."

"How did he wind up in Ventura?"

"He followed the oil." Burnett took a breath and blew hard, like he was trying to expel a couple generations' worth of hot air.

"It was beautiful at night. He'd take me when I was a kid.

The natural gas illuminated the sky. There were flares and shadows and machines pumping away. The old man was a real wildcatter. All those guys were gamblers, making crazy bets on what lay hidden beneath the dirt. Everybody had a system. But nobody's could beat his. He knew where there'd be a strike. And he was never wrong."

"So what was the big secret?"

"You had to be patient. You had to wait for late summer, when the seedpod was good and sunburnt. In the sunshine, grass over oil will turn red. Look for the red grass, my grandfather said, but don't tell a soul what you're looking for."

I hadn't thought of Burnett before as someone who'd been circumscribed by his family, by who they were, what they'd accomplished, what they expected of him. He was the classic poor little rich kid. And I knew that no matter how much sympathy I had for him, I could never pity him as much as he pitied himself.

As if he could read my mind, he sprang up from the bed, uncomfortable. "I've got to go down the hall and check on the balcony. It needs some repair work. Come find me when you're ready. You look happy stretched out there. Why don't you take a catnap or something?"

I nodded, though I wasn't very tired. I watched him walk down the hall. When the coast was clear, I tiptoed over to his mother's closet. I owed that much to Bridget.

Closetry, she had once explained to me, is a dying art. True connoisseurs are few and far between. In these days of disposable everything, few can be bothered with matching padded hangers, acid-free paper, customized double rods, and Polaroid-enhanced shoeboxes for identificatory purposes. An innocent in such matters, I could only nod dumbly.

Perhaps someday I'd try to arrange my sweaters according to tonal gradations. Things being what they are, however, my sweaters, acrylic and cashmere alike, have been smashed into my bad joke of a closet along with everything else I own. As for my shoe collection, those beauties live with my surplus toilet paper, napkins, and trash bags in the ignominious netherworld of my service porch. I don't know where anything is. If you asked me to produce my lavender twin set, I'd have to kill you.

I approached Meredith Allan's closet with reverence. People made pilgrimages to lesser sites. I knew it would smell like roses. Except it didn't. It smelled musty. And it looked as bad as my closet. Only a thousand times bigger.

There were chiffon scarves strewn around like crepe paper. Evening dresses thrown over chairs. Beautiful mohair sweaters popping out of drawers like jack-in-the-boxes. I touched a real Fortuny dress, which was falling off a bent wire hanger. And I saw something that would've made Bridget's skin crawl: a champagne-colored Norell suit, lying on the floor, turned inside out.

There was a big oak desk at the far end of the closet that the woman had transformed into a monster jewelry box. A gold necklace with a moonstone as big as a baby's fist was lying on top. Next to it were a couple of chunky coral rings and an onyx brooch encrusted with silver. The top drawer was open. There were bracelets inside—three or four turquoise ones perfect for a Navajo princess, a deco piece with diamonds sprinkled across the surface like fairy dust, a spiny silver thing that looked like something James Bond would deploy under water.

Without even thinking about it, I slipped a large gold filigree cuff onto my wrist. Well, I didn't exactly slip it on—I broke a sweat trying to work it over my knuckles. It was part of a pair, so I had to put the other one on, too. Then I held my hands up to the mirror. They were beautiful things, those bracelets, but I think I looked less like an oil heiress than Wonder Woman.

Suddenly, there was a tremendous crash from down the hall. What had happened? The balcony? It needed fixing, Burnett had said. Could it have given way? I rushed into the guest room and toward the open French doors. I stopped short. The spindly wooden railing was smashed to bits, and I didn't see Burnett anywhere.

"Burnett!" I cried. "Where are you?" There was no answer. My heart started to pound. Oh, god, maybe he was down there, in the garden, unconscious or worse. Slowly, I stepped onto the balcony. It seemed secure enough. I walked over to the edge and peered down. Nothing out of the ordinary. The grass below was spread out before me like a bolt of green velvet. So where was Burnett? I turned to go and all of a sudden the floor shifted beneath my feet, then fell away. And I was falling, too, down, down, down, through the pale blue sky.

32

Cece? Can you hear me?"

There was a row of Burnetts leaning over me, so pretty.

"Her eyes are open, Mr. Burnett! Look!"

There were many small men with garden shears fanned out next to him, like Victorian paper dolls.

"Cece, do you remember what happened? You fell when the balcony collapsed. Mr. Esposito here found you. You landed on a pile of leaves he'd been raking."

"The ground is so hard, miss," Mr. Esposito said. "Thank goodness my leaves made a cushion for you. You were lucky today!"

I struggled to get up.

"You stay right there," Burnett said. "I'm calling an ambulance."

"Don't be absurd," I managed. "I'm perfectly fine." As I rose to my feet, every joint in my body creaked. Mr. Esposito looked concerned.

"Don't worry. Nothing's broken. See?"

I twirled around with what little grace I could muster.

I wanted to throw up. Everything hurt. Oh, the bruises. They were going to look just great with my sarong. Well, it was no big deal. I brushed some plaster off my pants, which had ripped at the knee, and plucked some green things from my hair. I had to get out of there.

"I had no idea the balcony had rotted so badly," Burnett said. "The wood was ancient. It should've been taken care of years ago. God, I'm sorry. What a mess."

It looked as if someone had stage-designed a demolition site. There were leaves and branches strewn all over the place, scraps of wood and chunks of plaster. All that was missing were some hard hats and squashed beer cans.

"I thought you had fallen," I said, still a little confused about what had happened. "The railing was smashed. That's why I went out there."

"No, no. I never even went into that room. You were napping, so I decided to go down to the kitchen to get something to eat. I didn't hear a thing until Mr. Esposito called me."

Burnett looked miserable. I looked at my watch. It was already one P.M. If I didn't dither around trying to make him feel better, I could make it back to the title company in less than an hour.

"Listen, I've got to go," I said, heading across the grass. This was too weird for me.

"Slow down, Cece, please!"

"I have some more research to do this afternoon, and then I'm going to relax at the hotel. And we'll see each other on Sunday, right?" I gave him a reassuring smile.

"Right," he said, nodding. "Are you sure you don't want to have a doctor look you over?"

"Stop. I'm fine. Look at this gorgeous garden," I said, changing the subject.

Mr. Esposito rode up next to us on his lawn mower. "I hear you talking! I am good at my job! Please tell the lady of the house I need a raise. Ha-ha!"

He deserved one. Javier needed to see this. The garden was long and thin, but ingeniously planted. Distractions made the eye swerve and pause: a painted table tucked into a formal arbor, a magnificent spiky yucca. Even the stripes produced by Mr. Esposito's lawn mower drew the eye to the edges of the vista, where there were lush spills of bougainvillea and webs of golden foliage climbing the walls of the house.

Burnett took my arm as we walked down a flight of steps, through a somber arcade of cypresses, then into the brilliant light of the automobile court.

"Wait, wait," shouted Mr. Esposito. I turned around and saw him chasing after us. I also caught a glimpse of something else, parked behind Meredith Allan's Bentley. It was a black SUV. Just like the one that had followed me.

Mr. Esposito handed me my purse.

"You can't leave without your keys, miss."

"Thank you," I said, stepping into my car. Burnett kissed me on the cheek and I drove off in a trance. Had the SUV I'd just seen been black or dark blue? Or dark green? I had no idea. The sunlight had been blinding. My god, had Meredith Allan been the one tailing me the other day? And what the hell was her Bentley doing there anyway? She was supposed to be taking a drive up the coast. Damn it. I couldn't be sure of anything anymore.

Except that I was now officially a felon. I merged onto the

freeway heading back to Ventura, looking mighty fine in
Meredith Allan's matching gold bracelets.

They ran a tight ship over at that title office. Two P.M.
means two P.M., and not 1:47. I took a seat and waited. I felt
like I was riding the subway in New York City. All the people there looked a little crazy, like they might spit on me for
no good reason.

Maybe it was the bracelets. They were awfully showy. I
pulled my sleeves over them as best I could, but they stuck
out all over the place. I'd return them at Burnett's party. How
mortifying. It was that woman's fault. If her balcony hadn't
collapsed, none of this would've happened. Well, that wasn't
true, but blaming her made me feel a little better.

I stared at the clock over the counter. It was 1:54 P.M. I
picked up an old copy of *Esquire*. I used to read that magazine
when I was in high school. I thought it would help me understand the male of the species.

The man in the next chair over was staring at me openly.
My hand flew up to my hair, which must've looked like a
bird's nest, but there were no leaves left. I gave him a nasty
look. He stuck his head back into his *Reader's Digest*. An
article about prostate health, no doubt.

I plucked a copy of *The Case of the Lonely Heiress* from my
bag. Those Pocket Books editions from the fifties were the
best. This one had a sexpot with a blond bouffant and a bored
expression on the cover. She was sticking her long legs
through the inside of a huge letter "Q," which started the sentence "'Quite obviously,' Perry Mason said . . ." Yeah, it was
always so obvious for Perry Mason.

"Cece Caruso?"

For whom it wasn't always so obvious.

The clock read 2:00 P.M. on the nose.

"Here you go, honey. Have a good one."

By the time I got out to the sidewalk, I was already deep into the report. East-West Title Company. Property Profile. Although care has been taken in its preparation, the company assumes no liability for its accuracy or completeness. Blah, blah, blah. Please note that concurrent trust deed information may not show all encumbrances of record, nor all liens, defects, and/or restrictions. Well, for god's sake, what was I paying these people for?

I sat down in the car and opened the windows to let in some fresh air. June 17, 1944. Morgan Allan assumed title to Parcel 66 of Lots 11 and 13, Buenaventura Palisades Tract, no encumbrances on the property. The seller was Ava Anderson Albacco, Joe's mother. I knew that part already. I wanted to know when Joe's father bought the land, and from whom. October 22, 1928. Joseph Albacco Sr. took sole title to the property in the form of a transfer. A transfer? Was that the same as a sale? I didn't think so. I kept reading. October 17, 1921. Here it is. Prior title to the property was held by Joseph Albacco Sr. and a partner, as tenants-in-common. A partner? Joe's father had had a business partner? I read his name, then read it again. Oh, man. This was the return of the repressed, or divine justice, or Greek tragedy, or something.

Joseph Albacco Sr.'s partner had been Morgan Allan.

I closed the window and started up the car, my mind reeling. Joe's father and Meredith's father. It wasn't possible. The two of them, partners, back in the day. Did Joe know about this? How could he have?

"Lady, watch it!" I'd almost run over a man pushing a shopping cart. At my local Gelson's, they're rigged so you can't take them off the lot. Very fascistic. I saw a parking space and decided to pull over.

Morgan Allan and Joseph Albacco Sr. I shut my eyes and imagined how it might have happened.

It was the early 1920s. Both of them were roustabouts, the oil boom was beginning, they had nothing. But Morgan was a fast talker, they were buddies, and maybe they conned some people into investing in a get-rich scheme. Maybe. According to Burnett, the old guy could get anything out of anyone. All that hokum about red grass, and the oil just waiting to bubble up.

They raised some money, they bought some land, some tidelands, and they waited. They must have had some leases; maybe they were getting ready to expire. Or not. Those were lawless times. It was the frontier. Then Morgan received word from somebody working in the legislature that tidelands property was going to be worthless. That was the letter Jean had found. Legislation was about to be passed that would prohibit drilling. Whoever owned the land and/or leases would be stuck with a bunch of nothing. So Morgan gives his share up to Joe's father. Why does Joe's father want it? Does he know what's about to happen? I guess he doesn't. Maybe he thinks he's getting a great deal. But what does he give up in return?

Joe's father winds up killing himself. And years later his wife sells the supposedly worthless property back to her husband's former partner, who's become an oil billionaire in the meantime. But the property isn't worthless, never really has been. After World War II, offshore drilling explodes. Morgan gets richer. But somehow, somewhere, sometime, Jean Albacco gets ahold of the letter that set the whole plot in motion. She blackmails Morgan. And he kills her.

He kills her. Morgan Allan was the one. The father, not the daughter. His initials were M.A., too, after all.

But why exactly? Why does he have to kill her? To protect . . . what? What did Jean actually know? What had he actually done?

I needed to look at that letter again. The answers had to be in there, somewhere. But first I was going back to the historical society. I had a hunch. And for once I was going to make a librarian happy.

33

*H*ere's the last box, Cece," Mr. Grandy said, setting it down on the floor with a grunt. Sweat was pouring off his brow, but he didn't mind a hoot. The man had finally triumphed.

The big boss, Mrs. Murphy, looked like a punk-rock mother hen. Her auburn hair was organized into plumes. Actually, that made her more of a rooster.

"What happened to you, dear?" She gaped at my ripped pants and multicolored bruises.

"I had a little fall," I said. "Nothing to worry about."

She made some clucking noises.

"Well, let us know if you need new pencils or an eraser. Promise?"

"Oh, Cece's going to be here for a long time," Mr. Grandy said with an evil smile.

The boxes formed a barricade. I was surrounded. I wasn't out of there until they decided I was. And that was fine with me, because I had no intention of leaving the job unfinished. I was going to go through every scrap of paper in every one of those twenty boxes until I found what I was looking for.

ESG's legal files. Mr. Grandy was right. This was a treasure trove. None of the other biographers had had access to this kind of material.

I bent over the first box and pulled out a file. *Arnetta Hill v. Oxnard*. Sounded official. I skimmed the pages. Gardner's firm had been hired by a little old lady who was royally pissed at the City of Oxnard. In 1880, she'd planted fifty-five walnut trees along a road on her own land. When she donated the road to the city years later, she stipulated that they not touch the trees, a promise on which they were preparing to renege. After losing the case the first time around, ESG saved the trees on appeal. Noticing that three of the jurists were elderly, he played on their sympathies for sweet Arnetta. It worked brilliantly. My mother swears up and down this is the Century of the Senior. She and ESG both.

Magby v. New York Life Insurance Company. Now here was a guy who really wanted to off himself. He ingested poison, slashed his throat with a bedspring, and was finally found dead in his garage with the motor of his car running. The family hired Gardner's firm to prove it wasn't suicide because the insurance company would pay out only in the case of accidental death. Gardner produced a weather report which indicated that on the day of Magby's demise there had been a brisk wind, strong enough to blow the garage door shut and inadvertently do the guy in. The jury bought it. Actually, I remembered this one. Gardner pulled out the same argument in the A. A. Fair novel *Double or Quits*.

Brown v. Becker. Joseph Becker agrees to sell a tractor to his neighbor, Benjamin Brown. Later, the tractor turns out to have been in poor repair. Becker claims he knew nothing of the problems with the machine, and the contract is voided because of a mutual mistake in fact. But Brown is not satisfied. He feels duped. He has been delayed in planting his fields and is convinced Becker knew the truth about the tractor all along. He hires ESG's firm and sues. Notes in the file indicate that the five requirements for fraud, all of which must be present, are: 1. Misrepresentation of a material fact; 2. Made knowingly; 3. With intent to defraud; 4. Justifiably relied upon; 5. Causing injury to the other party. ESG finds a neighbor who overheard Becker's wife gloating to the postmistress about her husband's business acumen. Apparently, that was enough to satisfy the jury. Wonder if ESG handled the Beckers' divorce?

I had to get serious here. I had to keep my eye on the prize. I needed to go further back, back to the teens. Gardner had first hung out his shingle in 1911, in Oxnard, when he joined I. W. Stewart's law office. In 1916, he formed the law firm of Orr and Gardner in Ventura, which became Orr, Gardner, Drapeau, and Sheridan, and later Benton, Orr, Duval, and Buckingham, and who knows what else in between. The papers that had been donated to the historical society dated from 1912 to 1926, which was when Gardner's law offices had moved to the new building on the corner of California and Main. What I was looking for was in there, I knew it.

More files. Divorce cases, petty thefts, slander trials, property disputes; 1924, 1917, 1925, 1920. The files were in no particular order. Not chronological, not alphabetical. These people could've used a crack secretary like Allison. I looked up at the clock. It was after five P.M. Not much time left.

Mr. Grandy tiptoed over. "How's it going, Cece?"

"Fine, I guess, but I've only gone through one box and you're about to close and I haven't found what I'm looking for."

"Do you have a date?"

"Oh, not tonight. But I'm busy tomorrow and Sunday," I said quickly. I could've sworn Mr. Grandy was gay.

"No, no," he said. "I'm spoken for, silly. I meant, do you have a date you're looking for? And/or a name? I forgot to give you this." He handed me a slim folder. "It's an index we put together."

I grabbed it and tore through the pages. And there it was. Box 16. Mr. Grandy helped me hoist it onto the desk. My hands were trembling as I began to page through the files. "Abbot," "Ackerman," "Anderson." Shit. It wasn't there. How could this be? I flipped back to the front and started again, more calmly this time, as if I did this sort of thing every day. And then I found it, right where it was supposed to be, a thick file bearing the name "Albacco," typed onto a yellowed label. The "c" key must've stuck a little. The letters floated above the others like a pair of lovebirds.

I opened the file. *City of Ventura v. Albacco,* November 1916. Joseph Albacco's grandfather, William, is accused in an assault. The incident occurs around ten P.M., in an alleyway not far from his place of business, Elvie's Trophy Company, on Main. The victim, who suffered a broken arm and a concussion, identifies William Albacco in a lineup. There is no corroborating evidence. Albacco maintains his innocence throughout. During the trial, Gardner asks the victim to remove his glasses and to identify his wife in the courtroom. He cannot. Gardner then produces evidence that the victim had lost his spectacles the week before the incident and was still waiting for a replacement on the day the assault took place. How could a nearsighted person make a positive ID? Good question. Albacco was acquitted. A classic Perry Mason gambit.

One year later, October 1917. William Albacco's son, Joseph Albacco, gets in touch with Erle Stanley Gardner, the lawyer who'd exonerated his father. Here it is. I knew it. I *knew* this family's relationship to ESG was complicated. Joseph Sr. hires ESG to set up a limited-partnership agreement between himself and his friend Morgan Allan. Oh, this was amazing. Erle Stanley Gardner got the two of them together. ESG, the lawyer of choice "of all classes except the upper and middle classes." He was there from the beginning. No wonder Jean's murder rang a bell.

The agreement was executed the following month, in the city of Ventura, state of California. The documents noted that each of the limited partners was free from any liability beyond what they had contributed to the partnership. Joseph Albacco contributed five hundred dollars; Morgan Allan, five hundred. Their assets consisted of two pieces of property. Two? I kept reading. There were two parcels of land. Each man owned a 50 percent interest in each parcel as tenants-in-common. One was the tidelands parcel I already knew about. What about the other one? Parcels 17–22 of Lots 8 and 9, map of the Ventura Avenue Field, filed January 11, 1902, Map Book A, page 33, Ventura County Hall of Records. That was the legal description. But what did it refer to?

The Ventura Avenue Field. I remembered that name. It was a famous oil field. It was the oil field where records were broken in the mid-twenties, ten thousand barrels a day, fifteen thousand, extraordinary numbers like that. Jesus. The most valuable piece of land in the state. They owned that? No wonder Morgan Allan became a billionaire.

But why didn't Joe's father become a billionaire, too?

34

*E*llie, it's Cece Caruso, I'm calling from my car. How are you?"

"Oh, god. I can't talk to you now. My daughter's here, and she doesn't know anything about what went on back then, and that's the way I want to keep it."

"You were a kid, Ellie. He took advantage of you."

"It was a little more complicated than that. Ever read *Lolita*?"

"Listen, I don't care about your relationship with Bill Winters—I really don't. That's your business. But I need to know about something else. Please. It'll only take a second."

"One second. That's it. Hold on, I'm closing the door."

"You said something about Bill's family, about how they helped get the oil industry going in Ventura."

"And?"

"And there's this letter Jean had, from someone I think may have been Bill's father, Oliver Winters?"

"Oliver was his grandfather."

"The letter was written to Morgan Allan, advising him to sell some property he owned."

"So you found it."

"You knew about the letter?"

"That's one very valuable piece of paper."

"Wait, I can't hear you. Shit."

"Is that better?"

"Yes. So how did Jean get that letter?"

"Cece, I don't have time, my grandkids—"

"Ellie, please. I'm asking you, I'm begging you, to tell me what you know."

"I've got to hang up."

"Have you ever visited a jail cell? Do you realize Joe is an old man now? I want to help him. I know he didn't kill Jean."

"I'm hanging up. My daughter just walked into the room."

"My daughter is having trouble in her marriage," I blurted out. Was I really pimping my family to gain this woman's sympathy? Hell, I'd kissed Burnett Fowlkes to find out more about his family. Well, not that first day in the car. I was making myself sick. Perry Mason had never gone this far. Actually, he had. The TV Perry was a choirboy compared to the pulp Perry. In the early books, he'd punched people out, tampered with witnesses, broke the law whenever it suited him. But, somehow, he'd always maintained his dignity. Not me. Oh, well.

There was a pause, then Ellie let out a breath. "You can call me back in two hours. I'll be alone then. Good-bye."

She hung up just as I pulled into my driveway. My house. My velvety front lawn. It felt like I had been gone for months. It was hard to believe it was only yesterday that Joe had called me from jail and sent me scurrying off to Ventura and careening through thin air. My brain felt like it was going to explode.

I needed sleep. Food and sleep. And that was the end of my favorite black pants. Why was it that every time I came home from Ventura I had to throw away what I'd been wearing?

It was quiet and dark on the porch, and I almost tripped over a large wicker basket stuffed with little cakes. I peered through the green cellophane. Brownies, too. I picked it up and tucked the mail under my other arm. I could hear my babies mobilizing by the door. As soon as the key turned in the lock, they were all over me. I dropped to my knees, scooped them up in my bruised arms, and reciprocated with slobbery kisses of my own. There's nothing like family.

The light on the phone machine was blinking insanely, trying to catch my eye. Where were you? What were you doing? Who were you with? I had thirty-three messages. Let me guess: thirty-two from my mother, one from Lael, and none from Annie. I'd play them later.

I opened the card. Burnett. "Hope you're better. See you Sunday." Hope you're better, see you Sunday? It was insulting. You'd write that to a maiden aunt who'd just had an appendectomy. Where were the flowers and the champagne truffles? I guess I was supposed to be convalescing. That was me, a convalescing jewel thief.

I changed into sweatpants and a tank top, downed two glasses of milk and a mini–lemon poppyseed loaf, opened the mail, tossed all the catalogs except for American Girl, which I saved because Lael's daughter Nina's birthday was coming up, and watched a documentary on the History Channel about Madame de Pompadour. It was nine P.M. Two hours had passed. It was time to call Ellie back.

The first thing she said was how sorry she was about my daughter. I felt like a heel.

"My daughter's been divorced for three years," she continued. "She's raising two kids on her own. It's really hard on her. Does your daughter have children?"

Did Vincent's son, Alexander, count, even a little?

"No."

"It's a good thing, really."

"Yeah, I'm not sure I see myself as the grandma type."

"Oh, you'd be surprised, Cece."

"I know you're busy, so let's finish this."

"Sorry," she said frostily.

"I didn't mean it like that."

"It's fine. It's just that I don't exactly feel like strolling down memory lane, you know? So the letter."

"The letter."

"Don't interrupt me, Cece."

"I'm not saying another word."

"Bill's dad was a big guy. Bill was not. He was short. Handsome, but short. And he had the hard luck of having a dad who was big and tall and great at everything, especially getting his loser son out of trouble. The dad had fantasies that Bill would go into politics, like his granddad. I told you that part the other day. So when Jean went too far, threatening to ruin Bill over our affair, wanting more and more money, Bill went to his dad, like he always had. His dad said not to worry, that he'd fix everything up. He said he had something in his safe that would make Jean a happy girl."

"The letter."

"That's right. It was a copy of a letter his own father, Oliver, had written to Morgan Allan decades earlier. You see, Morgan and Jean, they were two peas in a pod. Morgan was a blackmailer, too. Oliver had been cheating on his wife and

Morgan knew it. He'd made it his business to know every-thing that happened in every sleazy bar and motel in town. What he wanted in exchange for keeping quiet was informa-tion about oil legislation, before it was made public. Oliver didn't think he had a choice. So he did what Morgan asked. But before he died, he gave a copy of the letter you found to his son, Bill's father, saying he might need it someday. And he turned out to be right."

"So Bill gave the letter to Jean?"

"Yes. He told her there were bigger fish to fry. And she agreed."

"When was this?"

"Oh, when we were sophomores in high school, I guess."

Why had Jean waited so long before using the letter against Morgan? According to her bankbook, she hadn't started blackmailing him until well after she'd married Joe. It was odd. She didn't seem like the patient type.

I thanked Ellie profusely and wished her well. She was a good egg.

I crawled into bed after that, but I was too exhausted to sleep. Curling into a ball seemed like an impossible expendi-ture of effort, so I stared at a water spot on my ceiling instead. It was shaped like a jack-o'-lantern, with a triangle nose and pointy teeth. I loved carving jack-o'-lanterns. I think it was because I was born on Halloween. Annie had always insisted to all her little friends that I was a witch. Some of them believed her. Their parents, too. Maybe Meredith Allan and I had something in common after all.

So where was my magic now? How was I going to make the bits and pieces of information fit together? One of the things ESG had been best at was teasing out relationships between the most disparate characters. I'd read enough of his books. Now I had to do it for real.

I sat up.

One last time: Joseph Albacco and Morgan Allan are partners. They have two assets between them, Asset A and Asset B. Morgan finds out Asset A will soon be worthless. And all of a sudden, according to the title report, he no longer owns it. It is owned 100 percent by his partner. Well, of course. Why hadn't I seen it before? The whole thing was exactly like a divorce.

The two of them dissolved their partnership—I don't know why, maybe because Joseph Sr. discovered what a prick Morgan was. Or maybe Morgan started something to precipitate a breakup, who knows. They wanted to go their separate ways. And Morgan came up with the solution. What good ideas old Morgan always had. How logical it must have seemed at the time. Joseph Sr. would get Asset A, and Morgan would get Asset B. What could be more equitable? Oh, I knew that song and dance so well.

It's all about splitting the assets. I got full custody of Annie and my ex got our savings account. So who got the better deal? He thought he did, but I knew better. Morgan got the Ventura Avenue field and became richer than God, and Joe's father got the tidelands and a fat lot of nothing. No wonder the man killed himself. But what he didn't know was that Morgan withheld the information Oliver Winters had so kindly provided. Morgan misrepresented the facts. And that, as I recently learned courtesy of Mr. Grandy's files, spells fraud, a felony offense in every state in the Union.

I may not know my torts from my tarts, but you didn't have to be a lawyer to understand that the Allan family was going to owe the Albacco family a shitload of smackeroos.

35

Gambino took me to Buffalo to meet his parents. We drove to a matinee of *Romeo and Juliet* in a beat-up blue Camaro. On our way back to the car we were caught in a sudden downpour, and I offered Gambino's mother, who was wearing a grass skirt, the umbrella I had been using as a walking stick because I had only one leg. Annie was using the other leg as a hatrack. But the umbrella blew inside out and we all got soaked. Just as we were about to strip down to our skivvies, I woke up to the clap of thunder. What a nightmare. At least I wasn't the one wearing the grass skirt.

I went to get my robe from the closet and stepped right into a puddle of water. I looked up. The jack-o'-lantern on my ceiling had spread into a Volkswagen Rabbit. Not a very auspicious start to the day. Poor Lael. She'd be frantic about her Labor Day barbecue.

"I knew it was you," she said, picking up on the first ring. "I'm watching the Weather Channel right now, and it's good news! The storm is supposed to clear before noon."

I looked out the rain-spattered window. The sky was as black as coal.

"It's already clearing on this side of town," I said. "I think I see some sunlight peeking through the clouds."

"That's great! Everybody's going to mope around all morning and by one o'clock they'll be ready to put on their swimsuits and chow down on burgers! And I'm making Jell-O molds in honor of Joe Hill and the Wobblies! Union Forever!"

I had to hand it to her. A sunny disposition can carry you through the worst of times.

"So, I have news, Cece. You'll never guess who's coming."

"What?" I couldn't hear her. Buster was howling. He was afraid of thunder. I headed to the kitchen, thinking I'd distract him with food.

"I said, you'll never guess who's coming to the barbecue."

"Who?" I asked, hoisting the bag of kibble.

"Your daughter, your son-in-law, your son-in-law's girlfriend, and their little boy."

The kibble went all over the floor. "You've got to be kidding."

"Nope. Annie called last night and asked if I'd mind, and of course I said it was fine."

"You should've said no, Lael!"

"Why?"

"Annie is trying to play matchmaker. Does she really need to bring those two together?"

"Maybe they should be together."

"Vincent should be with Annie. They love each other."

"And what about Vincent's son?"

"Lael, you of all people should know that the nuclear family isn't the only option."

"I never know how to take your comments. Are you trying to piss me off?"

"No, I'm sorry. I shouldn't have said that."

"How about you don't say anything, and trust those around you, feeble as they may be, to work out their own lives! Try that, Cece, why don't you?"

She hung up. And I hadn't even had time to tell her that Gambino was going to be my date. I got the broom and started sweeping up the little bone-shaped pieces of kibble. I must've been hungry, because they smelled good.

Once she got over being mad, Lael was going to be happy about Gambino. She liked him. He'd come to one of her barbecues a few years back, when we were first dating. Late in the afternoon, she'd been poking around behind the garage looking for some starter fluid when she'd caught Tommy and one of his friends smoking a joint. She'd sent the friend home and begged Gambino to haul Tommy off in handcuffs, to teach him a lesson, but Gambino took him for a long walk instead. To this day, neither of us has any idea what he said to the kid, but it was the last time Tommy ever got into trouble.

I finished cleaning up. I wouldn't have bothered, but it was that or work. Now I had no choice. I put on my slippers, grabbed an umbrella, and was about to dash out to the office when I remembered that I always have my best ideas in the shower. I draped a towel over the shower door and put a fresh legal pad and a pencil on the sink, within easy reach. I'd learned through bitter experience that mnemonic devices are not to be trusted.

The hot water beat down on my back. It was heavenly.

I didn't want to think about the Albaccos and oil rigs and murder. I wanted to think about Gambino and the cleansing rays of the sun and piña coladas. I daydreamed until I got to the cream rinse stage. Gambino and I were under a palm tree, eating guacamole and laughing. I daydreamed a little more. But I really did need to pumice my heels.

Usually I time it perfectly, but I was off by a couple of minutes today so I wound up shaving my legs in ice-cold water. Shivering, I draped another towel over my pillow and lay down carefully, so as not to get my jojoba-infused hair-restructuring gel all over the bed. Mimi sniffed me curiously, but she was enamored of kibble, not plant extracts.

So enough with the guacamole. I propped my legal pad up on my lap. Back to the matter at hand. What did Jean have on Morgan Allan?

Jean knew about his stooge in the legislature, but that wasn't enough. It was bad, but not bad enough to destroy a man like Morgan. She had to have known more. The really damning bit was the partnership agreement with Joe's father. Joe's father should've shared in Morgan's billions. Equally. It had to be that. Jean had to have known. That would have been enough to make Morgan sweat, enough to have made him pay her, week after week, month after month, enough to have made him realize that if he was ever going to be rid of her he'd have to kill her. But how could Jean have known when her husband, Joe Albacco Sr.'s own son, had no idea whatsoever? Why didn't she tell him? Wouldn't she have wanted all that money for herself?

I grabbed the phone to call Father Herlihy. While I waited, he found Joe. Chaplains, I'd discovered, have a lot of pull.

After about five minutes, Joe got on the line. We exchanged a few pleasantries. He asked how I was. I asked how he was. It was all so weirdly civil.

"I'm nervous about my parole hearing on Monday," he said finally. I tried not to hear the expectant note in his voice.

"Listen, Mr. Albacco. There's a lot you don't know, and I'm not sure where to begin."

"I can't talk long, Ms. Caruso. I work all day Saturdays."

"Well, then, here it is. Meredith's father and your father were business partners, and Morgan cheated your father out of billions of dollars."

He started to laugh. It did sound sort of implausible.

"Listen to me. What I'm trying to say is, when you get out of jail, you are going to be an extremely wealthy man."

"Hey, I don't want to be rude or anything, but this garbage isn't what I hoped to be hearing from you."

"Hey, I don't want to be rude, either, but don't you dare talk to me about garbage!"

"Excuse me?"

I paused a beat. "Erle Stanley Gardner never called you, did he?"

He didn't say anything.

"No, I didn't think he did. Why are you so quiet? Why don't you say something?"

"I knew you were smart, Ms. Caruso."

"Oh, I'm not half as smart as you are."

"I'm not smart. Look, I didn't mean to lie."

"You didn't mean to lie? That's pathetic!"

"Come off it. You and I both know you'd have never

started all this up without the right reason. Would you have looked into my case if I were just another unanswered letter to the Court of Last Resort? Would you?"

"I suppose not."

"So how'd you know he never called me?"

"ESG's history with your family goes way back. He couldn't have gone as far as you said without remembering your name. He would've remembered that he had set up the original partnership agreement between your father and Morgan Allan."

"What partnership agreement? You keep dreaming this stuff up. My father was a loser, I told you. You don't know what you're talking about."

"I believe you. I have no idea why, considering how you've jerked me around, but I believe you. You didn't know anything about this. But your wife sure as hell did."

"What are you going on about? How?"

"That's what I want to find out. Were she and your mother close?"

"No, Jean only met her once. My mother got sick after that and died very quickly. It was lung cancer. It had spread all over her body. She was in terrible pain. Jean helped me a lot after that."

"How did she help you exactly?"

"I wasn't good for much. Jean was just a kid herself. But she helped with all the arrangements, emptying out the house, everything. She was amazing."

That she was. Someone like Jean would know just how to empty out a house. What to keep and what to throw away. She must've found something in that house that tipped her off. Something neither Joe nor his mother even realized they had. And she knew just what to do with it.

I told Joe I'd see him at the parole hearing Monday morning. After I hung up, I looked out the window. The sky was blue, as if it had never been otherwise. I rinsed out my hair and decided to let it air-dry. I was going for sexy and tousled and vowed not to look in the mirror until bedtime for fear of encountering evidence to the contrary. I stuffed my bathing suit into an old beach bag, pulled on my jeans and a striped T-shirt, and sat on the couch waiting for Gambino. But that wasn't such a good idea. He wasn't coming for hours. So I picked up *The Case of the Glamorous Ghost*.

I was about halfway through. The main characters were Perry's spectral client, Eleanor Corbin, an exhibitionist, opportunist, and liar, and Olga Corbin Jordan, the well-heeled, well-groomed half sister of the ghost. Poor Olga was scandalized because Eleanor appeared to be involved not just in naked dancing in the park, which was bad enough, but illegal gems and narcotics.

Families. I had been thinking about them a lot lately, and they were all scary, every last one of them. Eleanor and Olga. Murderous Morgan Allan, his spooky daughter, Meredith, and her son, Burnett. Joe the liar and his dead wife, Jean, who thought it would be fun to blackmail her sister's lesbian lover, among others. There was Ellie, who was afraid her daughter would find out about her past, and the Winters clan: a cheating legislator, a fix-it son, and a screwup grandson. Then there was my family—my mother, who could still wound me with a word; my father, who had died before I could prove myself to him; and my daughter, who regarded me as superfluous. What did Tolstoy say?

Happy families are all alike. Unhappy ones are each unhappy in their own way.

Lael's barbecues were like that, come to think of it, each its own unique species of disaster. I hoped this year's would be the one we'd all forget. That it would be blissfully uneventful. That the highlight of the afternoon would be one of the children catching sight of a rainbow. That we'd eat, drink, and go home to our wide-screen TVs, those of us who have wide-screen TVs, that is. You never can tell.

36

Tomas, the default architect of Lael's rabbit warren of a residence, opened the front door.

"Hi, Cece!" he said, jolly as all get-out. I gave him a hug. We were old friends. He and his brother had master-planned my office.

Tomas's wife, Rosario, smiled warmly and handed Gambino and me little flags with pictures of Emma Goldman silkscreened onto them.

"Emma Goldman was a major figure in the history of radicalism and feminism. Lael told us," said Tomas. "Very interesting."

"Emma Goldman spent some time in Buffalo," Gambino said. "It was there that she first insisted that higher wages and shorter hours were an integral part of the revolutionary transformation of society."

"Buffalo," I mused. "The cradle of civilization."

"Everyone's in the back," said Rosario. "I'll take your things."

We followed the bluesy strains of "John Henry" out to the pool.

"Cece!" Lael shouted, making her way through the crowd. The place was packed with Lael's kids, most of their dads, their dads' wives and girlfriends and boyfriends, a few neighbors I recognized, Tomas and his crew and their wives and girlfriends and boyfriends, and, over by the bar, the tamale-eating agent from the farmer's market, wearing a different baseball hat.

"You're a sight for sore eyes, Detective Gambino," Lael said.

"I can't believe the tamale guy is here," I whispered.

"You think you're the only one who can pick somebody up?" she asked gaily.

Before I could open my mouth, she slipped her arm through Gambino's and said, "I'm being mean. Cece's got eyes only for you."

I wasn't sure if I should thank her or slap her.

Lael gave me a squeeze. "You know I love you," she said.

"Me, too," I answered. "I'm sorry for before."

"Forget it. This is a party, right? Get some drinks and mingle, you two."

We strolled over to the bar and helped ourselves to a couple of Coronas.

"I guess Annie's not here yet."

"Nope."

"I'm going to be calm, cool, and collected when I see her."

"Of course you are," said Gambino, taking a slug of his beer.

"Are you being sarcastic?"

"I know better."

We sat down on a slightly moldy wooden bench.

"I dreamed about you last night, Peter."

"I dreamed about you, too," he said, scooting a little closer and risking a splinter.

"Actually, it was more about your mother."

"That's so romantic."

"Gambino, why are you always so . . . what's the opposite of nonplussed?"

"Can I have your attention?" Lael ushered everyone over to a little stage she'd set up behind the pool. "The kids have prepared something on the Labor Day theme, if we can give them our attention for a minute or two. They've been working on it all week."

"Come with me," Gambino said, taking my hand.

The kids filed behind the stained red curtain. There was muffled laughter. Zoe peeked her head through and stuck her tongue out at no one in particular. After yanking her backstage, Tommy made his entrance. In classic adolescent fashion, he looked too big and too small at the same time.

"Voltaire," he announced. " 'Work spares us from three great evils: boredom, vice, and need.' "

Everyone clapped.

"Man, they ought to post that at the station house," Gambino said.

"Zoe, your turn," prompted Lael.

All smiles now, she took her place next to her brother. "Tennis, anyone?" she lisped.

"No, Tennyson," Tommy whispered in her ear.

" 'Death is the end of life,' " she recited, giggling. " 'Ah, why should life all labor be?' "

She hopped off the stage into Lael's arms.

"Hi, Mom," said a voice behind me.

"Annie!" I turned around and gave her a hug. "Hi, baby. I'm so happy you're here. You remember Peter, don't you?"

"Sure. How are you?"

"I'm great," he said. "It's good to see you again, Annie."

"So," I said, craning my neck, "where's the rest of your group?"

"Cece," Gambino cautioned.

"They're helping Alexander change into his swimsuit," Annie whispered, pointing to the stage.

"My turn," said Nina, with all the dignity a ten-year-old could muster. She took a deep breath.

" 'Most men in a brazen prison live/Where in the sun's hot eye/With heads bent o'er their toil, they languidly/Their lives to some unmeaning taskwork give/Dreaming of nought beyond their prisonwall.' By Matthew Arnold, a famous poet of the Victorian era." She gave a little curtsy.

"I will recite baby August's for him," Lael said, smiling down at him, fast asleep with his pacifier in his mouth. " 'Honest labour bears a lovely face.' It's from Thomas Dekker, and I have no idea who he is, so don't ask. Now let's eat!"

Tomas and Rosario were poised at the grill. Gambino went over to place our orders. Nina ushered the kids over to the side yard and passed out printed menus.

"They're eating better than we are," I said to Annie. "Spaghetti and meatballs, roasted baby potatoes with sea salt, green salad with tomatoes, and coffee."

"Oh, get a load of this, Mom," she said, as Tommy marched out with the plates.

The pasta was a heap of bubble gum tape, generously topped with malted milk balls and strawberry fruit roll-up for sauce. The lettuce and tomato salad consisted of a pile of gummy spearmint leaves and Swedish berries. The potatoes were balls of marzipan rolled in cocoa. And the coffee, served in gleaming white teacups, looked suspiciously like melted chocolate.

"Are you sure you covered all the food groups?" Annie asked Lael.

"I covered chocolate, didn't I?"

"Alexander's a chocolate freak already. C'mon, Mom," she said, taking my arm. "I want you to meet him."

Vincent was heading our way, with a tiny Vincent in tow.

"Hello, Alexander," I said, putting out my hand. He was clutching a speckled Superball as if his life depended on it.

"Is that your special toy?" I asked.

"No," he answered solemnly.

"*No* is his favorite word," Vincent explained. "No, no, no, all day long. You can ask him if he wants ice cream, and he'll say no. But he doesn't mean it, do you, little guy?"

"No," he said, clambering into Vincent's arms. He buried his face against his father's chest.

"He's a little shy sometimes."

"He's beautiful, Vincent."

"I'm really lucky. Roxana's in the bathroom, changing. I hope you have a chance to meet her, too, Cece."

"Of course," I said, looking to Annie for guidance. I had no idea what I was supposed to say or do or think. But Annie seemed happy, and that was good enough for me.

Gambino appeared with two plates piled high with hot dogs, pickles, and potato salad and propelled me toward a table in a shady corner.

"Excuse me," he said to two women who were going at

their corn on the cob like there was no tomorrow. "Can we sit here?"

They nodded, tight-lipped. I've never understood why people serve corn on the cob at parties.

We sat down.

"I'm proud of you, Cece," he said. "That was hard."

"Thanks," I said, leaning into him. His sweater felt soft against my bare arm. "Let's talk about something else."

"There is something, but I don't know if I want to get into it here."

"C'mon, Gambino, you can't stop now," I said, sitting up.

"Man, this potato salad is good. I think there's horse-radish in it."

"Gambino."

"There've been a couple of breaks in the Flynn case," he said, chewing enthusiastically.

"What?"

"Well, for one thing, they finally picked up Gil, the missing twin. He had a lot of cash and not a lot of alibi."

"Alibis are overrated."

"They also got a fingerprint."

"You have something on your lip."

He dabbed at his mouth with his napkin.

"No, there, I got it." He had very nice lips.

"Thanks."

"So they got a fingerprint," I prompted, excited now.

"Yeah."

"And it doesn't match Gil's, does it?"

"No, it doesn't."

"I told you," I said triumphantly.

"That doesn't rule him out by a long shot, Cece."

"Wait a second. I thought the place had been wiped clean."

"Yeah, well, for some reason Moriarty had the crime scene guys go back in for another look around. And lo and behold, on the dresser in the bedroom they found some prints they'd missed the first time around. Can you believe that?"

The dresser? They couldn't be mine. We'd worn gloves. I thought back. Damn. I must have already taken the gloves off when I remembered about putting Mrs. Flynn's ring back.

"That's not all, Cece."

"There's more?"

"They got some footprints in the mud out in the back-yard. One of them was a woman's boot."

I started panicking.

"Size nine Jimmy Choo with a three-and-a-half-inch spike heel. Ring any bells?"

"I must try that potato salad," I said.

"What the hell were you doing there?"

"I found the body, remember?"

The corn enthusiasts were hanging on our every word now.

"Excuse me, this is a private conversation."

"Cece!" said Gambino.

The ladies went beet red and moved next to a hedge of diseased eugenias.

"You know, you really are something."

"Is that a compliment?"

"No."

"Thanks a lot."

"You can't scam me, Cece. I know you too well."

"And you call yourself a cop?"

"What's that supposed to mean?"

"Oh, come on. The easiest people to scam are the ones who think they know you."

"Are you telling me I only think I know you?"

"I didn't say that."

"What did you say?"

"Ohmigod, that's it!" I cried.

"What's it? What the hell are you talking about, Cece?"

"Jean scammed Joe from the beginning, that's what I'm talking about!" I grabbed Gambino and planted a kiss on his lips. A big fat one.

"I'd ask for seconds," he said, "but you look a little scary. Like the cat who ate the canary."

"Yeah, me and Jean," I said, grinning.

"I don't get it."

"It was a perfect scam, Gambino. Jean was blinking dollar signs when she realized exactly what she'd found among Joe's mother's papers. If she could just make him fall in love with her—Joe, I mean—if she could actually become his wife, she'd be sitting pretty when he claimed what was rightfully his. She'd be rich, like she'd always dreamed of. That's why she sat on the information for so long! Blackmail, man, that was small potatoes compared to this!"

"Compared to what?"

"Poor Joe never even knew what hit him. All of a sudden, he was a married man. But the jig was up when Jean found out about Joe and Meredith. She realized Joe might very well leave her before the whole story about the fathers and the oil partnership came out, netting her precisely nothing for her years of trouble. And even if Joe didn't wind up leaving her, could she have convinced him to institute a suit against his lover's father? Probably not. So Jean fell back on old habits, trying to squeeze whatever she could out of Morgan."

"You lost me," Gambino said.

"Listen, I have to go, Peter. I have to settle this."

"That sounds ominous."

I sprang up from the table, knocking over both our plates of food in the process.

"Cece, don't be foolish," Gambino warned.

"I have one stop to make before going home, that's it. Don't worry."

A woman with a purpose, I caught Lael's eye and waved good-bye. But I wouldn't be leaving just yet. Because as I sailed through the sliding glass door, little Alexander fell into the deep end of the pool.

37

*I*t was like watching a movie on fast forward.

First, there was the splash. Then, somebody, I think it was Rosario, yelling, "The little boy! The little boy! He's fallen in!" Then someone was jumping in after him. It was Annie.

Before I had even allowed that to register, Vincent was there, at the edge of the pool. And then he was diving in. When he came up for air, he was smiling. He had them both in his arms.

"Vincent!" Roxana yelled. "What on earth are you doing? You know Alexander's been able to swim since he was three months old! Give me my son," she said, reaching out for the little boy. "So much fuss. Ah, don't cry, love," she murmured into his ear.

"Alexander can swim, but Annie can't," Vincent replied. "She needed me. And I need her. I need you," he said, looking into her eyes.

"I need you, too," she said, crying.

They struggled out of the water, their arms wrapped tightly around each other.

"What on earth is going on?" I asked Roxana. "Aren't the two of you back together?"

"Me and Vincent?" she asked, laughing. "No way. He's a nice guy, but please. It's always been Annie for him. And I'm engaged," she said, waving a stupendous diamond in my face.

"Watch it!" I said. "That thing's dangerous."

"Sorry. Anyway, my fiancé's in Canada until November, cutting an album. Christian rock. He's gonna be huge."

You never can tell. Well, maybe certain people can, if they aren't running around like certain other people, jumping to conclusions. I looked over to where Annie and Vincent were standing. Annie was my hero. She was sopping wet and shivering. I wanted to go to her, to tell her how much I loved her. But her husband was taking care of her, and everything was going to be fine.

Gambino came over and put his arm around me.

"Let's go home," he said.

"One stop first, okay?" I batted my baby blues.

Gambino didn't stay long. He said he didn't want to rush things, the way we had last time. I knew he was right, but that didn't keep me from missing him the moment he turned to go.

I watched him pull out. And watched a beat-up blue Camaro pull in. Right into my driveway, like he owned the place. The guy stepped out of his car and started up the walk toward me, cocky as hell.

"Don't take another step," I said, brandishing Mimi as a weapon.

"Hey, I'm harmless."

"I've heard that before." He did look a lot skinnier than I'd remembered. And younger.

"I'll pay anything."

"How dare you?"

"I'll do anything."

"Don't even think about it."

"That *Testament* shirt you were wearing the other morning. I have to know. Is it from the show's first season? It is, isn't it? Oh, man, I have to have it. I'm a Govian, a total Commander Gow freak."

Never assume.

After the kid left with the T-shirt and an autographed script I'd found lying around, I put a pot of coffee on and sat down at the kitchen table. There was a stack of mail to open, most of it bills, but that didn't seem very enticing. There was always shopping. Luckily, it was too late. Only the malls were still open and I had standards, thank you very much. With a dramatic flourish I swept the mail into a drawer and headed out to the garden. Time to euthanize my vegetables. They'd lived a good life. What more can any of us ask for?

I pulled on a pair of dirt-encrusted gloves and went to work. Big hunks of earth went flying. Buster was sitting ringside, hoping to find a snail to torture. There were plenty of those to choose from. Up went the remains of my once glorious eggplants, polished to an inky sheen, as beautiful to behold as to savor in a cheesy moussaka. Up went the garlic chives, which had begun to confound me midway through the season. Up went the parsley, which I'd had the misfortune to plant a day before a heat wave. Up went the carcasses of my four tomato plants, which had served me so long and so well. That latter operation took the better part of an hour.

Darkness fell, and I was done. Covered in sweat, I dropped my loppers and my pruning shears and peeled off my gloves. I have to say I found the whole experience, scrapes and all, even more satisfying than planting the seedlings in the first place. Maybe it was because the slate had been wiped clean. Next spring, I'd have another shot at it.

The tomatoes would be red and unblemished, every one of them. The cilantro would thrive for more than two weeks. I'd conquer those fleshy green hornworms, those squash bugs, and those Mexican bean beetles who attack the underside of leaves, devouring all but the stringy veins. I wouldn't neglect my oak leaf lettuce such that its tender, thick midribs grew skyward while the outer leaves crumbled into dust. My novelty cucumber plant would yield more than a single deformed specimen. I'd do everything right next time. Why not?

When I was a little kid, my mother told me I'd learn how hot the fire was only by burning my finger. I remember thinking that she wanted me to burn my finger. Perhaps my ambivalence toward her dated back that far. But she'd been right, of course, and I'd tried to impress the same thing on Annie. There is no substitute for experience. It is possible to get smarter, to do better, to figure out a thing or two. I'd learned something valuable by walking a couple of weeks in Perry Mason's shoes. I'd learned that guilt is not the issue. Everyone's guilty of something, for god's sake. What matters is that someone is innocent. And that that person not suffer more than he is supposed to, by which I mean we all suffer, to one degree or another. That's just the way it is.

I still didn't know exactly what had happened all those

years ago in that bungalow in Ventura. But as of a couple of hours ago, I had a good idea. What I did know for sure was that Joe had suffered enough. And that I would be able to help him. I didn't have proof, not exactly, but I had enough to shed doubt on his guilt.

Of course, it wasn't over yet. Only Monday would tell, and there was still Sunday and Burnett's party to get through before that.

38

*L*et's say you're Clark Gable, and you need a new suit. Do
you grab Carole Lombard and head on over to Sears? I don't
think so. Off-the-rack is not your style. This is what you do.
You take Carole by the arm and walk through the silvery star-
burst doors of the Oviatt Building. You linger in the lobby for
a moment or two, admiring the *très moderne* appointments.
Then you take the elevator up into the waiting arms of James
Oviatt, haberdasher to the stars. And you settle Carole on the
divan with a Manhattan and some cocktail nuts.

Which is to say it didn't much surprise me that one of the
most beautiful buildings in Los Angeles started its life as a
shrine to the well-cut trouser. James Oviatt was an aesthete.
He went to the 1925 Paris Exposition and flipped out. So
when it came time to build the headquarters of his presti-
gious haberdashery, Alexander & Oviatt, nothing less than a
gothic deco skyscraper with thirty tons of glass by Lalique
would do.

The place almost put my dress to shame. Almost, but not
quite. I was a vision. Carlos the hairdresser had said so, and

the man never lies. His Russian assistant, Annie, confirmed it. I'd given myself over to them. They were gifted, that pair. Burnett gasped when he saw me open the door. Not that I cared. My mind was on Gambino. And vanity is a deadly sin. Still, that kind of appreciation nourishes the soul. I felt like Annie after a pot of Kombucha mushroom tea.

Burnett took my hand as we stepped into the elevator. "Hold the door for Louella Parsons!" bellowed a heavily made-up woman in a broad-shouldered suit and an even broader-shouldered fox-fur jacket. It looked like a chubby Bridget owned, from Yves St. Laurent's forties-inspired collection of 1970. A chubby is a garment, not a person. You learn that sort of thing over time.

"Happy birthday, Burnett!" she rasped, her voice laced with nicotine. "You've aged divinely."

"Where's Hedda Hopper?" I cracked.

"Hedda who? I work for William Randolph Hearst, toots, and I wear the pants around here. If I don't like you, you might as well hop on the bus back to Podunk, because you'll never be anything more than a waitress or a hooker!" She gave me the once-over. "But you're good, honey. Oh, yes, you'll more than do."

Some of us were more into this than others.

The elevator doors opened onto the penthouse. Soft music was playing and cocktail glasses were clinking and tall men in slouchy suits were lighting cigarettes for sleek women with crimson lips. A burled mahogany hatrack stood in the corner of the living room. Someone had tossed a fedora onto it. I picked it up and glanced at the label. Mossimo for Target.

"This place was acquired by a developer in the late seventies," Burnett explained. "He restored it, but the penthouse isn't entirely finished. It was originally decorated by Saddler et fils, a French interior design firm. Lots of mahogany, very masculine. Look at the floor." It was parquet, laid out in wild geometric patterns.

"Can you imagine living like this?" I asked him, wide-eyed. Wrong question. He did live like this.

"Oviatt was a longtime bachelor. He got married at fifty-one," Burnett said, "so I've got six years to go."

Six years to go? That meant he was turning forty-five. The man was older than I was! How the hell could I have gotten that wrong? At least it made my crow's feet seem less egregious.

We wandered into the formal bathroom, which featured carved maroon plaster walls depicting jungle scenes. "This room makes me want to hunt wild game or something."

"I didn't know you had it in you," he said.

"Remember, you're not supposed to underestimate me."

"Why is that, again?"

I was getting the distinct feeling I had gotten more than one thing wrong lately.

"Burnett, finally! The photographers are waiting for us. You will excuse him, won't you, dear?"

My visual field was obfuscated by a swath of black satin. It was Meredith Allan, who insinuated herself between us. No wonder the man had never married. He belonged to his mother and, if you asked me, wasn't putting up much of a fuss.

She looked extraordinary. I needed Bridget to be sure, but her dress looked like vintage Balmain. It was a one-shouldered creation with a flirty peplum falling over a sleek column of black. She was wearing diamonds: in her ears, up and down her bare arms, and on her shoulder, a huge diamond-encrusted pin in the shape of an octopus. Its tentacles slithered down her back. Must've been a family thing.

"Good evening, Miss Allan. Why is it we're always meeting in bathrooms?"

"I can't say I detected a pattern, dear."

"Well, before you get away, I have something I need to return to you. I feel terrible about it." I reached into my purse for her gold bracelets.

"Not now," she said, taking her son by the arm. "We have a few things to attend to. I'm sure it can wait. Why don't you pop downstairs and check out your table? Everyone at Table Eleven despises each other. Except you, of course. No one knows you. It'll be fascinating."

They went off to immortalize themselves. My plan was to start drinking.

Out on the terrace there was caviar, mountains of it, and waiters bearing flutes of champagne. Champagne flutes always made me think of chimney flues. They should've called them champagne piccolos. Anyway, I got one, and then another. The waiter was looking at me funny.

"Do I remind you of someone?" I asked, hoping he'd say Dorothy Lamour.

"No, not really, but I love your dress! I go to FIT," he said. "The Fashion Institute of Technology? I'm into surfwear, neoprene, that kind of thing, but you're making me think more broadly about synthetics."

"That's quite a compliment."

He was the only person who had spoken to me, so I felt a pang of regret when he moved on to a guy in a zoot suit. He had the whole thing down perfectly, that guy: swooping chains, high-waisted pants, and a jacket hanging down to his knees. Talk about attention-getting fashion. Of course, the original zoot-suiters learned the hard way that self-expression can be a dangerous thing.

I walked over to the buffet and downed as many caviar-smeared blinis as I could without attracting attention. A dark-haired woman engaged me in a scintillating conversation about period makeup. Apparently, it was all about Revlon's Cherries in the Snow. I was trying to figure out how to make my escape when someone tapped me on the shoulder.

"I didn't mean to startle you," Burnett said, "but they're serving dinner downstairs now."

"Honey, I've been startled by experts." I stole that line from a Barbara Stanwyck movie. I guess Burnett wasn't a fan. He looked bemused, like he had no idea what to do with me, but that worked out just fine because his thoughtful mother had arranged for us to be sitting in opposite corners of the room.

Burnett walked me over to the dread Table Eleven and introduced me around. My tablemates were already slurping up their oysters Rockefeller. They certainly didn't appear to despise each other. Maybe it was the calm before the storm.

I sat down in an empty chair. Burnett promised to check on me before the floor show began. Yes, there was going to be a floor show.

"And what do you do, Cece?" asked Phoebe Something-or-other, who was seated to my right.

I tore apart a warm dinner roll and spread butter all over its plush interior. I was starved.

"I'm a biographer," I answered, taking a bite.

"William," she said turning to her husband, "they've seated me next to a pornographer."

"No, no," I sputtered, spraying little bits of roll around. "I'm a biographer. I write biographies. Stories of people's lives."

"I collect photographs of Gypsy Rose Lee and Sally Rand, the bubble dancer," offered Samuel, a distinguished-looking gentleman from across the table. "Do you ever publish those?"

"I have no involvement in pornography, personally or professionally," I insisted.

"Excuse me," Samuel said, "but my pictures are very tasteful. I just had an appraisal last year. Worth a bundle. Very rare. I have one of Sally posing with officials from the War Department. She fronted the money so they could develop a transparent balloon sixty inches in diameter. The biggest ones up to that point were thirty inches in diameter and used by the army for target practice."

I think Hedy Lamarr was also some sort of scientific genius. You never know. Meanwhile, I was getting worried about the fate of my dress. What if I left perspiration stains? Would I have to pay for it? Maybe I could stuff some Kleenex under my arms.

I downed my glass of Merlot. "I'm off to powder my nose before the beef Wellington arrives," I announced to no one in particular. On my way out to the foyer, I stopped at the head table.

"Miss Allan," I began.

"Your food will get cold, dear," she said, barely turning around.

"Yes, but I don't know when I'll have another chance to return these."

I reached into my purse and pulled out the bracelets.

"Here," I said, handing them to her. "My apologies."

She took one look at them, and the color, natural and otherwise, drained from her face.

"Why are you showing those to me?" she whispered. "What do you want from me?"

"Nothing," I said, puzzled. "I just—"

"You just what? You've been out for blood from the moment you laid eyes on me, you and that ridiculous story you concocted to get in to see me! And now this. What are you planning to do?" she asked, her eyes wild.

The floor show was about to begin. The emcee was making his way to the stage, and the eight-piece jazz band was warming up.

"Planning? I'm not planning anything," I said, my voice low. "I want to return these to you. I took them by accident the other day, and I'm giving them back."

Why was she acting like this? I didn't get it.

"Meredith, is there a problem?"

Pale skin, crooked teeth, impeccable Savile Row suit. This had to be Burnett's father, Mason Fowlkes. I recognized him from Burnett's description the other afternoon. No costumes for this fellow. No sense of humor, either. He looked down his nose at me and placed a proprietary arm on Meredith's shoulder.

"No, no, Mason dear." She was putting tremendous effort into unclenching her teeth. As the woman smiled up at her ex-husband, her face softened into something that resembled beauty. That trick must've taken years of practice.

I closed my purse. Whatever. I could give the bracelets to Burnett later. There was a line a mile long at the powder room, so I gave up on that, too, and headed back to my table.

I was just in time for the comedy routine. The top banana was in tie and tails—his sidekick, too.

"I'm going to Tampa with your daughter," the first guy said.

"You tamper with her and I'll break your neck."

Bada-bing.

"Actually, it looks like you're already pretty messed up."

"I was living the life of Riley," he answered. "Then Riley came home."

Next up was the Oyster Girl. She came on wearing a white chiffon robe. After some tasteful writhing the robe came off, then the marabou-trimmed negligee. When she was down to her bra and panties, she stepped into an enormous oyster shell, wheeled in by the comedians. A classic from the great age of burlesque, I guess.

The finale was an explosion of feathered headdresses, fringed skirts, and beaded gloves, which were removed from female bodies of every possible configuration in synchronized beats. Then, the ladies did an energetic cancan. My eyes were glued to the tassels on their pasties, which were whipping around as if powered by turbo engines. One poor girl, however, had made the mistake of settling for a cheap pair instead of the high-end models favored by her coworkers. They wouldn't stay in place, and, in despair, she finally ripped them off.

"So, what do you think?" murmured Burnett, who had pulled up a chair next to me.

"She should have shopped at TwirlyGirl.net, home of extraordinary pasties for the discriminating nipple."

"Are you kidding?" he said, laughing. "Is there such a place?"

"That's for me to know and you to find out."

Burnett thanked everyone at Table Eleven for coming to his party and sat through a long-winded toast by Samuel. Then he whispered, "Finish your glass of wine and then let's get out of here. I want to show you something."

He took my hand and led me to the elevator.

"Next stop, the thirteenth floor."

39

That would be the roof.

It was just another night in downtown Los Angeles. The only thing marring the quiet was the sound of helicopters making a drug bust somewhere nearby. When you've lived in L.A. long enough, you learn how to tune the whirring out.

We walked over to the edge. Burnett stood behind me as we gazed at the city lights.

"Look at that view," he said with a sigh. "I love the city after dark. In the day, it's so benign somehow. But at night! At night, I can feel the electricity shooting through my veins, can't you?"

"Burnett, we have to talk." I had to explain about Gambino.

"Not now, Cece. Everything's the way it should be."

"Burnett—"

"Sssh. Don't say a word." He wrapped his arms around my waist, and I felt something hard poke into my back.

"Is that a gun in your pocket or are you just happy to see me?"

"I'll bet you say that to all the guys."

I tried to extricate myself, but he held on tight. I felt like I had led him on, but people change their minds.

"Burnett, I'm sorry, but this isn't going to happen."

"Yes, Cece, I'm afraid it is."

Surprised, I wheeled around and saw something shiny and black pointing at my gut. Jesus. The one time I utter that stupid line, and it really is a gun. Why does that figure? I got ahold of myself. Now was not the time for irony.

"Everybody's waiting for us downstairs, Burnett. It's time to cut the cake. They'll wonder where we are."

"Relax, Cece. This isn't going to take long."

"What isn't going to take long?" I asked, willing myself not to panic.

Burnett pushed me a little closer to the edge. I looked up and saw the neon numerals of the clock tower. It was a quarter past nine. All over the city, mothers were putting their children to bed. Truck drivers were crowding onto the I-10, heading for destinations unknown. Waitresses were serving that last cup of coffee. Friends were becoming lovers. Lovers were figuring out how to stay friends. I looked down and everything was sparkling, from the tips of my sandals, covered in tiny copper beads, to the sidewalk a hundred feet below, still slick from the brief afternoon rain. How beautiful it all seemed. The colors were vibrating, pulsing, spinning in circles. Fuschia, chartreuse, midnight blue. It was 9:16 P.M. now. Burnett Fowlkes was going to push me off of the roof of an art deco landmark before another minute passed, and I was going to fall through the night sky into nothingness.

Like hell I was.

"You're too smart to do this, Burnett. Stop while you're

ahead. Or not too far behind. Dozens of people saw us leave the party together. And besides, I have evidence, and it's in a safe place. The police know what to do in case anything happens to me."

I could feel my sweat stains spreading from tiny half-moons into something the size of buffet plates.

"You have nothing, Cece. You have some wild ideas about a murder that's half a century old and has nothing to do with me. I wasn't even born yet."

"You were born in plenty of time to kill Theresa Flynn," I said, shaking my head at my own blindness. It had been him all along. Him stalking that poor woman; him breaking in to her house to look for her sister's lockbox; him there, in the backyard, the night Lael and I had broken in; him in the black SUV. He was on to me from that very first day, when I showed up at his mother's house on my cockamamie quest to save a condemned man. The minute his mother told him I'd been asking about the Albaccos, he'd known they were in for trouble. God, had he seen me go into the locksmith's shop? Had he been following me for weeks? What a fool I must've seemed, kissing him that day in the car.

"Why would I kill a woman I don't even know?" he asked calmly.

"To protect your fortune. To finish up what your family started fifty years ago."

"You're obsessed with history, Cece. You think too much in terms of the past. The past is dead. There's no legacy to protect."

"There's a hell of a lot of money," I said.

He pushed me still closer to the edge. It would be so easy for him to claim I'd lost my balance and fallen. I'd been drinking up a storm. Wine, champagne, you name it. But maybe, after I was dead, somebody would notice this unfortunate habit I'd developed of falling into thin air whenever Burnett Fowlkes was in the vicinity.

"You know, this birthday thing, Burnett, it would get anybody down. Who needs a big party? We could've just crawled under the covers and hidden from the world until it was over."

"Cece. Stop. Your prattle is annoying me."

Now, that was really insulting. And look at him. Not a hair out of place. I was just a minor prattling problem he was going to take care of before blowing out the candles on his birthday cake. There was only one thing I had ever seen rile him.

"Your grandfather killed Jean Albacco."

He reddened. "Leave my grandfather out of this."

"I can't. It's just like you said, Burnett. You said he was an octopus. His tentacles reached everywhere."

"That was a stupid metaphor."

"Your grandfather killed Jean, and you killed her sister. God, talk about family legacies."

"Shut up."

"Jean knew he had defrauded Joseph Sr. out of his share of a fortune. She got her hands on a copy of a letter from a state legislator advising him of impending legislation about the tidelands. And more damning yet, she had a copy of the original partnership agreement between him and Joseph Sr. One plus one makes jail time, doesn't it?" I'd found that particular piece of evidence yesterday, when Gambino and I had paid a visit to my safe-deposit box on the way home from Lael's. I'd missed it the first time I went through the papers in Jean's lockbox. It was folded up into a tiny square and tucked between two yellowed photographs. Too bad—it would have saved me a lot of time.

"That's not proof of anything. Certainly not murder."

"Oh, I think it's enough to reopen the case. Detective Gambino of the LAPD agrees with me. He knows where all the relevant documents are."

"You bitch."

"You bastard. You killed a woman."

"I'm not done yet."

He smiled that smile at me. I melted despite myself. It was lethal, that smile, the kind of smile that made you complicit in a great big secret, the kind you'd sell your very soul for. I blinked. Oh, Jesus. I knew I knew that smile. Only I didn't know from where until this very second.

It was Joseph Albacco's smile.

Burnett Fowlkes was Joseph Albacco's son.

I started laughing. There was no escaping the irony this time.

"Is something funny?"

"You didn't have to do this, Burnett," I said. "You didn't have to do any of it. It was all for nothing. Don't you see? You would've gotten the money anyway. The oil fortune was yours, Burnett. Even after the truth came out, it still would've been yours."

"What are you talking about?"

"Why don't you ask your mother?"

"Ask me what?"

Meredith Allan had appeared, as if by magic. But she was no gossamer vision, no Fairy Queen. She was as solid, as cold and hard, as steel.

"Everyone's waiting downstairs, dear. Everyone's been

looking for you." She appeared entirely unperturbed by the sight of her son about to murder his dinner date.

"Tell Burnett who his father is," I said.

"Burnett knows who his father is." She was walking toward us slowly.

"I don't think so," I said.

"Burnett knows how much I love him. That's what matters. And that I would never lie to him."

"Then tell him what he needs to know. Tell him he's Joseph Albacco's son. Tell him how you were already pregnant with him when you married Mason Fowlkes."

"Ms. Caruso, give me those bracelets."

Now she wanted the bracelets. And I knew exactly why. Thank goodness she had dismissed me so curtly when I'd tried to give them back earlier.

"Why does Cece have your bracelets?" Burnett asked, confused. Meredith Allan had spent a lifetime confusing her son, smothering him or ignoring him according to her mood. But that was good. I wanted him to be confused. All I needed was for him to forget about me for a second and to think about her. To think about her and get all mixed up. It had to be a reflex by now. Then, maybe, he'd loosen his grip a little and I could make a dash for the stairwell. It would lead me straight to the elevator. It was my only chance.

"She stole them, and I want them back. Will you get them for me, dear?" she asked.

"No."

Had he ever defied her before? The look on her face said he hadn't.

"I don't want to talk about your bracelets, Mother. I don't give a shit about them."

"Burnett! Don't you dare speak to me like that!"

"Tell me who my father is. Tell me what I need to know." The hand holding the gun was shaking now, but the other was still squeezing me tight.

Meredith smiled encouragingly. "I'm not angry. Please don't worry. Just give me the gun, Burnett. I'll take care of it. Don't let this woman ruin everything for you."

"Don't you mean for you?"

For her. He'd done it for her. It was always about her. I'd had it right the first time. Meredith wasn't Joe's alibi; Joe was her alibi. It wasn't her father who had killed Jean. It was Meredith herself. Her father had been the one who didn't want to get his hands dirty. They were dirty enough. There was oil under his fingernails, a bad, bad smell he couldn't wash away. Morgan had done his share. He'd left the mop-up work to them, to his daughter and his daughter's son and whoever else would follow. Meredith knew that the only one who could be hurt by Jean, or by Theresa, for that matter, was her. Her son would inherit everything anyway. Because he was Joseph Albacco's son, too. Did Joe know? I had no idea. I knew only this: it always comes down to money, just like Gambino said.

All of a sudden, Burnett let me go. I didn't matter to him anymore. The money didn't matter, either. There was no one in the world except the two of them. I tripped as I ran toward the stairs, ripping my silk stockings.

Meredith walked toward her son, her arm outstretched.

"I did it for us, Burnett, don't you see? I did it to protect us. Jean would've destroyed everything, destroyed our name, twisted everything around."

"You didn't do it for me."

"Oh, Burnett. You're just like Joe. Your brain's in a

muddle, thoughts moving in every direction at once. The shortest distance between two points is a straight line. See the world clearly, for once."

"I do," he said, then shot her dead. And before I could say or do a thing, he flew off the side of the Oviatt Building, another fallen angel with painted wings.

40

I did finish my biography of Erle Stanley Gardner, by the way. I don't know if I ever figured out my subject, but I think I came close, which is the most I'd hoped for in the first place. Like I said, a person can never really know another person, not really, not deep down. We're lucky enough if we figure ourselves out. It can take years, for example, to know whether to go with the music or the alarm in the morning, to know what to fix for breakfast so you don't crash by eleven A.M., what attitude to adopt in what situation to achieve maximum success as opposed to ritual humiliation. And choosing the right makeup base, not to mention learning how to put it on so there's no demarcation along the jawline—well, that's a life's work, especially because once you've aced the whole thing they're guaranteed to discontinue your color. But that's another story.

My ex will tell you that biography is a minor genre, best suited for those more enamored of gossip than history. I pretend to take offense, but I suspect he's right, though in ways he hardly intended. Gossip is the purest form of human communication. It's how Perry Mason always got his best information, for one thing. He couldn't always verify it, not right away, but he could smell the truth. He could taste it. Moral of the story: trust feelings over facts. Of course, that assumes that unlike Tinker Bell you can juggle more than one feeling at a time. I'm constantly juggling a million—that's my whole problem.

Actually, that's not my whole problem. My whole problem is that I'm always hoping for a happy ending, even when I know there isn't a chance in hell of one. I had no idea.

Lisette Peterson Johnson was finally elected to the school board, no thanks to me. Interesting thing is, she, too, had a past with ESG. I discovered that one rainy afternoon when I was proofing my book. I'd pulled out my copy of Joe's heartbreak file to double-check something and had taken another look at the note ESG had clipped to that dog-eared letter on lined paper: "L.P.: follow up. Rings a bell/ESG." I checked with the archivist, and lo and behold, there she was, in 1958, when she was supposed to be in Hollywood trying to become an actress; one Lisette Peterson, on the payroll of the Court of Last Resort.

The archivist had also found a letter to ESG from Lisette's grandfather, asking for a favor from an old Ventura buddy for his "wayward" granddaughter. ESG had always been loyal to old friends. So what I figure is the reason ESG had never contacted Joe in jail was that Lisette had buried Joe's letter, misfiling it under "J," where I'd come across it all those months ago in Austin, Texas. She'd been more calculating than I'd given her credit for. When I confronted her about my suspicions, she admitted nothing. She said only that she'd been put on this earth to do God's work and that there was never any sense in looking back.

Then there was Joe's parole hearing. It went well, on paper, at least. Father Herlihy met me at the prison entrance first thing Monday morning and ushered me up two flights of stairs and down several corridors into a fluorescent-lit room where three men in dark suits were sitting behind a desk opposite Joe.

Joe looked strange—not happy, not sad, just strange. Detectives Moriarty and Lewis were standing in the back. Moriarty gave me a little wave. Since the events of the night before, he'd been eating humble pie all over the place.

The parole commissioners introduced themselves and stated that hearings such as these were intended to determine if the inmate in question was ready for release from incarceration. But in this case, there were extenuating circumstances. Important matters had come to their attention. They glanced at me. Father Herlihy patted my arm encouragingly. They would not be considering parole for Mr. Albacco today. Thanks to certain individuals, they said, they would instead be referring this case to the Board of Prison Terms, which would be investigating and making a recommendation on Mr. Albacco's application to have his sentence vacated. They believed a positive outcome would be the result.

Joe would see the ocean again.

"Thank you, Ms. Caruso," he had said when it was over. I shook my head. It was over, yes, but I was only beginning to understand what his freedom had cost him. He had spent his life in jail protecting the woman he thought he loved from having to admit she was sleeping with a married man. Forty-five years ago, that must've seemed like a big deal.

Of course, he hadn't had any idea what he'd really been protecting her from. It was probably a good thing that chivalry was dead. And now *she* was dead, killed by the son her long-ago lover, Joe, never even knew he had.

Fairies, as it turns out, don't always elude capture.

There were a few things I still didn't get. I didn't want to burden Joe further, but I had to know.

"That afternoon, after we'd made love, Meredith sent me out for cigarettes," he explained. "The same as always, Camels, unfiltered. When I came back with them, she had already left. Gone. She was gone. I figured she was sick of our little game, that she went to see her fiancé, Mason—I didn't really know. I was so messed up I punched through a window. That's where the blood came from. Then I lay back down and fell asleep thinking of her beautiful face. When I woke up, I realized how late it was. That it was my wedding anniversary, and I needed to get home, to my wife."

"And your keys?"

"They'd been gone a week," he said, his eyes dead from the inside out. "Meredith must've taken them."

I couldn't hear any more.

Gambino was waiting for me in the hallway.

"Only you would wear a red dress to a parole hearing," he said.

I twirled around. "Do you like it?"

"Versace, pre-Donatella, am I right?"

I looked at him with new respect.

"And yes, I like it. A lot."

He took my hands and was about to kiss me, when Detective Moriarty came over.

"You don't need to apologize again, Detective," I said, trying not to sound too pleased with myself.

"I wasn't going to," he replied.

"Oh."

"I just wanted to give you an update, Ms. Caruso. But when you and the detective are done with the personal stuff."

"We're done," Gambino said, embarrassed.

"We are not," I said.

He grinned at me. "Please go ahead, Moriarty."

"Well, we found out about the money from the Bank of Santa Barbara. It's gone. It went to the state in the early sixties, when the account went inactive."

So Jean's blackmail money paid for the time her husband served at Tehachapi for not murdering her. It was perfect, in a sick sort of way.

"And we put in a call to that girl you told us about at the law offices in Ventura."

"Allison," I said.

"Right, Allison. She got back to me right away."

I'd counted on that.

"There's a guy there who's supposed to be a genius at this stuff. Allison explained everything about the Albacco family's long involvement with the firm, and the guy's looking forward to sinking his teeth into this one."

"And his percentage of a billion dollars," added Gambino.

Moriarty laughed. "Speaking of lucky, good thing the filigree work on Ms. Allan's bracelets was so intricate. Those babies'd been scrubbed within an inch of their lives, but the lady wasn't too skilled at the housewifely arts, shall we say. Our guys found skin and hair embedded all up in there. Jean Albacco must've taken quite a pounding. But they're not going to have to dig her up. The lab'll be able to make an ID by comparing her DNA with that of her sister, Mrs. Flynn, whose stay in the morgue may have to be extended a few more days. It's like I always say, you gotta love modern technology."

Actually, as I told Gambino the next morning, when the doorknob came off in his hand, I'm low-tech all the way.

Turn the page for a sneak preview
of the next Cece Caruso mystery

NOT A GIRL DETECTIVE

by Susan Kandel

Coming soon in harcover from
William Morrow
An Imprint of HarperCollinsPublishers

1

When I couldn't tell the rain from my tears I knew it was time to pull over. I laid my arms across the steering wheel and choked back a sob. I had gone through the first four stages of grief: denial, anger, bargaining, depression. Now I was stuck on stage five—damning the mechanic. But what good was that going to do? My Toyota Camry was dying. Not peacefully but spectacularly, with great plumes of smoke emanating from the rear and strange wails coming out of the air-conditioning vents.

Yesterday, the tape deck shredded Frank Sinatra's greatest hits. The day before, the cup holder snapped off in my hands, sending Diet Coke all over my favorite beaded sweater. Hell, if I had known it was going to end like this, I would've leased a Jaguar in the first place.

If only I were the cheerful sort, like my best friend Lael. It's unseemly how cheerful Lael is. That's all I'll say. Or conniving, like my second best friend, Bridget, who knows just what to say when, and to whom. Scary. Or better yet, the resourceful type, like teenage supersleuth Nancy Drew. I spent my entire youth idolizing that girl. I'm pushing forty now, but some fantasies die hard.

If only I were Nancy Drew.

I'd pull some Vaseline out of my handbag and fix those windshield wipers lickety-split. I'd solve the mystery of the air-conditioning vents with my superior knowledge of dehumidification, say. And if I couldn't get the car to stop smoking by any other means, I'd ask my daddy to buy me a new one. A pretty blue roadster to match my pretty blue eyes.

Self-recrimination has long been a favorite pastime. I could keep it going forever, but I had someplace to be. I opened the car door and stepped directly into a puddle. Damn. With my raincoat pulled up over my head, I waded around back and stared at the exhaust pipe in wonder. How could it betray me? Vexed, I gave it a kick. It belched, evil thing. Then it occurred to me that it could explode any second—the whole car, I mean. These things do happen. But I was such a sodden mess I probably wasn't combustible. And they say it never rains in Southern California.

I fished my cell phone out of my purse and was about to call for a tow when I realized the bookstore I was heading to was only a few blocks away. I decided to make a run for it. That would be the end of my spike-heeled boots, of course, but they were already halfway to kingdom come. Maybe I could claim them as a business expense. I'd been taking a more aggressive approach to tax deductions lately. My accountant's thinking was that I made so little money they'd never in a million years bother auditing me. I wasn't sure that was sound reasoning, but Mr. Keshigian had managed to keep all his gangster relations out of the hands of the IRS, so I could hardly question his expertise. And god forbid he should fix me up with one of the cousins again.

Dodging the mud puddles, I sprinted down Melrose Avenue. No one sipping organic coffee at the Bodhisattva Café today. What a neighborhood. On sunny days you could drop your car with the Bodhisattva's valet, pick up a soy latte to go, and in the space of a single city block have your palm read, buy a New Age tome, get your colon cleaned, and take a ceramics class—not necessarily in that order. It wasn't my thing. I grew up in New Jersey. I live for synthetics.

Frederick A. Dalthorp Rare Books and Bindery was just around the corner, and talk about synthetic. It had fake gothic spires poking into the sky, stained-glass windows, turrets. No serving wenches, however. Too bad. I could've used a tankard of ale right about then. Nope, just the Dalthorp twins. They'd inherited the business from their father, Frederick, a smooth operator who'd sweet-talked the building out of some morticians who'd been there since the thirties. The Dalthorps were cousins of my purported boyfriend, Peter Gambino. A few weekends ago we'd had brunch together and they'd made a big to-do over Gambino's mocha chip pancakes, which I found impossible to stomach myself. But those girls were clearly addicted to sugar. They were eating marzipan at their desks when I pushed open the massive wooden door.

"Heave ho!" I said.

"For god's sake, don't spray the books!" yelled Dena, the older of the two by seventeen minutes and accustomed to milking every one of them.

"What do you think I am, a Saint Bernard?"

"Oh, Cece," murmured Victoria, Dena's more politic sister, "look at your turtleneck! It shrank in the rain!" She handed me a wad of paper towels.

"It's cropped," I explained, drying off. "It's supposed to be that way. It matches my cropped toreador pants."

"Good god," said Dena. Dena did not appreciate fashion. She was wearing a shapeless woolen sweater, a longish kilt, and brogues. Perfect for stomping through the heather.

Victoria gave me a sympathetic look. "I'm sure you looked lovely."

"Thank you," I said, crushed by her use of the past tense.

"The seventies, right?"

"The fifties, actually. Gina Lollabrigida goes beatnik?"

I was used to being misunderstood. My mother, a rummage-sale diva, never met a pot holder she couldn't love. Or a TV tray table not worth saving. She'd happily plunk down five dollars for a moribund blender, ten dollars for a card table with three legs. Yet she was unable to figure out why I'd want to wear old clothes. Worse yet, somebody else's old clothes.

"So what's this about Nancy Drew?" Dena asked.

The chitchat was over.

"Cece's writing a book about Nancy Drew!" Victoria exclaimed. "Remember how much we loved Nancy Drew when we were kids? Twisted candles flickering at midnight! Blood-curdling screams and secret passageways! But we didn't have an attic," she said, sighing. "Nobody in L.A. does. And how could we be detectives without a musty attic to explore?"

"There are plenty of mysteries to solve around this moldering old relic," Dena snapped. "Like why the pipes are always backed up. And where my favorite coffee mug went. Why don't you solve them?"

Thank god I had brothers. They just slugged you.

I slid into a leather club chair. "Actually, my book isn't exactly about Nancy Drew. It's a biography of Carolyn Keene, the author of the series."

"There is no Carolyn Keene," Dena said with a smirk.

"Technically, that's true."

"Dena was the one who told me there was no Santa Claus," Victoria whispered.

"A number of different people wrote the Nancy Drew books," I continued, "based on detailed outlines they were given by the publishing syndicate that originated the character. The Stratemeyer Syndicate was an actual writing mill. They put out the Hardy Boys, the Bobbsey Twins, dozens of children's series. Anyway, the real identities of the writers they hired were unknown for decades. Everybody took oaths of secrecy. It was pretty cloak-and-dagger. Carolyn Keene was just a made-up name."

"So you're writing a biography of a pseudonym?" Victoria asked.

It did sound perverse when you put it that way.

"Look, why don't we show Cece what we've got, okay?"

"Good idea, Dena. I don't want to keep you." There's your sister's ego to crush and marzipan bananas to finish and it's already four in the afternoon.

She pointed me toward a rickety glass-fronted bookcase in the corner of the room. "We don't usually handle children's books. We had a beautiful first edition of *Robinson Crusoe* that sat here collecting dust for years."

"Well, you did scare off that buyer from Baltimore, remember?"

Dena glared at her twin. "He was a big phony."

"Was not."

"Was too."

As they continued bickering, I opened the cabinet and reached for the white dust jacket. I ran my finger over the

familiar emblem on the spine, a tiny silhouette of the blond
sleuth from River Heights, looking through a magnifying
glass, a scarf thrown jauntily around her neck. The girl could
definitely wear clothes.

The Mystery of the Ivory Charm. If I remembered correctly,
The Mystery of the Ivory Charm featured a strange woman
who was trying to deny a rajah his throne. She could go into
a hypnotic trance at the drop of a hat, but Nancy saw through
her, of course.

I pulled the book off the shelf and turned to the front
cover. There she was, Nancy Drew, looking typically surrepti-
tious. She was inside an old shed, sneaking some yellowed
documents out of a coffeepot and trying not to get caught.
The bad guy was just outside the open door. You knew he
was the bad guy because he was going after a mangy hound
dog with his leather whip. In Nancy Drew books—as in life,
I suppose—you can always identify evildoers because they're
the ones who mistreat animals.

Most of the dust jackets I'd seen were tattered, missing
bits and pieces. This one was in perfect condition. I ran my
fingers over the pages. They felt rough. This was definitely
wartime paper, which meant it couldn't be a first edition. The
other tip-off was the silhouette, which didn't appear on the
spines until 1941, with the second printing of number 18, and
subsequent reprintings of numbers 1 to 17.

Dating and assigning valuations to these books was tricky.
The first Nancy Drew mystery, *The Secret of the Old Clock,*
has been reprinted more than one hundred and fifty times
since its original appearance in 1930, with minute variations
each time—different paper stocks, boards, endpapers, fron-
tispieces, etc. You'd have to be obsessive-compulsive to keep

track of all the details. I'd love to be obsessive-compulsive but I'm too lazy. Still, I was pleased that some of my research had stuck.

"Do you have a buyer already?"

Victoria took the book out of my hands. "Yes, someone local. He wants everything we can get, first edition or not."

"Sticky fingers!" reprimanded Dena.

"You've eaten more candy than I have," Victoria said with a sniff. She turned toward me. "This would be a great thing to own, wouldn't it? A piece of American history! The first role model for teenage girls, ever!"

It seemed churlish to mention Joan of Arc.

"Say, Cece, why don't you deliver it for us?"

"Did you forget to pay the courier service again, Victoria?"

Victoria ignored her sister and started wrapping the book in brown paper. "I bet he'd love to hear about your research. And it would give you a chance to see his collection. It's amazing. I believe he has the only complete set of Nancy Drew first printings in the world!"

How interesting that it would be a man. "I'd be happy to deliver the book."

"Hold your horses," Dena said, squinting at me suspiciously. "Are you bonded?"

This time, it was me who ignored her.

Tucking *The Mystery of the Ivory Charm* under my coat, I stepped out into paradise. Double rainbows streaked across the sky. A soft wind caressed my cheeks. The Bodhisattva Café was packed, the laughter of hemp-clad sybarites filling the air. It was as if the rainstorm had never happened. As if it were a bad dream some colon hydrotherapy had dissolved. This is why people move to Los Angeles. You can live in a permanent state of denial here. Except when it comes to meter maids. They are the hardiest of all urban tribes and one of them was eyeing my Camry. Once her pen touched paper it would be too late. I ran toward her, screaming at the top of my lungs.

"Back off, sweetie," she said, putting her pad back into her pocket. "You made it." Then she shook her tightly coiffed head. "You got enough trouble with those sorry-ass boots."

I was blessed, I think. But there was only one way to know for sure. I held my breath, got in, and turned the key in the ignition. It wheezed and spat and quaked and shook, but my car was alive. Alive! I knew I should probably drive straight to the dealership on Hollywood Boulevard, but I had so much to take care of, and that would be the end of my day. Once those guys get you in their clutches they just keep on talking. No, I'd take the car home and go to the dealer first thing in the morning. They'd probably need a few days to whip it into shape, which was fine. It gave me a perfect excuse to rent a car for the weekend.

A convertible.

I could see it now.

Me and Lael and Bridget, gunning down the 10 toward Palm Springs, the wind whipping through our big hair. We all had big hair. Maybe we'd put the top up if it got too windy. Wind strips the hair of moisture. I guess we could wear scarves.

The three of us were taking a business trip. Well, at least for me it was business. I'd been asked to deliver the keynote address at the annual Nancy Drew fan convention. Some persons in my life had found the very idea amusing. Like my daughter, Annie, and her husband, Vincent, who about choked on their Kombucha mushroom tea when I told them. And a certain Detective Peter Gambino of the LAPD, whom I might have mentioned earlier. But Mr. Keshigian had nodded, pleased. I was to deduct everything.

It was a paycheck, for god's sake. When you write biographies of dead mystery writers for a living, you need as many of those as you can get. And it would be great publicity for the new book, which was almost finished. But I was nervous. Those fans knew a hell of a lot, and they'd probably love to catch me in a mistake, like not knowing that the spine silhouette for number 24 was missing the scarf. Or that early printings of number 18, *The Mystery at the Moss-Covered Mansion,* made reference to the forthcoming volume as *The Quest of the Telltale Map* when it was actually printed as *The Quest of the* Missing *Map.*

Fan is short for fanatic.

Bridget was going to take the opportunity to raid the Palm Springs thrift shops, hoping to find a couple of Bob Hope's wife's discarded Adolfo suits, maybe something with a mink collar and jeweled buttons. Or a Galanos caftan, very Nancy Reagan on holiday. Bridget owned On the Bias, L.A.'s top vintage clothing shop.

Lael was a master pastry chef and oblivious to clothes, vintage or otherwise, but she didn't have any gigs until late next week, and her children's fathers (that would be four for four) were taking the kids for spring break, so she was coming, too.

Not for Nancy Drew. My lusty friend had no patience for professional virgins.

Not for the sunshine. Lael was a Norwegian blonde who freckled like crazy.

I think she wanted an adventure.

Me, too.

We should have remembered that when it rains, it pours.